Alice-Miranda
at the Palace

Books by Jacqueline Harvey

Alice-Miranda at School
Alice-Miranda on Holiday
Alice-Miranda Takes the Lead
Alice-Miranda at Sea
Alice-Miranda in New York
Alice-Miranda Shows the Way
Alice-Miranda in Paris
Alice-Miranda Shines Bright
Alice-Miranda in Japan
Alice-Miranda at Camp

Clementine Rose and the Surprise Visitor
Clementine Rose and the Pet Day Disaster
Clementine Rose and the Perfect Present
Clementine Rose and the Farm Fiasco
Clementine Rose and the Seaside Escape
Clementine Rose and the Treasure Box
Clementine Rose and the Famous Friend
Clementine Rose and the Ballet Break-In

Alice-Miranda
at the Palace

Jacqueline Harvey

RANDOM HOUSE AUSTRALIA

A Random House book
Published by Random House Australia Pty Ltd
Level 3, 100 Pacific Highway, North Sydney NSW 2060
www.randomhouse.com.au

Penguin
Random House
RANDOM HOUSE BOOKS

First published by Random House Australia in 2015

Random House Books is part of the Penguin Random House group of
companies whose addresses can be found at global.penguinrandomhouse.com.

National Library of Australia
Cataloguing-in-Publication Entry

Author: Harvey, Jacqueline
Title: Alice-Miranda at the palace/Jacqueline Harvey
ISBN: 978 0 85798 272 8 (paperback)
Series: Harvey, Jacqueline. Alice-Miranda; 11
Target audience: For primary school age
Subjects: Friendship – Juvenile fiction
          Queens – Juvenile fiction
          Anniversaries – Juvenile fiction
          Detective and mystery stories
Dewey number: A823.4

Cover and internal illustrations by J.Yi
Cover design by Mathematics www.xy-1.com
Internal design by Midland Typesetters, Australia
Typeset in 13/18 pt Adobe Garamond by Midland Typesetters, Australia
Printed in Australia by Griffin Press, an accredited ISO AS/NZS 14001:2004
Environmental Management System printer

Random House Australia uses papers that are natural, renewable and recyclable
products and made from wood grown in sustainable forests. The logging
and manufacturing processes are expected to conform to the environmental
regulations of the country of origin.

*For Ian, who is full of wonderful
surprises and good ideas, for Holly and Catriona,
who have worked so hard, and for Sandy, as always.*

Prologue

A man in a bowler hat and charcoal overcoat dashed out of the alley and through the pounding rain. Just as he did so, a sleek black car pulled up to the kerb. He glanced left and right, then quickly folded his umbrella and jumped into the passenger seat.

The driver gave a swift nod. 'Good evening, Sir.'

'I'd hardly call it that, old chap,' the passenger replied, brushing the droplets of water from his shoulders.

The windscreen wipers swiped at the deluge as

the driver checked his side mirror and pulled out into the deserted street. Without a word, he handed the passenger a manila folder.

The man scanned the contents, a row of frown lines settling on his forehead. 'Why her?' he asked. 'She's not a relative.'

'No, but she makes perfect sense. Rich parents, adored by all and apparently just about the sweetest child you'll ever meet. She's a natural target.'

'Do you think this is enough to force Her Majesty's hand?' the passenger asked.

'That, and this.' The driver passed the man a plastic sleeve containing a single document. 'Everything we need is there.'

The passenger nodded. 'So it's true, then?'

'Yes. It was never witnessed and countersigned. It should never have been *her* and it most certainly won't be *him*.'

'How did you get this, or do I not want to know?'

'I have someone on the inside. Very reliable and even more ambitious,' the driver replied.

'It's not the original, is it?'

'Heavens, no. But don't worry, I'm sure we'll have it when we need it.' The driver slowed down as the traffic lights ahead turned red.

'When do we begin?'

'The first letter will arrive tomorrow, then there's no going back.' The driver swallowed hard. 'Are you ready?'

'Since I was fifteen years old,' the man in the bowler hat said.

'Very good, Sir.' The driver pulled up outside a row of Georgian townhouses.

The passenger shook the other man's hand. 'No going back,' he said firmly and opened the car door. The man popped up his umbrella and scurried away towards the yellow glow of a porch light.

Chapter 1

'Ooh, she gives me the creeps,' Millie whispered, glancing at the new teacher sitting at the end of their row. The tall woman with a pixie hairdo, dressed in a sensible beige pants-suit, looked up just at that moment and their eyes met. Startled, the child quickly turned back to the front.

'Who?' Alice-Miranda asked, peering around her friend. 'Miss Broadfoot?'

'Miss Bigfoot more like it. Don't look!' Millie cringed as she noticed the teacher giving them a death stare.

'You shouldn't be so hard on her,' Alice-Miranda chided. 'She only started a week ago.'

But Alice-Miranda had a strange feeling about the woman too, though it was nothing she could put her finger on exactly. Miss Broadfoot just seemed to be popping up all over the place. She'd taught Alice-Miranda's English class and then Science and even PE. She was also helping out in the boarding house. And there had been a strange incident that Alice-Miranda hadn't told anyone about yet – not even Millie – mainly because she wasn't sure if it was real or if she'd been dreaming.

'Quiet,' Miss Broadfoot hissed.

The clacking of high heels echoed as Miss Ophelia Grimm walked to the podium in the middle of the stage. Immaculately dressed in a striking red suit, she cleared her throat and waited until all eyes were focused her way.

'I'm so thrilled to have everyone together for the final assembly of the term,' she began. 'And after a slightly patchy start, I can't tell you how pleased I am with the way things are going over at Caledonia

Manor with the year seven girls. You are doing yourselves proud, and Miss Hephzibah and Miss Henrietta tell me they haven't felt this young and happy in years.'

The two old women were sitting up on the stage, having been specially brought over for the occasion by Charlie Weatherly, the school gardener. Both of the ladies nodded and grinned, and Hephzibah gave a little wave. Alice-Miranda waved back.

'It now gives me great pleasure to announce this term's citizenship awards, as voted by the teachers and girls,' Miss Grimm continued. 'These awards are very important. Knowing that you have won the admiration and respect of your peers is quite something – and I must say there is one name here I would never have guessed. It just goes to show that all of us are capable of being better versions of ourselves.'

Miss Grimm glanced at Caprice Radford, who wasn't paying the slightest bit of attention. As the girl wasn't in the running for the award, she couldn't have cared less. Ophelia knew she had a challenge and a half on her hands with that one but, fortunately, Caprice's parents were well aware of their child's foibles. It made for a nice change compared to some of the monsters and their completely hoodwinked parents that she'd dealt with over the years.

The girls waited quietly while Sofia Ridout, the Head Prefect, picked up the badges and certificates from the table at the side of the stage and handed them to the headmistress.

'Congratulations to Essie Craven in year three, Lilian Banks in year four, Matilda Suttie in year five and Susannah Dare in year seven.' The announcement of each name was followed by a loud burst of applause. 'Please come up to accept your award.'

'What about year six?' The words tumbled from Millie's mouth before she had time to stop them.

Miss Broadfoot sent a thunderous look her way.

'Don't be so impatient, Millie,' Miss Grimm said, a strange smile perched on her lips. 'Without further ado, I am *very* pleased to announce that the citizenship award for year six goes to –' Miss Grimm paused and looked out at the students – 'Sloane Sykes.'

The mention of Sloane's name sent the children into a frenzy. The girls stamped their feet on the floor and cheered loudly.

Sloane looked as if she'd been bitten by a bedbug. 'Me? Really?'

Alice-Miranda grinned while watching the girl practically float down the centre aisle. 'I don't think she can believe it.'

'Who'd have thought?' Millie said, shaking her head. 'But, you know, she totally deserves it.'

Sloane bounded across the stage and, to everyone's great surprise, launched herself at Miss Grimm and hugged the woman tight. There was an audible gasp from the students as they watched to see what Miss Grimm would do next.

'I couldn't be any prouder of you if you were my own daughter,' the headmistress said quietly, embracing Sloane.

'Thank you for giving me a second chance, Miss Grimm,' Sloane said, positively beaming.

Miss Grimm stepped back and shook Sloane's hand vigorously. 'Thank *you* for proving you deserved one.'

Miss Reedy smiled as did Mr Plumpton and the other teachers who were sitting on stage beside Sofia Ridout. Miss Grimm stepped back up to the microphone.

'Please give our award-winners another round of applause,' she said as the girls exited the side of the stage, and the hall erupted again. The headmistress waited for the noise to die down before she continued. 'Girls, I'd like to wish you all a wonderful term break. Whatever it is that you're doing, be sure to do it well. Mr Grump and I are looking forward to a very special holiday in Italy, and I know that some of the other staff are off on grand adventures too.' Miss Grimm arched an eyebrow in Miss Reedy's direction.

Miss Reedy's cheeks flushed and Mr Plumpton's nose glowed bright red.

'Did you see that?' Alice-Miranda whispered to Millie. She smiled, hopeful that there might be another special announcement when they returned to school.

Millie giggled. 'I think Miss Grimm must know about Mr Plumpton and Miss Reedy.'

The assembly finished with the school song, and the girls filed out into the sunshine to the sound of Mr Trout playing the organ.

Alice-Miranda spotted Sloane and rushed over to give her a hug. 'Well done!'

'I still can't believe it,' Sloane replied, shaking her head.

'How many of those little kids did you have to bribe for their votes?' Jacinta teased.

Sloane's jaw dropped. 'I was going to say I miss sharing a room with you but maybe not so much after that comment.'

But that wasn't true at all. Sloane was having a far

more difficult time with the school's newest student, Caprice Radford.

'You know I'm joking,' Jacinta said, holding her hands up in surrender. 'Seriously, Sloane, congratulations. I've never won a citizenship award.'

'Wait until I tell Mummy. She'll probably take out a notice in the newspaper.' Sloane grimaced at the thought.

The other girls grinned.

Millie's stomach let out a strangled gurgle.

Sloane stared at the girl. 'What's going on in there?'

'Sorry – I must be hungrier than I thought,' Millie apologised.

'I wish we could stay for lunch but we have to head back to Caledonia Manor,' Jacinta said with a frown. 'But I'll see you all tomorrow. I think Mummy is even more excited than I am.'

'I can't wait to meet the twins,' Alice-Miranda said. Her Aunt Charlotte had recently given birth to two bouncing babies, Marcus and Imogen. 'I'm so glad that they've been given the all-clear to travel.'

None of the group noticed the girl with the long copper-coloured hair lurking behind them. 'What are you all fizzing about?' she asked, barging into their conversation.

The girls had agreed not to mention their invitations to Aunty Gee's jubilee celebrations to their classmates. Millie had been desperate to share the news but Alice-Miranda convinced her that it might sound as if she were boasting, and they didn't want anyone to feel left out.

Alice-Miranda turned around and smiled at the girl. 'Hello Caprice. I was just saying how much I'm looking forward to meeting my new cousins.'

Caprice wrinkled her nose. 'Babies are boring. All they do is eat, sleep and poo.'

Millie glared at the girl. 'And you'd know that because . . .?'

Since the incident during camp at the beginning of the term, when Caprice had blackmailed Millie into some behaviour she was less than proud of, things hadn't improved much at all between the two girls. Although there were times when Caprice seemed relatively normal, she still let her competitive streak get the better of her more often than not.

'What are you doing in the holidays, Caprice?' Alice-Miranda asked.

'Mummy's in charge of the catering for some stupid party for the Queen,' the girl began.

Millie, Sloane and Jacinta gulped in unison and stared at one another.

'I don't know why she has to do it. Doesn't Queen Georgiana have a thousand servants? Mummy says that it's an honour, but I say it's ruined our holidays,' Caprice blathered.

'Are you going?' Alice-Miranda asked as the other three girls' faces contorted.

'Of course not!' Caprice snapped. 'Children aren't allowed to go and, besides, Queen Georgiana's mean.'

Jacinta shook her head. 'That's not true. We're –'

'Looking forward to having a break,' Alice-Miranda quickly finished.

Caprice eyed the two girls suspiciously. 'What were you going to say?'

'Nothing,' Jacinta replied, relieved that Alice-Miranda had stopped her. Who knew what Caprice might do if she found out they were all attending the Queen's jubilee weekend.

Miss Grimm had begun ushering students to the dining room. She walked over to Alice-Miranda and her friends, a huge smile plastered on her face.

'Make sure you take lots of photographs, girls,' Miss Grimm said, lowering her voice conspiratorially. 'I want to know *everything* about the palace.'

The headmistress then pointed towards Miss Reedy, who was rounding up the year seven girls to walk back to Caledonia Manor.

'You'd better get moving, Jacinta,' the woman warned before hurrying away towards some of the younger children who had started an impromptu game of chasings over by the library.

'What would you know about the palace?' Caprice narrowed her eyes at Alice-Miranda and her friends. She remembered the way Queen Georgiana had been so cosy with them at the end of their school camp. 'Are you going or something?'

Millie nodded smugly.

'But my mother said children weren't allowed.' Caprice's porcelain face grew red and steam could almost be seen pouring from her ears.

'I thought you didn't like Queen Georgiana, anyway,' Jacinta said.

'That's not the point. Why should you all get to go? I'm going to make Mummy take me. You wait and see,' the girl hissed and stormed away.

'You shouldn't have said anything, Millie,' Sloane scolded. 'What if Caprice convinces her mother to let her come? She'll ruin our whole weekend.'

Millie sighed.

'She must be terribly lonely,' Alice-Miranda said. She watched the girl push her way into a younger group of students.

'Well,' Millie said, drawing herself up as tall as she could, 'it serves her right after what she did on camp. Anyway, I'd prefer not to think about her. I'm starving and that smells like Mrs Smith's chicken casserole to me. Come on.'

The girls waved goodbye to Jacinta and charged off to the dining room.

Chapter 2

Queen Georgiana looked daggers at Thornton Thripp. The man cleared his throat and adjusted his right cufflink, hoping she would say something – anything. But it was Marjorie Plunkett who spoke first.

'Your Majesty, our intelligence is credible.'

Queen Georgiana removed her glasses from the tip of her nose and looked at the woman. 'I should hope so. Someone in your position wouldn't want to get it wrong.'

'No, Ma'am,' Marjorie replied with a sharp shake of her head. As the Head of the Secret Protection League of Defence, she prided herself on her impeccable track record.

'Why wasn't I told about this earlier?' the Queen demanded. 'The two of you have been sitting on this information for at least a week!'

Thornton Thripp swallowed loudly, his right eye beginning to twitch. 'You've been so busy with preparations for the jubilee —'

'Thripp, as my chief advisor, it is your job to inform me of all threats made to the Crown. And, Marjorie, I expected much more from you,' Her Majesty huffed. 'I don't care which one of you made the decision to keep me in the dark. You are both at fault.'

'Yes, Ma'am.' The pair looked like two naughty schoolchildren in the headmistress's office.

The Queen took a deep breath, trying to calm herself. 'Well, now that you've finally told me what's going on, what do you suggest we do about it?'

'There was a recommendation not to make any sudden changes to routine,' Thornton Thripp offered. The man sat bolt upright, his hands resting one on top of the other on the table in front of him.

Queen Georgiana arched an eyebrow. 'Upon whose recommendation?'

'Mine, Ma'am,' Marjorie said quietly. 'I've organised for there to be a significant security detail at Evesbury this weekend. We'll be able to keep a good eye on her at the jubilee celebrations.'

'Yes, but that's just this weekend,' Her Majesty said impatiently. 'What about afterwards? What about *now*?'

'I'm sure Her Majesty can use her considerable powers of persuasion to achieve the best outcome.'

'For heaven's sake, Thripp, I'm sitting right here. You don't have to talk about me in the third person. It's frightfully annoying. And what do you mean by "achieve the best outcome"? Get them to stay? Is that what you're saying?' Queen Georgiana sighed loudly.

'Yes, Ma'am,' he replied.

'Then jolly well say it, Thripp. We're not playing "Guess that Tune", are we?'

'No, Ma'am,' the man mumbled.

The Queen turned to Marjorie. 'What have you been doing for the past week?'

Marjorie bristled at having to explain herself. As Chief of SPLOD, she thought she'd earned Her

Majesty's trust. 'I made all the necessary arrangements, Ma'am,' Marjorie replied.

'Well, I hope these *arrangements* of yours are more than adequate,' Her Majesty replied. 'And that security detail had better be invisible. I don't want the guests thinking that we've got anything to worry about. Let's leave the worrying to me and the two of you. Come to think of it, with the amount I pay you both, you should be doing the worrying for all of us.'

There was a hesitant knock on the door. Her Majesty's constant companions, Archie and Petunia, raised their heads and growled from beneath the table.

'Stop it, you two,' Queen Georgiana scolded. Upon hearing their mistress's voice, the two beagles ceased their objections and lay back down again. 'Come in,' Her Majesty boomed.

Mrs Marmalade poked her head into the room. A slender woman with an immaculate grey bob held back by a black velvet headband, Her Majesty's lady-in-waiting favoured floral prints, A-line skirts and sensible mid-heels. She was never seen without a pearl choker around her neck and, over the years, had been described in various magazines and newspapers as the Queen's reliable upper-crust offsider. The daughter of an earl, she had in fact gone to school with Queen Georgiana and Her Majesty's close friend, Valentina Highton-Smith.

While Valentina had knocked back the offer of the position in favour of raising a family, Marian Marmalade had chosen to spend her life by Her Majesty's side. Her husband had been aide to King Leopold, and when both men died within months of one another, it didn't occur to Marian that she would do anything other than stay. Truth be told she sometimes wondered why she did, given Queen Georgiana's frequent disdain, but there was an underlying affection between the two women.

'E-excuse me, Your Majesty,' the woman stuttered. 'I'm afraid we must get going if you're to make the hospital opening on time.'

'Oh, yes, I'll be there in a minute. Thank you, Mrs Marmalade.'

Her Majesty's lady-in-waiting cast Marjorie and Thornton snarky looks before retreating and closing the door. The woman had been frightfully annoyed to learn that Dalton, the Queen's personal bodyguard, had been granted long service leave at the very same time she'd requested a couple of weeks off to visit her sister, who'd recently had surgery. Marian wasn't sure which one of them had approved Dalton's leave over hers, so as far as she was concerned they were both in her bad books.

Queen Georgiana eyeballed the man and woman sitting across the table. 'May I leave this in your allegedly capable hands, then?'

Marjorie nodded. 'Of course, Ma'am.'

'Certainly,' Thornton added.

The Queen pushed back her chair and stood up. The others, including the dogs, were quickly on their feet too.

'Oh and, Marjorie, congratulations on your engagement. He's an honest fellow and good company at cards when we can drag him away from that workshop of his. I've never understood what he does but others tell me he's quite a genius with electronics and the like. It's a lovely story, isn't it – my milliner and second cousin falling in love?' Queen Georgiana winked knowingly.

Marjorie Plunkett blinked in surprise. 'Thank you, Ma'am.'

'Keep me informed,' the Queen said.

'Absolutely,' Marjorie replied, smiling broadly. 'You'll be the first to know when we've set the date. I should imagine sooner rather than later.'

Queen Georgiana smothered a chuckle. 'That's

not what I was referring to, dear. I believe we have far more pressing matters than your impending nuptials.'

'Of course. My apologies, Your Majesty.' The young woman's porcelain cheeks blushed a deep shade of red as she reprimanded herself for being so thick. Marjorie took pride in her professionalism but clearly love could do silly things to a person.

'Well, I'd better get going or Mrs Marmalade will be spinning herself into a migraine,' Queen Georgiana tutted. 'You know you're both off her Christmas card list.'

Marjorie and Thornton looked sheepishly at one another, then bowed as Her Majesty left the room with Archie and Petunia trotting alongside her.

Chapter 3

'Is it much further, Daddy?' Alice-Miranda asked as they drove past emerald fields dotted with ancient oak trees and little flocks of sheep.

They'd entered the palace grounds about a mile back, through a grand set of gates where a uniformed sentry had checked them off his list. Several gardeners had been busy at work just along the perimeter wall, which Hugh thought to be odd timing when Her Majesty was in residence and having guests for the weekend. Then again, it had been raining during the week and weeds stopped for nothing.

'I wonder if someone washes them,' Millie said with a grin.

Hugh Kennington-Jones glanced at the girl in the rear-vision mirror. 'Washes what?'

'The sheep – they look like cream puffs,' Millie replied. 'Ours are always sort of grubby around the edges.'

Cecelia Highton-Smith's jaw dropped in mock horror. 'I can't imagine Aunty Gee would have her staff washing the sheep.'

'She might,' Hugh said, a glint in his eye. 'Aunty Gee could have anything she wanted, really.'

'I'd have someone to deal with earwax,' Millie said. 'It's disgusting.'

Alice-Miranda laughed.

Hugh smiled. 'Bellybutton fluff for me. What about you, Alice-Miranda?'

The child thought for a moment. 'Someone to floss my teeth,' she decided. 'I always get the string caught at the back.'

Cecelia giggled. 'Oh, stop it, you lot. I'm sure that Aunty Gee deals with her own earwax and belly-button fluff and flossing.'

'I don't know, darling. It might explain why Mrs Marmalade is always in such a bad mood.' Hugh winked cheekily.

Alice-Miranda gasped as the car rounded a bend. 'Look, Millie!' she said, pointing towards the mansion in the distance. 'It's like a painting.'

Millie leaned across the seat and stared. 'Wow!'

Hugh and Cecelia smiled at one another.

'I remember the first time I saw the palace I thought it was a dream,' Cecelia said. 'Breathtaking, isn't it?'

The road snaked through more open fields peppered with stands of trees, some clustered in groves, others towering majestically on their own. They drove over a beautiful stone bridge that crossed a flowing crystal-clear river and continued on towards the palace.

'I just counted twenty-six windows in the front of the house!' Millie exclaimed. 'It's even bigger than your place.'

'It's about four times the size of Highton Hall,' Cecelia confirmed. 'If you're not careful you could be lost in there for days.'

'I wouldn't mind that,' Millie breathed. 'That way I'd get to see everything.'

The cream stone walls glinted in the sunshine. Beyond the house and rear gardens was a steep slope covered in a dense wood, creating the perfect backdrop to the palace.

'What's that?' Alice-Miranda pointed to the top of the hillside.

'It's the hunting tower,' Cecelia replied. 'In the old days, royal hunting parties used it to see what was going on across the estate.'

'Do you think we could go up there?' Alice-Miranda asked. 'Imagine the view.'

'I'm not sure if there will be time, sweetheart,' Cecelia said. She pulled an envelope from her handbag and unfurled an elegant white page which had the initials 'GR' embossed in gold at the top.

'If I know Aunty Gee, she'll have the weekend planned right down to the very last minute,' Hugh said.

Cecelia scanned the page in front of her. 'I think you're right, darling. Almost immediately after we're settled into our rooms, there's a garden party in the early afternoon, followed by games on the lawn, and then we're allowed a couple of hours to rest before tonight's ball.'

'Will there be dancing?' Millie asked.

'Absolutely, and Aunty Gee will be the first one on the dance floor,' Hugh said with a grin.

'What about tomorrow?' Millie asked.

'Just as busy, I'm afraid. Aunty Gee has planned a picnic brunch by the river with fishing, clay shooting and buggy rides,' Cecelia explained. 'And we'll have to leave early in the afternoon so Hugh can catch his flight to New York.'

'I wish we could stay longer,' Alice-Miranda said, gazing out the window.

'Me too,' Millie sighed. Her brow furrowed as a thought occurred to her. 'Do I have to curtsy? I can never remember who to curtsy for. I thought maybe I'd just do it for everyone.'

Hugh chuckled. 'Random curtsying – I like it. That will surely have everyone confused.'

Cecelia looked at her cheeky husband. 'It's all right, Millie, I'll help you. It's a lot more relaxed here than at the castle.'

'How many houses does Aunty Gee actually have?' Millie asked. 'And why are some called castles and others are palaces?'

'I used to wonder about that too until Aunty Gee explained it to me,' Hugh said. 'Apparently, a palace is a beautiful home used mostly for fun and entertaining, while castles are a bit like forts, built to withstand an enemy attack.'

Cecelia frowned. 'Mmm, let me see if I can remember them all. There's Chesterfield Downs near your school, then there's Brackenhurst and Hillsdon – they're both castles – and Swanston Hall and, of course, Evesbury Palace.'

'Have you been to all of them, Mummy?' Alice-Miranda asked.

Cecelia thought for a minute. 'I've been to the five I can remember but I suspect there might be more. I think Aunty Gee would love to be able to stay here at Evesbury all the time. But when you're the Queen you don't always get to do what you want. At least it's not that far from Brackenhurst in the city.'

Hugh drove the car up to an enormous pair of sandstone gateposts, where two more guards stood sentry. But this time he was waved through the open iron gates without having to stop.

'Look at the waterfall.' Millie almost swooned at the sight of a rectangular pond that cascaded down the slope for a couple of hundred metres and pooled in the centre of the vast rear garden.

A sign labelled 'guests' directed them to a court-yard behind the massive building. Hugh steered the vehicle around the circular cobblestoned driveway and pulled up outside an imposing pair of black doors. Four footmen dressed in red-and-white livery opened the car doors simultaneously and bowed.

'Good morning, Mr Kennington-Jones,' one of the men said.

Hugh smiled at the man. 'Good morning, indeed.'

Alice-Miranda leapt to the ground. 'Hello, my name is Alice-Miranda Highton-Smith-Kennington-Jones,' she announced, holding out her hand to the young man who had opened her door. 'It's very nice to meet you.'

The fellow glanced uncertainly at the footman beside him.

'Well, go on,' the older fellow whispered.

'Likewise, miss,' the young footman said to the girl, extending his gloved hand.

Just as he did so, the head butler marched out through one of the palace doors. Dressed in black tails and with his hair slicked into a perfect side part, the elderly man exuded an air of importance. He was followed by a much taller and younger blond fellow with a dimple in the middle of his chin.

'Good morning, Ms Highton-Smith, Mr Kennington-Jones,' the first man said. He glared at the young footman, who looked as if he'd just been caught with his hand in the lolly jar.

'Langley!' Hugh said with surprise. 'It's good to see you, old chap. I thought you would have retired by now.'

The blond man snorted, then coughed and covered his mouth.

Vincent Langley shot him a withering look before turning back to Hugh. 'I assure you, sir, I plan to be here for many years yet.'

'Good for you. I don't much believe in retirement, either. This is our daughter, Alice-Miranda, and her friend Millie,' Hugh said, introducing the girls.

Alice-Miranda smiled. 'It's lovely to meet you, Mr Langley. We're so excited to be here.'

The man gave a stiff nod, his face seemingly set in stone. 'This is Braxton Balfour, the *under* butler,' Mr Langley said.

The younger fellow broke into a wide grin and waggled his eyebrows playfully.

Millie giggled. She much preferred this under butler to the cranky old one.

Mr Langley scowled at Balfour, whose smile melted like an ice cream in the Sahara, then quickly turned his attention back to the family. 'I'll see you to your rooms,' he said. 'There is only a short space of time to freshen up before the garden party commences at one o'clock.'

Millie looked across the back lawn. There was no sign of any preparations out there. 'Where's the party going to be?' she asked.

'It's in the secret garden, miss,' the man replied.

'Oh,' Millie said. 'I suppose that was meant to be a secret.'

Braxton Balfour chortled and was immediately silenced by another dark look from the head butler.

'Have Aunt Charlotte and Uncle Lawrence arrived yet?' Alice-Miranda asked. She couldn't wait to meet her new cousins.

The head butler pursed his lips, his left eye twitching in the process. 'If you are referring to Ms Highton-Smith and Mr Ridley, no, they haven't. But I believe Mrs Headlington-Bear and her rather excitable party are upstairs.'

Alice-Miranda clapped her hands together. 'This is going to be the best weekend ever!'

Vincent Langley shuddered at the thought of all those children together.

'Would you like to follow me?' he asked the group, turning to lead the way inside before any of them had a chance to answer.

Chapter 4

Marjorie Plunkett read through the document again, hoping that something would leap out at her. Whoever was behind this thought themselves terribly clever.

> *Dear little girl so small and sweet,*
> *to meet you would be such a treat,*
> *Soon enough we'll take you away,*
> *I hope that you won't have to stay,*
> *but that all depends on how much they'll pay . . .*

The silly, lilting rhyme hardly sounded threatening at all, and yet the words were absolutely menacing. The phone buzzed, interrupting her train of thought.

Marjorie reached across and pressed the loudspeaker. 'Yes?'

'Excuse me, Ms Plunkett, but I have Agent Treadwell here to see you. She says it's urgent.'

'Give me three minutes then send her in.' Marjorie snapped the file closed and placed it back in the bottom drawer of her desk. She shut the drawer and pressed her thumb against it until she heard the whir of the lock.

'Thank you, Ms Plunkett. Your documents are now safely returned,' a cheery voice informed her.

'Thank you, Fi,' Marjorie said.

The door to her office opened.

'Good afternoon, Agent Treadwell.' Marjorie nodded at the woman as she strode into the room. 'What have you got for me?'

'Afternoon, Chief.' Rowena Treadwell reached inside her coat pocket and handed Marjorie a piece of paper in a plastic envelope. 'They've made contact again.'

'I see.' Marjorie opened a timber box on her desk and pulled out a pair of white gloves. She put them on and then removed the letter from the sleeve. 'How was it received?'

'Same as last time,' Agent Treadwell replied. 'Unmarked envelope, in among the rest of the palace post. There's a stamp but no postmark, so we have no way of knowing where it was sent from.'

Marjorie's heart thumped as she scanned the page. 'All right, leave it with me,' she said calmly.

'Would you rather I take things straight to the lab in future?' Rowena offered.

'Agent Treadwell, I shouldn't have to explain the extremely sensitive nature of this investigation,' Marjorie snapped, her words underlined in ice. 'We don't know exactly what we are dealing with yet, but we do know there is a child at risk. And for some reason, whoever this monster is, they've chosen to involve Her Majesty. Everything comes to me first, do you understand? Everything!'

The tall woman cleared her throat. 'My apologies, Chief.'

'I suggest you go home and get some rest. It's all hands on deck this weekend.'

'Will I be part of the palace detail?' Agent Treadwell asked.

'Yes. You'll receive your instructions at oh-six-hundred,' Marjorie replied.

Rowena Treadwell was about to say something when she stopped herself.

'Is there anything else?' Marjorie looked at the woman.

'So you're really going to marry him, Chief?' Treadwell asked.

Marjorie Plunkett frowned. 'Yes, of course. Why do you ask?'

'Does he know what you do?'

'Absolutely not, and it will stay that way,' Marjorie retorted. 'Do you have a problem with that?'

'Not at all, I'm just in awe,' Agent Treadwell replied. 'I suspect I'll be single for the rest of my life. I wouldn't trust myself – pillow talk and all that.'

Marjorie smiled thinly. She'd imagined the same sort of life for herself until Lloyd had swept her off her feet. Getting married had never been on her agenda, and now here she was planning a wedding and wondering if she might even have children.

Rowena smiled. 'You'll be a beautiful bride, Chief.'

Marjorie's demeanour softened. 'Thank you,

Agent Treadwell. Sorry if I was tetchy earlier. I've got a lot on my mind.'

'I understand. We need to catch this one as soon as possible. She's such a sweet girl. I can't imagine why anyone would want to harm her,' Rowena said.

Marjorie nodded. 'I'm sure they'll slip up soon. See you tomorrow.'

Rowena Treadwell turned on her heel and headed for the door.

'Oh and, Treadwell,' Marjorie called after her.

The woman spun around. 'Yes, Chief?'

'I like the new do,' Marjorie said, patting her head.

'Thank you, Chief. Not sure what I think of it yet but it takes no time to get ready in the morning,' Rowena replied before leaving the room.

Marjorie chided herself for being so hard on Treadwell. The woman was a wonderful asset and had proven herself most reliable over the years. There had been some tension between them when Marjorie had been promoted to Chief three years ago, but Treadwell had come to understand that the best woman had been given the job. Marjorie pressed her thumb against the drawer. It whirred open.

'Hello Chief,' Fiona trilled. 'What may I do for you?'

'I need you to run some tests on this.' Marjorie dropped the letter into the third compartment in her desk drawer.

'Of course, Chief.'

'Thank you, Fi. That will be all for now.' Marjorie closed the drawer and held her thumb against the lock. She took a deep breath and picked up the phone.

'Yes, Chief?'

'Miss Betts, please get Thornton Thripp on the line for me.'

Chapter 5

'Gosh, look at that staircase!' Millie gawped as they followed Mr Langley into the rear entrance foyer. 'I wonder if Aunty Gee would let us have races.'

Vincent Langley recoiled at the idea.

'Perhaps we should save those for the Highton Hall rollercoaster,' Cecelia suggested, noticing the man's reaction. 'Not everyone appreciates their banisters being polished by speeding bottoms.'

'No, ma'am, they most certainly do not,' Mr

Langley said, shaking his head. 'Mrs Wellesley, for one, would not be amused.'

'Who's that?' Alice-Miranda asked.

'The head housekeeper.'

Just as Mr Langley spoke, a dark-haired boy whizzed backwards down the rail. He leapt off before the last step and landed with a thud on the flagstones below. Seconds later an identical lad did exactly the same thing. Without a word, they both charged out the back door.

'Who are they?' Millie asked, her eyes bulging.

'You've just met Edgar and Louis, Her Majesty's youngest grandchildren,' Langley replied flatly.

Hugh grinned. 'Good to see they haven't changed.'

Vincent Langley's lips twitched. 'I can assure you, Mr Kennington-Jones, they haven't changed a bit.'

'Maybe we can challenge them to a race,' Millie whispered to Alice-Miranda.

'That would not be wise,' Mr Langley said.

Millie looked at him in disbelief. The old man had bionic hearing, just like Miss Grimm. 'How come?' she asked.

'Apart from suffering the wrath of Mrs Wellesley,

those boys are quite possibly the two most competitive lads you'll ever meet. They'd take out their own grandmother to win.'

'Sounds like someone else we know.' Millie looked at Alice-Miranda and mouthed Caprice's name.

'How unfortunate,' Mr Langley said, proceeding up the staircase.

The group followed the man up two flights of stairs and down a long corridor to the left.

'Please remember that you are in the West Wing. The children are all in rooms on the right-hand side of the hall and the adults are on the left. Ms Highton-Smith, your mother is in her usual suite on the first floor. Her Majesty said she didn't think you'd mind.'

'Much better having Valentina down there,' Hugh said with a wink. 'Otherwise she'd be up here giving orders and making sure we're not a second late for anything.'

'That's my mother you're talking about, darling,' Cecelia admonished.

'Granny's not bossy, Daddy,' Alice-Miranda said. 'I can't wait to see her.'

'No, she's not bad for a mother-in-law,' Hugh admitted.

'Who's not bad for a mother-in-law?' a voice boomed from behind the group.

'Granny!' Alice-Miranda turned around and raced to the woman, leaping into her arms.

'Oops!' Hugh looked at Millie and pulled a face.

Valentina Highton-Smith gave her granddaughter a kiss and then greeted the rest of the group. She arched an eyebrow at Hugh. 'So, what have I done to upset my formerly favourite son-in-law?'

Hugh held out his arms. 'Formerly favourite? I thought I'd always be your number one, Valentina. Although, I suppose I didn't count on having a movie star as my competition.'

'Good grief,' Vincent Langley muttered under his breath.

'Oh, stop it, Hugh,' Valentina said, flicking her hand. 'You know I can't resist those puppy-dog eyes of yours. Lawrence might be one of the most handsome men on the planet, but you're a pretty close second. Besides, I've known you a lot longer and he's still in the probationary phase.' Valentina embraced the man. 'Speaking of Lawrence, I wonder how far away they are. I'm bursting to see those babies again.'

41

'Excuse me, Ms Highton-Smith, I'd rather like to show you to your rooms if I may.' Vincent Langley tapped his foot impatiently. The man was mentally ticking off some of the hundred and one things left to do before the garden party and he was eager to get back downstairs to see if Braxton Balfour had managed to get through his long list of duties.

'Yes, of course. Sorry to hold you up, Mr Langley,' Cecelia said.

'I'll leave you to settle in then,' Valentina Highton-Smith said. 'I think I'll hunt down a cup of tea before I change for the party. See you all later.'

'Bye, Granny.' Alice-Miranda gave a wave and the others said goodbye too.

Vincent Langley unlocked a door and pushed it open. 'Mr Kennington-Jones, Ms Highton-Smith, this is the Tulip Suite.' He motioned for them to enter. 'Children, would you like to follow me?' Mr Langley asked, turning on his heel. 'Your room is directly opposite, across the hall.'

'I'll go with the girls,' Cecelia said. 'Darling, why don't you have a lie down for half an hour before the garden party?'

'You read my mind, Cee,' Hugh said gratefully.

'What's our room called?' Millie asked.

'It's the Daffodil Suite,' Mr Langley replied. He'd barely opened the door when Millie rushed past him and into the room.

'Whoa!' she exclaimed. 'Look at that ceiling. How did they make all those flowers in the plaster?'

Alice-Miranda smiled. 'Very carefully, I'd say.'

The wallpaper was the softest of yellows and imprinted with a delicate white fleur-de-lis pattern, and there was a huge spray of daffodils in a vase on the wide mahogany dressing table. The room had twin double beds with white duvets, and each bedside table held a lamp with a pale yellow shade in the shape of a daffodil. A pair of floral yellow armchairs with high wingbacks sat either side of the double-hung windows with their billowing striped lemon-coloured curtains.

Alice-Miranda walked over to the window. 'Millie, we can see the hunting tower from here,' she called.

Millie raced over to join her, and the two girls were soon pointing at this and that and making plans about all of the things they wanted to see.

'Shall I leave you to settle in?' Cecelia asked.

Alice-Miranda turned and nodded. 'Mummy, it's all so beautiful. I can't wait until the party.'

'Why don't I come and help you get ready in a little while?' Cecelia suggested.

'The garden party starts at one o'clock,' Mr Langley reminded them. 'Everyone is meeting downstairs in the rear entrance hall at ten to one, and Her Majesty does not appreciate tardiness.'

'Thank you, Mr Langley,' Cecelia said. She turned back and grimaced at the girls, before following him out the door.

'Goodbye, Mr Langley, we'll see you soon,' Alice-Miranda called out, and Millie gave a wave, but the man did not respond.

'Someone got out on the wrong side of the bed,' Millie remarked as she ran her fingers along the top of a cherry-wood writing desk. 'He reminds me of Mr Winterstone from the *Octavia* but with better hair. Well, not really better, just *more* hair – except that he obviously dyes it. I think grey would look much better than that purple-black colour.'

Alice-Miranda grinned. 'Please don't tell him that. Remember what happened when Jacinta asked Mr Winterstone about his hair? The poor man looked as if he'd never recover,' she said. 'And Mr Winterstone turned out to be lovely in the end.'

'Well, I think Mr Langley takes his job *way* too seriously. He could smile once in a while. I mean, if I lived here, my face would be aching from smiling so much. That other butler – the under one – seemed a lot more friendly. Anyway, bags this bed.' Millie executed a high scissor kick, landing on the mattress with a bounce. She laid back on the pillow with her hands behind her head, gazing at the intricate ceiling detail. 'I still can't believe we're really here,' she sighed.

'It's pretty amazing, isn't it?' Alice-Miranda sat on the edge of her own bed and looked around the suite.

There was a sharp knock on the door. Alice-Miranda leapt up to open it.

'That's strange,' she said, finding no one there. She poked her head into the empty corridor. Just as she closed the door there was another sharp rap. She opened it again.

Millie hopped off her bed and walked over. 'Who is it?'

'No one.' Alice-Miranda closed the door and frowned.

Millie's eyes widened. 'Maybe it's a . . . ghost.'

'Millie, you know there are no such –' Alice-Miranda was interrupted by another knock on the door.

'Hey, it sounds like it's coming from in there.' Millie pointed and ran to the dressing-room. Alice-Miranda followed her.

The room had built-in drawers on either side and a circular gold velvet love seat which occupied the centre of the floor. In the middle of the far wall sat a large wardrobe. Millie wrenched open the door and discovered a small bolted door behind the hanging rail. It didn't even come halfway up the back of the cupboard and looked as if it had been built for a child.

Alice-Miranda peered over Millie's shoulder.

'What do you think? Narnia?' Millie turned and looked at Alice-Miranda before she slid back the lock.

Suddenly, the door burst open and Jacinta tumbled through, almost sending Millie flying.

Alice-Miranda giggled. 'Well, at least it's not a ghost or the White Witch.'

Sloane poked her head through the opening and crawled into the wardrobe, falling out most ungracefully onto the lemon-coloured carpet. 'Oh, that's disappointing,' she sighed. 'It's just you two.'

'Believe me, we were hoping for something more interesting too,' Millie retorted.

Alice-Miranda bent down to help the girl up. 'How long have you been here?' she asked them.

'About an hour,' Jacinta replied. 'Mummy was so excited, we left as soon as we finished breakfast.'

'Come and have a look at our room,' Alice-Miranda said, beckoning the girls to follow.

The girls walked out of the dressing-room and into the bedroom.

'It's exactly the same as ours, just the other way around, and ours has roses all over it instead of daffo-dils,' Jacinta said.

'And there's lots of pink instead of yellow,' Sloane added. 'It beats Grimthorpe House any day!'

'Just a bit,' Millie said. 'Have you been to the garden yet?'

Jacinta and Sloane shook their heads.

'We've had a bit of a look around this floor but we didn't want to go downstairs,' Jacinta explained. 'That scary butler, Mr Langley, told us that we'd have to pay for any damages and pointed out some priceless vase he said had been in the family for centuries. We didn't want to risk it.'

They were interrupted by another knock, but this time Alice-Miranda knew exactly where it was coming from. She ran to the bedroom door and opened it. 'Aunt Charlotte!' she cried. 'Uncle Lawrence!'

Charlotte Highton-Smith scooped her niece into her arms and peppered the girl's face with kisses. Lawrence Ridley bent down and hugged Alice-Miranda once she was back on the ground.

'Hello Millie, Jacinta, Sloane, it's lovely to see you all.' Charlotte smiled at the girls.

'Yes, good to see you all,' Lawrence said and gave a wave.

Alice-Miranda peered behind them. 'Where are the babies?'

'They're in our room, being watched over by two dutiful young men,' Lawrence nodded.

'Have you got footmen babysitting for you?' Sloane asked.

Lawrence grinned. 'Not quite. Your brother and Lucas volunteered their services.'

'Whoa, you're brave,' Sloane said. 'I don't think Sep's ever looked after a baby in his life.'

'He was doing very well for a beginner,' Lawrence

said. 'And as for Lucas, he's more gaga over them than I am, which I didn't think possible.'

Jacinta almost swooned at the thought of Lucas holding a baby. 'Lucas will be such a wonderful father one day.'

The girls giggled.

'When he's much older, of course,' Jacinta added quickly.

'Would you like to meet them?' Charlotte asked.

Alice-Miranda nodded. 'Yes, please. Can we all come?'

'Absolutely,' Charlotte said. 'But you'll have to be quiet. They're still sleepy.'

'Just the way I like them,' Lawrence Ridley said with a wink.

Chapter 6

The girls followed Charlotte and Lawrence down the hallway to their room. Lawrence held open the door as the girls and Charlotte filed in. A double pram was sitting in the middle of the room with Lucas and Sep standing over it, gazing at the babies.

'Hi Lucas,' Jacinta said, much more loudly than she'd intended.

The boy turned around and pressed a finger to his lips.

Jacinta blushed. 'Sorry.'

The girls walked over and peered into the pram.

'They're adorable,' Millie whispered.

'She looks just like you, Alice-Miranda,' Sloane said, pointing at the baby in a white jumpsuit with a pink trim.

Sep nodded. 'That's what we were saying. Imagine how cute it will be when she's a bit bigger. You'll have your own mini-me, Alice-Miranda.'

The children huddled around the infants, mesmerised by their tiny faces with rosebud lips and creamy skin.

'I think Marcus is waking up, Aunt Charlotte,' Alice-Miranda said as the little boy stretched his arms, his face contorting.

The children watched and waited to see if he'd open his eyes but his face just went red and his eyes remained shut.

'Pooh-wee!' Millie held her nose. 'I think he's done something evil.'

The other kids laughed.

'Bags not changing the nappy,' Sloane said, screwing up her face.

'I'll do it,' Lucas volunteered.

'Really?' Jacinta looked at him quizzically. 'You'll change his nappy?'

The boy shrugged. 'I have to learn sometime and I might as well practise on my baby brother.'

Jacinta sighed. Lucas would make an even better father than she'd first thought.

'Come on, then.' Lawrence leaned in and picked up the baby boy. 'Looks like it's us men on duty.'

Sep shook his head. 'Not me. I think I'll stay here if you don't mind.'

Charlotte and Lawrence didn't just have one room – they had a sitting room, where the children were gathered, and a bedroom through a set of double doors. There was a huge king-size bed for Charlotte and Lawrence, and twin cots for the babies.

Charlotte looked at Alice-Miranda. 'Would you like to hold Imogen?'

The girl's eyes widened. 'Could I?'

'I have to get her up for a feed before the party and I'd best make a start,' Charlotte said, reaching into the pram. She lifted the infant into her arms. 'Why don't you go and sit on the chair over there and you can all have a turn?'

The girls and Sep walked over to a large rocking chair and Alice-Miranda sat down. Charlotte placed baby Imogen into her arms.

'She's so little.' Alice-Miranda kissed the girl's downy forehead.

'You were even smaller when you were born,' Charlotte remarked.

'Really? I can't imagine it.' Alice-Miranda admired the tiny baby, breathing in her scent. 'I love her so much I think my heart is going to burst.'

Charlotte rested her hand on Alice-Miranda's shoulder. 'I know she'll adore you too, darling girl.'

Alice-Miranda wanted to hold her forever but Millie, Jacinta and Sloane were keen to have their turns. As she was passed around all of the children, baby Imogen slowly began to wake up, opening her eyes every few minutes before drifting back to sleep again.

'Well, that was gross,' Lucas said, walking out of the bedroom holding Marcus. 'Don't ask me to do it again.'

Charlotte smiled. 'You offered, remember?'

'I didn't realise that something so small could make such a disgusting mess,' the boy replied, clearly horrified by the experience.

Charlotte looked at Lawrence. 'Was it really nasty?'

'Nasty is an understatement, Char. Most of it wasn't even in the nappy and, just to top it off, he let loose on me with the sprinkler.' Lawrence grinned.

'Eww.' Jacinta and Sloane wrinkled their noses.

'But he is pretty cute,' Lucas said as Marcus's tiny fingers wrapped around his pinkie.

Lawrence nodded. 'Yes, I think we'll probably keep him.'

Charlotte glanced at her watch. 'Oh, goodness, it's a quarter past twelve. Sorry, darlings, but I need to start feeding these two,' she said, settling herself into the rocking chair with Imogen. 'It's a marathon effort and I don't want to miss all of the festivities.'

'Thanks for letting us meet the babies,' Jacinta said.

The children said their goodbyes and made their way to the door.

'Oh, and Alice-Miranda,' Lawrence called, 'I think you're up for nappy-changing duties next time.'

The girl turned and grinned. 'I don't mind. They could make the biggest, smelliest mess ever and I'd still love them to pieces.'

Chapter 7

The man opened the top drawer and took out a pair of thin white gloves. He carefully pulled them on then picked up a pair of scissors. It was a tedious business but it had to be done. He read over the words before he began to cut letters from the pages of the newspaper.

Soon enough *The Beacon* looked like something from a kindergarten craft class. He'd had it sent from the other side of the country so, even if they were able to trace the origins of this particular edition, there was nothing to lead them to him.

He hummed quietly to himself as he cut out the letters with military precision. There was a strange meditative quality to the whole thing. He arranged the letters on the blank page and unwound the glue stick. Then he carefully pasted each letter until the page was full. This time the words were fiercer, the threat more forceful. They had to be – there was a lot at stake.

A child so sweet and young and fair,
her spirit free, without a care.
Hugh and Cecelia must not know,
nor anyone else, or my wrath will grow.
I imagine you'd like to know what I seek.
Hold tight, old dear, you'll know next week!

A smug smile settled on his lips as he surveyed his work. He hadn't written poetry in years but it had always been something he'd excelled at. He threw the newspaper in the hearth, then struck a match and watched the pages burn.

He walked back to the desk and folded the letter carefully before placing it in an envelope. But he didn't seal it yet. He flicked open the locks on his briefcase and pulled three photographs from the rear compartment. He added them to the envelope and sealed it with his first mistake.

Chapter 8

'This is a much more adventurous approach to the garden,' Braxton Balfour said as he led the children through a tightly woven tunnel of trees. 'I just discovered it recently myself.'

'Have you been here long, Mr Balfour?' Alice-Miranda asked the man.

'A couple of months. I was previously a footman at Brackenhurst before I was promoted to the role of under butler here at Evesbury.'

'Congratulations!' Alice-Miranda smiled at him. 'Do you think you might be in charge one day?'

'Well, you never know. I suppose that's what I'm hoping for.' The man looked a little sheepish. 'Better not tell Mr Langley, though. I don't think he's ready to retire just yet.'

Alice-Miranda nodded. 'Don't worry, Mr Balfour, I won't say a word.'

The man grinned.

'Wow!' Jacinta exclaimed as the group emerged onto a viewing platform that overlooked an enormous sunken garden.

Large expanses of lawn were framed and crisscrossed by hedge-lined paths dotted with exquisite marble statues. In the centre of it all, a giant fountain guarded by four marble lions spouted water high into the blue sky. At the opposite end, a Palladian summer house was swarming with guests and waiters in black tail coats, carrying trays of drinks and delicious treats.

Braxton Balfour caught sight of Mr Langley glaring at him from down below. 'I should leave you now. Have a lovely afternoon, children.'

'Thank you for bringing us, Mr Balfour,' Alice-Miranda said.

'It was my pleasure.' The man gave a bow before he turned and walked back up the path.

The children stared out into the crowd. Alice-Miranda spotted her parents talking to Ambrosia Headlington-Bear, and waved.

'It's all so beautiful,' Sloane sighed happily.

Jacinta pointed to a woman's hat. 'Is that an umbrella on her head?'

'Jacinta!' Alice-Miranda chided, giggling.

'You have to admit it will come in very handy if it starts to rain,' Jacinta teased. 'I think we could all fit under there.'

Millie raised her camera and clicked away at the men dressed in top hats and tails, and the women in a kaleidoscope of pretty dresses, hats and gloves. The child paused and glanced down at her own mint-green ensemble, wondering if it was up to scratch.

'I love your dress, Millie,' Alice-Miranda commented, noticing her friend's hesitation. 'It's perfect.'

'Do you really think so?' Millie asked.

Alice-Miranda nodded. 'Of course.'

Her own dress was the palest of pinks with a delicate floral pattern. Jacinta was in powder-blue, and Sloane had decided on a yellow outfit. Together, they looked like a rainbow of pastels.

'I don't know about everyone else but I'm starving,' Sep said as he spied a plate of food circulating just below them. He led the way towards one of the two sets of stairs that fanned out from either side of the platform.

Sep and Lucas made a beeline for the waiter.

'You have to try these,' Lucas said to the girls while munching on a miniature pie. 'They're amazing.'

The children all reached in and the waiter handed each of them a tiny white napkin that bore the initials 'GR' in gold.

'Mmm.' Millie smacked her lips together. 'These are delicious.'

The group wandered further into the garden with Lucas charging ahead, eager to explore every inch of it.

'Hey, look at this,' he called out. In the middle of one of the outer walls, Lucas had found an opening to what looked like a cave. He could hear the sound of running water coming from within.

The children ran to catch up. Just as they were heading for the entrance, a statuesque woman in a white lace dress stepped out from a side path to block their way. She wore a wide-brimmed hat trimmed with the same delicate fabric and was on the arm of a tall, handsome man.

'You're not going in there, are you?' she barked.

Alice-Miranda and her friends looked at the woman, startled.

'It's just that it might not be safe,' the woman said, her voice softening.

'Marjorie, leave the poor children alone,' the man said, frowning at her. 'I'm sure there's nothing to be afraid of.'

Alice-Miranda smiled at the couple and held out her hand towards the man. 'Hello, I'm Alice-Miranda Highton-Smith-Kennington-Jones.'

'Oh, you're Hugh and Cee's little girl.' The man reached out and took her tiny hand into his. 'I'm Lloyd Lancaster-Brown and this is my worrywart fiancée, Marjorie Plunkett.'

'It's lovely to meet you both.' Alice-Miranda was thrilled to meet a member of the Lancaster-Brown family, and introduced her friends to the couple.

'Charmed,' Marjorie said stiffly. She turned to Lucas. 'You're Lawrence Ridley's son, aren't you?'

The boy nodded, wondering how she knew that since he and his father didn't share the same surname. 'How do you know Her Majesty?' he asked.

'Oh, I'm just a distant relative,' Lloyd replied.

'Hardly distant, darling,' Marjorie leapt in. 'Lloyd's a cousin of Queen Georgiana's. His grandfather and Her Majesty's father were brothers.'

Alice-Miranda's eyes grew wide. 'Was King George your grandfather?'

'Yes,' the man said with surprise, 'but how on earth would you know that?'

'I was reading something in the library recently about King George and how he abdicated to marry your grandmother Evelyn,' the child explained.

'Why did he do that?' Millie asked.

'Marry my grandmother?' Lloyd said with a cheeky grin. 'Oh, the old girl wasn't that bad. Then again, come to think of it . . .'

Millie laughed, shaking her head. 'No, why did he have to abdicate to marry her?'

Sloane frowned. 'I'm confused. What's abdicate mean?'

'It's when a king or queen stands aside and gives up their claim to the throne,' Alice-Miranda explained.

Lloyd nodded. 'Yes, that's exactly right. My

grandfather abdicated because my grandmother had been married before, and back then divorce was frowned upon,' he said. 'Grandmama Evelyn was the love of his life, although I always found her a little bit on the scary side.'

'So if your grandfather hadn't abdicated, would you be King now?' Jacinta asked, trying to work out the royal line in her head.

Marjorie nodded. 'Lloyd's father was the eldest son and he passed away some time ago, so you're right – Lloyd would have been King.'

'Cool,' Lucas said.

Lloyd grimaced. 'All those visits to factories and hospitals are not my thing at all. I'd much rather leave it to Cousin Gee.'

'At least you know exactly the right things to say and do at these parties,' Millie said.

'Oh, not at all.' Lloyd chuckled, shaking his head. 'Even after all these years I never know what to talk about or who I might offend. It's a bit of a minefield.'

Millie smiled with relief. 'I'm glad I'm not the only one who gets confused. I think there should be a guide to curtsying. I accidentally curtsied to one of the maids before, but she didn't seem to mind.'

'Perhaps you can give me some lessons in curt-sying,' Lloyd teased. 'I'm horrible at it. I wobble hopelessly.'

Millie giggled.

'Don't be so silly, Lloyd,' Marjorie rebuked. 'Of course you enjoy these parties. Who wouldn't?'

'It is fun to get dressed up,' Alice-Miranda agreed.

'How long are you staying at the palace?' Lloyd asked the group.

'Just until tomorrow,' Alice-Miranda said.

'I wish we could stay all week,' Millie added.

Marjorie smiled at the girls. 'Oh, well, you never know . . .'

'I would love to see the hunting tower,' Lucas admitted.

Sloane nodded. 'And everything else. I bet there are secret places all over the estate.'

Marjorie frowned. That very same thought had begun to dawn on her too.

'I used to play in the tower as a boy,' Lloyd said, staring into the distance. 'But it's been abandoned for years. I haven't been back there since . . .'

Marjorie looked at her fiancé. 'Since when?'

Lloyd shook his head, as if banishing a memory. 'It doesn't matter, dear.'

Marjorie wished he'd say something. It was awfully hard pretending she didn't know things sometimes.

'I don't think we're going to have much time to go exploring,' Alice-Miranda said.

Lloyd nodded. 'Perhaps on another visit, then.'

'There probably won't be another one, so we should make the most of being here now,' Millie said, brightening up. She pulled her camera out of the little handbag that was slung across her shoulder. 'Would you mind taking a picture of us?'

'Oh, that's a lovely camera, Millie,' Marjorie said. She'd hoped that one of the children would have one.

Lloyd reached out to take it from Millie but Marjorie intercepted him. 'Darling, you know you're terrible at taking photographs,' she scolded. 'I can do it.'

The children organised themselves into a huddle and smiled as the woman snapped away.

'Hang on, it's a bit glary,' Marjorie said, checking the screen. 'I'll just make sure they're as good as I think they are.'

She turned away from the others and, quick as a flash, pulled a small silver object from her handbag.

She popped open the battery case and within seconds had replaced the original battery with the one from her bag. She swivelled back to the children and passed the camera to Millie.

'They're perfect,' Marjorie said with a smile. She placed a hand on Lloyd's arm. 'Come along, darling. I've just spotted Lord Tavistock, and I'd like to ask him if he'd be emcee at the wedding.'

'Tavistock? Really?' Lloyd said, rolling his eyes. 'I'd much rather stay here.'

The children giggled as Marjorie hustled him away.

'Come and rescue me later,' he whispered over his shoulder.

Alice-Miranda nodded. 'We will.'

'I wonder why Miss Plunkett was so worried about us going into the grotto,' Sloane said, once the couple was out of earshot.

Millie and Jacinta shrugged. 'She looks like she's forgotten about it now,' Jacinta said.

'He seems like a great guy,' Sep said.

'And she's gorgeous,' Sloane added wistfully. 'Mummy would hate her.'

Chapter 9

A hand emerged from the bushes and tapped Lord Luttrell on the shoulder before quickly retreating into the hedge. The fellow turned around, smiling, expecting to see someone he knew. He paused, confused to find no one there, then shrugged and returned to his drink. Just as he took a large gulp, the hand darted out again and tapped him on the opposite shoulder. This time he sputtered and showered champagne all over the woman in front of him.

'Hubert, what on earth?' his wife shrieked. She glared at him as she dabbed her sodden apricot-coloured frock with her napkin.

'I'm sorry, Lisbeth. Someone touched me on the shoulder and startled me. I didn't mean it.'

'You must be imagining things.' His wife craned her neck to see over his shoulder. 'There's no one there.'

'But I felt it,' he whined.

A few metres away, Lucas and the rest of the group were about to explore the cave.

'Are you coming, Alice-Miranda?' Millie asked, noticing the girl hadn't moved. She squinted into the distance to see what her friend was looking at.

When Alice-Miranda saw the hand poke out of the hedge for a third time, she leapt into action, charging down the path and intercepting the offending limb.

'Hey!' a voice shouted as Alice-Miranda grasped the hand and yanked it from the bushes.

The victim spun around. 'What's all this?'

'I'm sorry, sir, but I think you've been the brunt of a practical joke.' Alice-Miranda held up the contraption – a long stick with a stuffed black glove attached to one end. She scanned the bushes for its owner.

'Good heavens, that's the last thing I'd expect to happen here,' Lady Luttrell said, still mopping up the front of her dress. 'Who on earth is responsible for such mischief?'

Millie, Jacinta, Sloane, Sep and Lucas ran to see what Alice-Miranda was up to. Just as they reached her, Aunty Gee approached from the other end of the path. She was flanked by Mrs Marmalade on one side, and Archie and Petunia on the other.

'Good afternoon, Hubert, Lisbeth, children. It's lovely to see you all. I do hope you're enjoying yourselves.'

There was a flurry of curtsies and bows.

'Hello Aunty Gee.' Alice-Miranda smiled at her.

Queen Georgiana leaned down and embraced the girl, kissing the top of her head.

Alice-Miranda grinned at Her Majesty's furry companions. 'Who are you two?' The child crouched down to pat the beagles.

'This is Archie and Petunia. They are a little wary of children, but perhaps that's just my grand-children.' The Queen pointed to the stick with the gloved hand. 'What's that you've got there, dear?'

'I think someone's been playing tricks on your

guests,' Alice-Miranda said, holding the hand upright.

There was a rustle in the hedge. Archie and Petunia shot off towards the greenery, barking.

A deep row of lines furrowed across Queen Georgiana's brow. 'That had better not be my missing Hermès glove, or two boys I know will be spending the rest of the weekend mucking out the stables. Edgar, Louis, come out of there right this minute!'

The hedge rustled again and two boys slunk out from behind the bushes. Their black suits were covered in leaves, and twigs were sticking out of their wild hair.

'Goodness me,' Queen Georgiana growled as loudly as the dogs. 'Archie, Petunia, heel,' she commanded, and the two pooches ran and sat behind their mistress.

The lads said nothing, but it was obvious they were working hard to suppress smirks.

'How old are you now?' Queen Georgiana demanded.

'Fourteen,' they answered in perfect unison.

'Old enough to know better.' Her Majesty shook her head. 'I believe you owe Lord and Lady Luttrell an apology.'

'It was just a joke,' one of the boys muttered.

'We didn't hurt anyone,' the other boy added sullenly.

Lady Luttrell pointed at the wet patches on her dress. 'Well, I'm not very happy about this.'

Millie smothered a grin. She wouldn't have been either if she was wearing such an ugly dress.

'Oh, Lisbeth, I hadn't realised,' Queen Georgiana said. 'You boys are incorrigible. And I thought your sisters were bad when they were younger. I can't say I'm sorry that they're all away studying at the moment, but at least they seem to be growing into decent human beings. I can only hope that one day you might do the same.'

'Sorry, Grandmama,' the boys said flatly.

'Don't apologise to *me*.' Queen Georgiana glared at the lads and nodded at Lord and Lady Luttrell.

The boys reluctantly mumbled some words of regret.

'I'll look after that, Alice-Miranda.' The Queen took the stick and passed it to Mrs Marmalade, whose face was set into a very nasty scowl.

'What am I supposed to do with it?' the woman muttered under her breath.

Queen Georgiana frowned at her. 'I'm sure

you'll think of something. Come along, Lisbeth. I'll organise for a dress in your size. Boys, I suggest you stay out of trouble, or that threat to muck out the stables will very quickly come true.'

Alice-Miranda had only just met the twins, but something told her that those two would not be staying out of trouble for long.

Once the adults were safely away, one of the twins looked accusingly at Alice-Miranda. 'Thanks for that.'

'Do you know how long it took to work out how to attach that glove to the stick so it looked real?' the other boy added.

'I'm sorry to have ruined your game,' Alice-Miranda replied. 'It just didn't seem like a very nice trick, especially when Lady Luttrell ended up covered in champagne.'

'Who made you the fun police?' the first boy huffed.

The pair were the most identical twins Alice-Miranda had ever seen. They had thick heads of curly dark hair and blue-black eyes, were exactly the same height and wore completely matching outfits. She wondered how anyone could ever tell them apart.

'I'm sure there are plenty of things you can do that won't involve upsetting the guests,' Alice-Miranda said.

The first boy rolled his eyes. 'How dull.'

'Who are you lot, anyway, and how come *you're* at the palace?' his brother asked.

'I think we were invited because your grand-mother is godmother to my stepmother and step-aunt,' Lucas said.

One of the boys wrinkled his lip. 'Why haven't we ever seen you before, then?'

'I'm not sure,' Alice-Miranda answered, 'but we've spent lots of time with your grandmother in the past year or so, just not here. She hosted Aunt Charlotte's wedding onboard the *Octavia* and it was lovely to see her at the village fair. Her horse, Rockstar, and my pony, Bonaparte, have a bit of a bromance going on. I thi–'

'So *you're* the famous Alice-Miranda?' the boy on the right said disdainfully.

'I'm certainly not famous but, yes, I am Alice-Miranda,' the girl replied. 'It's lovely to meet you. I presume one of you is Edgar and the other is Louis but I'm afraid I don't –'

'That explains a lot then,' one of the lads said.

His brother nodded. 'It sure does.'

'What's that supposed to mean?' Millie asked. She didn't like their tone one bit.

'Grandmama is *always* talking about her.' The boy waved his hand dismissively. 'Alice-Miranda *this* and Alice-Miranda *that*, and if only you were as well behaved as Alice-Miranda and her goody-goody, snot-nosed, brat-faced friends.'

'I can imagine Aunty Gee saying that about Alice-Miranda,' Sloane said, 'but does she really say that about the rest of us?'

'I think they're joking, Sloane,' Millie whispered.

'Aunty Gee?' one of the boys scoffed. 'You know she's not really your aunt. She's the Queen and you should call her "Your Majesty". Seriously, who do you think you are?'

'A bunch of jumped-up little commoners, if you ask me,' his brother said.

'Who are *you* calling commoners?' Millie demanded, outraged.

'You!' The boy glared at her.

'Your grandmother asked us to call her Aunty Gee,' Jacinta retorted. 'And it would be impolite not to call Her Majesty by the name she requested.'

'Listen to you, Miss Goody-Two-Shoes,' one of the boys taunted.

'Me? I think you've got that wrong,' Jacinta replied. 'I used to be known as our school's second-best tantrum thrower.'

'Yeah right,' the boy sneered.

Jacinta nodded. 'It's true. I had some of the biggest tantrums you're ever likely to see and I was almost expelled from school too.'

Lucas reached out and touched Jacinta on the arm. 'But you're not like that anymore.'

'Come on, Jacinta. I'm hungry and I think I saw Aunt Charlotte and Uncle Lawrence arriving with the babies,' Alice-Miranda said. The last thing they needed was a scene.

One of the boys stepped out to block their path. 'You're not going anywhere.'

'You need to pay us back for ruining our game,' his brother agreed.

Alice-Miranda folded her arms. 'Well, that's just silly.'

The two boys looked at each other. Then one of them turned and pointed at Jacinta. 'She has to throw a tantrum,' he said, 'so that everyone sees.'

'What?' Jacinta frowned. 'No, I don't.'

'Yes, you do,' the boys snapped at the same time.

Lucas put an arm around Jacinta. 'Just leave her alone.'

'You can't tell us what to do,' Louis spat.

'Edgar! Louis!'

The group turned to see a rotund blonde woman rushing down the path towards them. She looked as if she'd raided a game reserve, with her zebra-print dress, leopard-print hat and a crocodile-skin handbag and shoes.

'I've been looking for you everywhere,' she puffed.

The two boys' shoulders drooped and their faces fell. 'Hello Mother,' they said in unison.

The woman peered past the twins at Alice-Miranda and the other children. 'Oh, have you made some new friends?'

The boys looked at each other and gave a half-nod.

'As if,' Jacinta muttered.

Alice-Miranda stepped forward. 'Hello, I'm Alice-Miranda Highton-Smith-Kennington-Jones,' she said, then proceeded to introduce the rest of the group.

'I'm Edgar and Louis' mother, Elsa. I'm so pleased the boys have met you all. They spend far too much time together, and I'm afraid that's not always a good thing.' She turned her attention back to her sons. 'The look your grandmother gave me a few moments ago – I was almost certain you were in some sort of trouble. You should come and say hello to Aunt Valentina and the rest of Granny's friends, or you'll definitely be in the bad books.'

'We should go and say hello to Granny too,' Alice-Miranda piped up, seizing the opportunity to escape.

'Oh, of course. Valentina's your grandmother. She's always had such a soft spot for my children. Anyway, it's lovely to meet you all. Look, there's Prunella Spencer. Prunella!' Elsa hurried over to a woman in a red-and-white polka-dot ensemble.

Alice-Miranda smiled. She couldn't remember Granny ever having a soft spot for Aunty Gee's grandchildren. In fact, she was sure it was quite the opposite. Her grandmother had often delighted in telling terrible stories about the older girls and the twins. Granny Valentina said that Aunty Gee avoided inviting her son Freddy and his wife Elsa and their brood of seven to anything as often as she could. Alice-Miranda had always wondered if Granny was exaggerating, but now she wasn't so sure.

'Just to be clear, we're not your friends,' Millie said.

'Ditto,' the twins chorused.

Chapter 10

Braxton Balfour looked at his watch. By his calculations he'd have just enough time to drive to the cottage and back before the afternoon games, provided the parcel was ready. He rushed down the path, through the woodland glade and across the lawns to the courtyard and then down to the kitchen, where he picked up the hamper that was waiting by the door.

He dashed to the garages behind the stables and jumped into a tiny red hatchback, then tore off down the driveway. As the crow flew, the cottage was just up and over the ridge, nestled in the valley below and shielded by a dense thicket. But on the ground it was a forty-five-minute round trip that involved negotiating six locked farm gates. There were days when Braxton happily made the trek over the hill, but not today. Mr Langley was already in a foul mood and the man didn't need any more excuses to bay for Braxton's blood.

It all began a month ago, when Vincent Langley had spent a short stint in hospital for an emergency appendectomy. Mrs Marmalade had taken Braxton with her to the cottage one afternoon and had given him explicit instructions to pick up a package from the gate every Saturday. He was to tell no one and, in return, Her Majesty would look favourably upon him. The trouble was that it had been a job previously assigned to Mr Langley, and it didn't go down too well when the head butler returned to service and discovered that a former role of his had been usurped. Though Langley never said as much, it was obvious he resented the younger man.

He frequently made outrageous demands on Braxton's time, often requiring that he complete jobs well after the rest of the household had gone to bed. But Braxton was determined not to let it get to him. He had wanted to be the Queen's butler ever since a very special visitor had taken tea with his parents when he was a boy. Langley was getting on, and although he said he didn't plan to retire anytime soon, Braxton was sure Her Majesty would insist upon it one of these days.

Braxton drove as quickly as he dared, hopping out to open and close the gates. He hoped the parcel would be there. If it wasn't, when he'd have time to go back later was anyone's guess, given that Langley had him on games duties in addition to finalising preparations for the ball.

He parked the car in the usual place next to the oak tree with a giant knotted branch and walked to the edge of an overgrown garden. To the naked eye the undergrowth was impenetrable, but Braxton knew where the vines gave up their stranglehold and pushed his way through. Once on the other side, the grounds opened up to a surprisingly pristine cottage that was bordered by a low stone wall.

There was something odd about the whole picture but Braxton had long ago come to understand that it was not his place to ask questions. He didn't even have an inkling about the contents of the packages he collected, nor of the inhabitants of the cottage. As a butler of the highest order, his job was to do as he was bid and ensure complete confidentiality.

Braxton walked over to the gate and looked inside the rusted metal cabinet. Annoyed to find the parcel wasn't inside, he paused to consider what to do next. Mrs Marmalade had been very clear that he was never to approach the house or try to talk to the inhabitants, but this was an emergency. If Braxton didn't get back soon, Langley would string him up.

'Is anyone home?' he called from the gate. 'I have to take the parcel to Her Majesty and I really don't have time to come back later.'

Braxton scanned the grounds then glanced up at the roof, where a beady-eyed raven was glaring at him. It was often there. He wondered if whoever lived inside had befriended the creature.

'Hello?' Braxton called out again.

He thought he could hear coughing coming from inside the cottage. It wasn't a small cough either, rather a desperate hacking that he didn't like the sound of at all. He waited and listened, then did something he'd been instructed never to do. Braxton opened the garden gate. He hesitated, holding the basket in his hand. What if the person inside was choking? He'd never forgive himself. Braxton ran towards the porch.

The raven dived at him, flapping and cawing, its beak snapping like castanets. Braxton fought it off, his arms flailing as he smacked it away. He dropped the basket on the path, its contents spilling everywhere. But the creature persisted. It came at him again and again, striking Braxton's cheek.

Braxton took one last swipe at the bird and pushed open the front door, slamming it hard behind him. A single shiny black feather fluttered down inside the hall.

'Where are you?' Braxton called urgently, his eyes scanning the hallway with its narrow staircase. The house was now eerily quiet. He turned to his right and saw a woman slumped on the floor of the sitting room, a bowl of nuts scattered beside her.

Braxton rushed over and picked her up like a rag doll, her long brown curls spilling behind her. The woman's dark eyes begged as she struggled for breath. He spun her around and laid her over his knee, bringing his hand down hard, striking her between the shoulderblades. All of a sudden a large walnut flew across the room, pinging against the glass-fronted bookcase on the wall.

Braxton stopped and turned her around to face him. He held her in his arms as he watched the colour slowly return to her ashen face. Then he gently set her down on a sofa. He couldn't help staring as a memory tugged at the corners of his mind.

'Water?' Braxton asked, giving a small sigh.

The woman shook her head.

'But you need something to drink,' he said softly. 'I thought you were going to die.'

Braxton decided the kitchen would likely be down the end of the hall at the rear of the cottage. He began to walk towards the door but the woman quickly gathered herself together and ran to block his path.

She held up her hand and motioned for him to stay where he was. Braxton did as he was bid, at the same time realising that just being inside the cottage could land him in desperate trouble.

The woman scurried down the hall and disappeared through a doorway at the end. Braxton could hear a tap running. He glanced back into the front room. Two comfortable-looking sofas sat at right angles to one another, while two matching timber bookcases sat in perfect symmetry beside an open fireplace with beautiful ceramic tiles. Braxton hadn't known what to expect when he entered the cottage, but this house could have been anywhere, on any street, in any village. Neat and well cared for, he couldn't understand why it was so deliberately hidden. For some reason he'd always imagined it would be untidy and cluttered, and quite simply strange.

Braxton spotted a small scrap of material on the floor and bent to pick it up. He studied its pretty peacock pattern, wondering what it was doing there. When the woman reappeared holding a brown paper package, he quickly stuffed the material into his pocket and took the parcel from her. It was the same size as every other one he'd ever collected, with almost no weight to it at all.

She glanced up at Braxton, studying his face.

'It's nothing,' Braxton said, touching his bloodied cheek. 'I'd better get going.'

'Wait,' the woman whispered, her voice catching in her throat. She raced away again and this time returned with a cloth and a small basin of water that smelt powerfully of antiseptic. She reached up and gently dabbed at the scratches on Braxton's face.

The man flinched. 'I know I'm not supposed to come past the gate. I promise not to tell anyone, but just so you know, I'm Braxton Balfour and I'm one of Her Majesty's butlers.' For a fleeting moment, their eyes locked and Braxton realised something. 'Lydie?' The name floated from his lips on the softest of breaths.

She looked at him like a lost child.

'Is your name Lydie?' he asked again.

She nodded.

'Don't you remember me?' Braxton frowned, his eyes searching her face for a glimmer of recognition.

She shook her head.

The way she stared at him, Braxton felt as if he were a ghost. There were so many questions. 'What happened to you?' he asked.

'Please go,' she whispered. 'I don't know you.'

'I'm sorry. I didn't mean to upset you,' Braxton said, backing away.

The moment he opened the front door, the raven flew past him into the hallway, where it perched on the woman's shoulder. Bewildered, Braxton stumbled down the path, past the basket and its spilled contents, and didn't once look back.

Lydie stood in the doorway, staring out. 'Who is he, Lucien?' she said, stroking the bird on her shoulder. 'And why can't I remember?'

Chapter 11

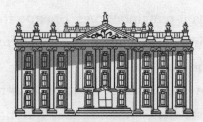

The children took turns wheeling the babies around the garden and soon enough they forgot about Louis and Edgar. They concentrated on exploring as much as they could and even revisited the grotto. It turned out to be an artificial cave decorated with the most beautiful mosaics they'd ever seen. Several little bridges led the way over a moat to a central island with an ornate wooden table and chairs. The children had found it charming and not scary at all, and Millie thought it would make the perfect picnic spot on a warm day.

Later on, while Jacinta, Sloane, Sep and Lucas were being introduced around by Ambrosia, Millie and Alice-Miranda took the babies for a final lap of the secret garden. As the pair rounded the end of the path they noticed Marjorie Plunkett disappearing into the grotto.

'What do you think she's going in there for?' Millie asked. 'She seemed pretty worried about us taking a look earlier.'

Alice-Miranda shrugged. 'I imagine she's just curious, like we were.'

'Perhaps she's having a romantic rendezvous with her fiancé.' Millie giggled.

As the girls drew closer to the grotto they could hear voices.

Millie stopped on the path to listen. 'That doesn't sound very romantic.'

'Come on, Millie,' Alice-Miranda whispered. 'It's none of our business.'

Millie knew that her friend was right but there was something about Marjorie Plunkett that intrigued her.

'Is there anything more to report?' she heard Marjorie say. Although the woman spoke in hushed tones, the grotto walls amplified her voice. She sounded anxious, not like someone who was having fun at a garden party.

Millie lingered a moment longer while Alice-Miranda pushed the pram further down the path.

'I've just received this,' a voice replied. 'Delivered with the palace post, same as last time.'

'Is the perimeter secure?' Marjorie asked.

'Yes, ma'am.'

'Thank you, uh, Bunyan. You know we can't be too careful. I've made some arrangements of my own to monitor their whereabouts.'

Millie's ears pricked up, but she couldn't hear what Marjorie said next. She raced to catch up with Alice-Miranda, glancing back to see if anyone had emerged. 'I just heard Miss Plunkett say the strangest thing,' Millie said.

Alice-Miranda looked at her friend.

'I know, I know, I shouldn't have been eavesdropping,' Millie conceded. 'But I heard Miss Plunkett say something about being careful and that she had made arrangements to monitor someone's whereabouts. What do you think that means?'

Alice-Miranda turned to look back up the path and noticed a bald man in a dark suit walking out of the grotto.

'Maybe she's nervous about the paparazzi getting into her wedding,' Alice-Miranda suggested. 'You know how much Aunty Gee hates being stalked by them. A royal wedding is bound to create a lot of interest.'

'Oh.' Millie's face fell. 'That's probably it. Now you mention it, I'm surprised there isn't more security inside.'

'I suspect there is but we just can't see them,' Alice-Miranda said with a knowing smile. 'For example, how would you know if that man over there was a guest or a secret-service agent?' Alice-Miranda pointed to a gentleman who was dressed the same as every other man in the garden. 'We wouldn't, would we?'

'I'd never really thought about that, but you're right,' Millie agreed, not knowing whether that made her feel better or not.

'Hello darling,' Lloyd said as Marjorie walked towards him. 'Where have you been?'

'I was just chatting to Lady Adams,' Marjorie replied, planting a kiss on his cheek.

Lloyd turned to see where she had come from and frowned. 'That's funny because I was just talking to Lord Robert and Lady Sarah a few moments ago, and she didn't mention you.'

'Oh, I meant Lady Luttrell.' Marjorie kicked herself for being so careless. If she'd checked to see where Lady Adams was, she would have known that Lloyd had just seen the woman.

'Lloyd, hello there.' Lord Adams appeared through the crowd with his wife on his arm.

Dressed in her trademark cerise pink, Lady Sarah refused to be missed. 'I didn't realise you were here, Lloyd. You could have saved me from an hour with Tavistock.'

Lloyd gulped, a red flush engulfed his cheeks. 'Robert, Sarah,' he said sheepishly as he reached out and shook hands with the man, then leaned in to kiss Sarah's cheeks. 'Where are your lovely girls?'

Marjorie flinched before she greeted the pair. She wondered why her fiancé had just lied to her.

'They're staying with their grandmother this week,' Lord Robert replied. 'Sarah and I are having a bit of a getaway. It's a special anniversary.'

'Congratulations,' Lloyd said. 'Marjorie and I

are looking forward to our own special day soon. Aren't we, darling?'

'Yes, of course,' Marjorie said distractedly, looking at something in the distance. She turned back to the group and smiled. 'Please excuse me, I must find the amenities – too much champagne.'

Lord Robert and Lady Sarah chatted away as Marjorie scanned the crowd and located her target. Fortunately, he was standing close to the edge of the garden near the toilets. Marjorie scurried along in her high heels and was pleased to see the woman he was speaking to walk away just as she drew close.

'We need to talk,' Marjorie whispered, pretending to wait for the loo.

'What? Now?' Thornton Thripp replied. The man had the skills of a ventriloquist the way he could speak without moving his lips, although it did seem to cause an odd twitch in his left eye.

'As soon as possible – with Her Majesty,' Marjorie said before walking away.

Thornton Thripp glanced across the garden and caught Lloyd Lancaster-Brown staring at him. He raised his champagne glass in the air and gave a nod. If he didn't know better he'd have sworn the man looked jealous.

Chapter 12

'Good afternoon, my dearest friends and family,' Queen Georgiana beamed at the crowd gathered at the front of the summerhouse.

'Notice how Mummy mentioned her friends before her family?' Freddy hissed into his wife's ear. 'Some would think she doesn't like us at all.'

Elsa shushed her husband. 'Don't be ridiculous, darling.'

Queen Georgiana glared at the woman before continuing. 'I do hope that you've enjoyed yourselves this afternoon in our secret garden. It's always been one of my favourite places here at Evesbury. In about forty minutes we will reassemble on the east lawn for some games and further refreshments. I am sorry about the rush, but I do like to pack as much fun into these weekends as possible. At my age you don't know how much longer you'll be enjoying them. Anyway, there are team lists available as you arrive – I believe Mrs Marmalade and Mr Balfour have them.'

Her Majesty's lady-in-waiting gave a decisive nod.

'And, Lord Tavistock, I'd recommend a change of attire – we wouldn't want a repeat of last year's unfortunate episode, would we?' Her Majesty arched an eyebrow.

There was a titter of laughter as some of the guests recalled how the man's suit pants had torn right down the centre seam during a particularly rowdy game of croquet. Lord Tavistock held his hand up to shield his eyes, his cheeks aflame.

Queen Georgiana waved and stepped away from the microphone.

Seconds later, Valentina Highton-Smith took to the makeshift stage. 'Oh, no you don't, Gee,' she said, wagging her finger. 'You're not getting away with things that easily.'

'What's Granny up to?' Alice-Miranda wondered aloud. She and her friends were standing with her parents, aunt and uncle and Ambrosia Headlington-Bear.

'Your guess is as good as mine,' Hugh whispered.

Valentina cleared her throat. 'I have known Georgiana since we were toddlers, which might surprise you to learn is quite some years ago now. I wanted to take this opportunity to congratulate her on twenty-five years as our monarch. While most think it is an easy job full of fun and frivolity, the truth is often far more complicated, and I couldn't think of anyone better suited to the role than this woman with an iron will and a heart of pure gold.'

'Valentina, dear, you do go on.' Queen Georgiana gave an embarrassed grin and shook her head.

'And I will continue to,' Valentina said, smiling at her friend. 'So, Gee, on this celebratory occasion, I'd like to personally thank you for serving our nation these past twenty-five years, and I wish you all the very best for the next twenty-five.'

A stream of waiters moved through the crowd

dispensing champagne flutes and glasses of lemonade for the children.

Valentina raised her glass. 'To the Queen.'

'The Queen.' Crystal glasses filled the sky.

Her Majesty grinned. 'Thank you, Valentina, my oldest and dearest friend. Sadly, I don't think we'll be celebrating fifty years together, but it's a lovely thought.'

At the mention of Valentina being her oldest and dearest friend, Mrs Marmalade's lips twitched.

'Another twenty-five years and I'll never get my turn,' Freddy muttered, garnering the glares of everyone standing within twenty feet.

'Steady on, Freddy, she's not dead yet,' Lord Tavistock tutted. 'And, quite frankly, I hope the old bird lives forever.'

Freddy slunk down, trying to make himself invisible.

Marjorie Plunkett and Lloyd Lancaster-Brown were standing behind Freddy and Elsa and had also heard every word. But Marjorie wasn't thinking about that. There were a million other things racing through her mind. She wondered how soon she'd be able to speak with Her Majesty and she was rattled about why Lloyd had lied to her earlier, though he seemed to be doing his best to make up for it. Lloyd squeezed Marjorie's hand and gave her a tender smile.

'What are you looking at me like that for?' Marjorie asked.

'It's a beautiful day, darling, and I'm engaged to an even more beautiful woman. Aren't I allowed to look happy?'

'Of course,' Marjorie said as Lloyd leaned across and kissed her cheek.

Alice-Miranda looked at the pair, who were standing a little way to the group's left. 'They're such a lovely couple,' she said.

'She's gorgeous,' Ambrosia commented.

'Yes, who'd have thought Lloyd would ever end up with a woman like that?' Hugh Kennington-Jones said.

'Daddy, that's not very nice,' Alice-Miranda chided. 'We met Lord Lancaster-Brown earlier and he seemed perfectly charming.'

'No, darling, that's not what I meant. Lloyd's love life has always been a bit of a mystery. I just wonder how they met, that's all,' Hugh clarified.

'You know he had the most beautiful sister,' Cecelia said.

'Really?' Hugh frowned. 'I don't think I've ever met her.'

'No,' Cecelia said. 'And you won't.'

'Why not, Mummy?' Alice-Miranda asked.

'There was some sort of terrible accident years ago, and not long afterwards she disappeared. No one's seen her for almost two decades,' Cecelia explained. 'I think it broke Lloyd's heart to lose her. She was a few years older than him and they'd been very close.'

'That's awful.' Alice-Miranda looked over at Lloyd Lancaster-Brown. It was hard to imagine such a terrible thing as losing a sister.

'Do you know anything about Marjorie?' Ambrosia asked.

'I bet she's a movie star,' Millie said.

Lawrence shook his head. 'I don't think so.'

'She's Aunty Gee's milliner,' Cecelia said. 'Mummy reminded me earlier when we were ogling her outfit.'

'Miller what?' Millie asked.

'Milliner,' Alice-Miranda said. 'She makes hats.'

'Beautiful ones at that,' Cecelia added. 'Aunty Gee always has gorgeous headwear. I absolutely adore that blue one she's wearing now.'

'Maybe I could interview Marjorie,' Ambrosia mused.

These days, Ambrosia was writing for Highton's in-house magazine and various publications under the pseudonym Rosie Hunter, and was earning quite the reputation as a journalist. Jacinta couldn't have been prouder of her mother, who had gone from serious socialite, whose only goal was to get herself in the social pages, to a woman with a career and little concern about being an 'it girl' anymore. Most people who knew her couldn't believe the transformation.

'We'd run the story, of course,' Cecelia said. 'But I don't think she's ever given an interview and I don't even know where her salon is. Come to think of it, I remember Mummy once telling me that she works exclusively for Aunty Gee.'

'Her Majesty must pay handsomely,' Ambrosia said.

Hugh finished his last sip of champagne and placed the glass on a nearby waiter's tray. 'Time to get going. We don't want to be late for Aunty Gee's games – she takes them very seriously, you know.'

'I wonder who'll be on her team,' Millie said.

'She'll stack it with all the best players because, although we don't like to say it out loud, *someone* is very competitive.' Hugh grinned cheekily.

'What was that, Hugh?' Queen Georgiana asked, appearing behind them.

Hugh grimaced. 'I'm getting myself into lots of trouble today. I was just saying that I hope I'm on your team for the games this afternoon.'

Aunty Gee shook her head. 'Not after last time, when you belted the croquet ball out of the park. I think I need some new blood.' She pointed at Lawrence and Jacinta. 'I can recognise talent when I see it.'

Lawrence gave her one of his megawatt smiles. 'Thanks, Aunty Gee.'

Jacinta beamed.

'And, besides, if he can't play, at least he's pretty to look at.' Queen Georgiana winked.

Hugh's jaw gaped open and the rest of the group's did too. Mrs Marmalade gasped.

'For heaven's sake, Marian. He's a good-looking man and I'm old enough to be his mother and then some. It's just human nature to admire lovely things.' Queen Georgiana rolled her eyes. 'Chop chop, everyone! I'll have points docked for tardiness.'

Chapter 13

'Caprice, if you're going to be here you have to be helpful.' Venetia Baldini washed her hands in the huge sink and reached over to grab a bag of onions for the sauce she was about to make.

'I have been,' the child complained, hovering behind her mother. 'I peeled loads of potatoes and look what it's done to my nails.' Caprice held a hand aloft and picked at the dry skin around her cuticles.

'I appreciate your efforts very much but there's

still a lot more to do.' Venetia sighed and wiped her brow with the back of her hand.

She'd brought in a whole team to assist her and had access to Her Majesty's own chefs too, but time would be tight nonetheless. Venetia knew that all the best dinners happened this way and, truly, she thrived on the stress of it all. She just hadn't been expecting to have to look after her daughter at the same time.

Plans had gone awry when her husband had received an invitation to take their children on a camping trip in Africa. Given Caprice's last camp experience, they'd decided it would be safer for the girl to stay at home for some mother-daughter time while her father and three older brothers went on a boys-only adventure. Venetia had made arrangements to leave Caprice with the nanny for the jubilee weekend but was thrown for a loop when the woman had telephoned to say that she had a family emergency and couldn't possibly look after the girl. Venetia had her suspicions about the real reason. She hated to think that Caprice could have put the woman off but, knowing what she did about her daughter, she couldn't help being concerned.

Venetia had had a hard time convincing Caprice

that, while she could come along to the palace and help out, she wasn't actually a guest and needed to keep a very low profile. That was perhaps going to be more difficult than she'd first thought.

'Mummy, please may I go for a walk outside?' Caprice begged. 'I promise I'll come back when you say I have to.'

Venetia shook her head. 'I can't afford for you to get into any trouble. You know this is the biggest job of my life. Never in my wildest dreams did I think I'd be catering for the Queen and yet here I am.'

Caprice pulled a face. 'It's not *that* big a deal. Everyone knows who you are, anyway.'

A chef in a white uniform and tall hat dumped another bag of potatoes on the edge of the sink beside the huge tub that were already peeled. He winked at Caprice. 'Looks like you're doing a stellar job with those.'

The child groaned.

'Caprice, please,' her mother said, turning her attention to the onions.

It was true that Venetia's television show, *Sweet Things*, was the highest-rating cooking program on earth. From her childhood in a tiny Tuscan village, Venetia Baldini had become one of the most highly regarded chefs in the world and had a growing empire to prove it. But cooking for Her Majesty was in another league altogether.

All around them, the kitchen bustled with activity. There were chefs preparing vegetables and others dressing meat while an entire section whirred with the sound of mixers and blenders as a huge group of pastry chefs worked on the evening's desserts. The menu was the most complicated Venetia had planned in her life and she was determined to oversee the whole lot personally.

'Something smells good in here,' a tall lad with a mop of black curls commented as he wandered into the kitchen.

Venetia looked up. 'May I help you?'

Before she could blink, an identical boy appeared. 'Are you Venetia Baldini?' he asked.

The woman nodded. 'Yes.'

Although they would never admit it, the twins loved watching her show, probably because Venetia happened to be outrageously beautiful as well as a great cook. Men the world over had fallen under her spell, and even those with absolutely no interest in cooking were often to be found enjoying an episode of *Sweet Things*.

'And who are you?' she asked the boys.

'I'm Louis and he's Edgar.'

Venetia looked at them blankly. She couldn't remember seeing either of those names on her list of staff for the evening.

'Well, you can start washing the brussels sprouts,' she instructed, then pointed at the other lad. 'You can dice the potatoes that are already peeled.' With that, she began to peel the onions on the bench.

'What did you say?' Louis asked.

Venetia exhaled. 'Really, I don't have time for this. I was told that the palace staff would take direction without question.'

'Palace staff?' Edgar was incredulous.

Louis nudged his brother. 'It's all right, Edgar. I'll take the sprouts and you can look after the potatoes.'

Caprice watched the pair from over by the sink.

'I want the sprouts washed and the stems cut like this.' Venetia grabbed a vegetable and showed the lads. 'And these potatoes need to be cubed for a salad. This size.' Venetia picked up a potato and, within seconds, had diced it into perfectly matching pieces.

Louis grabbed a sprout and picked up a large

knife. 'I think I'd rather do this with the sprouts.' He brought the blade down on the vegetable and proceeded to chop it into a mangled mess.

'What on earth do you think you're doing?' Venetia roared.

The boy grinned. 'I hate brussels sprouts.'

His brother nodded in agreement. 'Me too. They're like the Nigel No Friend of the vegetable world. They're ugly and horrid and were secretly created for the sole pleasure of punishing children.'

Caprice giggled.

Venetia looked at the pair again. It dawned on her that they weren't dressed for the kitchen at all. 'I gather you're not here to help?' she demanded.

'No, we're here to find something to eat,' Louis said, his eyes wandering around the benches to see if anything took his fancy. 'There was nothing particularly interesting at Grandmama's stupid party.'

Venetia swallowed. 'Grandmama? Oh, heavens, is Her Majesty your grandmother?'

The twins nodded.

'I am so sorry. It's just that we're missing a couple of staff members and I assumed . . . Of course I shouldn't have,' Venetia apologised.

All of a sudden there was a loud bang in the adjoining room and a spluttering of expletives.

'Oh dear, please excuse me.' Venetia raced away to see what disaster had befallen them.

Edgar looked at Caprice, who'd been enjoying the exchange between her mother and the twins. Louis stared at her too.

'You're very pretty,' Edgar said. 'Who are you, anyway?'

'Caprice,' the girl replied sweetly. 'Venetia's my mother and I'm sorry she's not very smart some-times. I knew who you were straight away.'

'How?' Louis asked.

'I've seen your pictures in *Gloss and Goss*,' Caprice said. 'Mummy's in it all the time. She never pays any attention but I do.'

'What are you doing here?' Edgar asked.

'Slave labour.'

The twins nodded. 'Is there anything to eat?' one of them asked.

Caprice thought for a moment then remembered that her mother had made some chocolate mousse earlier in the morning. 'Come with me,' she said, beckoning for the boys to follow.

They walked into a large room lined with

industrial-sized refrigerators. Caprice opened the door of the furthest one to reveal trays upon trays of dark-chocolate confections in crystal glasses lining the shelves.

'What about this?' She pulled one out and handed it to Louis.

The boy spotted a canteen of cutlery on a bench in the far corner of the room. He walked over and picked up a shiny silver spoon and dug it into the soft dessert, then quickly jammed it into his mouth. 'This is unbelievable,' the boy mumbled with his mouth full.

'Give me one,' Edgar said eagerly. He took a bite and was even more enthusiastic than his brother.

Caprice folded her arms and batted her eyelids. 'So it's okay?'

Edgar swallowed. 'Better than okay. This is the best thing I've ever tasted.'

'What's going on out there in the real world?' Caprice asked.

'Real world?' Louis rolled his eyes. 'That's a joke.'

'Grandmama is hosting one of her boring garden parties where everyone's swanning around making polite conversation about nothing, and they're all too nice to tell her that they'd rather be washing socks,' Edgar explained, waving his spoon in the air.

'It would be better than peeling a zillion potatoes down here.' Caprice examined her ruined finger-nails. 'So why aren't you out there?'

Louis shrugged. 'Some brat called Alice-Miranda spoiled our fun. We thought we'd come down here and get something to eat before the games – which will be much more interesting once *we* get started.'

The twins looked at each other and grinned.

'Alice-Miranda!' Caprice's eyes widened.

'Is she your pal too?' Edgar asked. 'She seems to be besties with everyone else out there.'

Caprice shook her head. 'She is definitely *not* my friend. She ruined everything for me at school this term. I can't stand her.'

'Maybe you should come out for the games this afternoon,' Louis suggested.

'I love games and I'm very good at them too, not to mention it would give Little Miss Perfect quite the surprise.' Caprice smirked at the thought.

'Come on, then.' Edgar scraped the last of the mousse from his glass and plonked it down on the bench. Louis did too.

'You'll have to tell my mother that you're inviting me properly or else she won't let me go,' Caprice said.

Edgar smiled. 'Don't worry, we can be perfectly charming when we want to be.'

Chapter 14

'Your Majesty, may I have a quick word?' Thornton Thripp intercepted the woman as she was on her way to get changed.

'Now?' she asked.

The man nodded. 'I'm afraid so.'

Queen Georgiana quickened her pace and charged through to her private apartments, where she was surprised to find Marjorie Plunkett waiting for her. The woman rose and gave a curtsy.

'This had better be important, Marjorie,' the Queen warned. 'I told you that unless it was an issue of life and death, today was off-limits. As far as I can see, everyone out there is hale and hearty and doesn't appear to be in mortal danger.'

Thornton waited for Her Majesty to take a seat before he sat down opposite her.

'Have you managed to persuade the parents to let the children stay on?' Marjorie asked.

Queen Georgiana exhaled. 'Goodness, is that all? I haven't broached the subject yet. I was planning to sort it out this afternoon during the games.'

The Queen pushed back her chair and stood up, quickly followed by Thornton and Marjorie.

'I'm afraid that's *not* all, Your Majesty,' Marjorie said with a shake of her head. 'Please, Ma'am, I think you're going to want to sit down.'

'Oh dear.' Queen Georgiana plonked back down onto the chair. 'I don't like the sound of this at all.'

Marjorie's gloved hand pulled a piece of paper from her white purse and placed it on the table in front of Her Majesty.

Queen Georgiana looked around for a moment. 'Thripp, don't just sit there. Find my glasses, man.'

Thornton scanned the room and soon located a pair of Her Majesty's reading glasses on a small table beside her favourite armchair.

Queen Georgiana popped the spectacles onto the tip of her nose and held the page at arm's length. She too was still wearing her gloves from the garden party. The woman's rosy cheeks turned pale and she sat back in her chair. 'Where was this found?'

'It was in among the palace mail. One of my agents brought it to me just now,' Marjorie explained.

Thornton Thripp poured a glass of water and set it down gently in front of the Queen.

'They obviously think themselves rather clever with all that dreadful poetry.' Queen Georgiana's face was ashen as she took a sip from her glass and looked at Thornton Thripp.

'Really?' Thripp said. 'I thought it rather clever.'

Queen Georgiana scoffed. 'Absolutely amateur – that's what it is. And what do they want? Why all the suspense? We know they're talking about Alice-Miranda but she hasn't been in any danger to date.'

'I'd be inclined to agree, Ma'am, if it weren't for these.' Marjorie produced three photographs from her handbag.

Her Majesty squinted at them. 'Good heavens! Are these what I think they are?'

Marjorie nodded. 'Yes, Ma'am.'

'Then we have to tell Hugh and Cecelia,' Her Majesty said decisively.

Thornton and Marjorie both shook their heads.

'You can't. Whatever these people want, they've stated very clearly that, should you inform the parents, Alice-Miranda will be kidnapped,' Marjorie reasoned. 'I have assigned a security detail to watch the children, which is why you mustn't let them leave.'

'But won't that look obvious?' Queen Georgiana wrung her hands together.

'Not if that person is a member of the palace staff,' Thornton pointed out.

'Who have you got in mind?' the Queen asked.

'A butler – someone who can blend in,' Marjorie said.

Her Majesty pinched the bridge of her nose and nodded wearily. 'Well, if it means that you can guarantee Alice-Miranda's safety I can hardly object, now can I?'

'Very well, Ma'am,' Marjorie said. 'Mr Thripp,

can I leave it to you to inform Mr Langley of his new staff member?'

Thornton Thripp groaned inwardly. The old man was so particular about his staff, the news was guaranteed to go off like a pot of pâté in the midday sun. 'You know the old boy won't be happy about it. What am I supposed to tell him?'

'Tell him that I'm doing a favour for a friend and the young man is perfectly well-trained and will live up to all his expectations,' Queen Georgiana said.

Thornton looked at Marjorie. 'How soon can you arrange the assignment?'

'My man is here now, ready as soon as I give the order,' Marjorie replied.

'I'd better hunt down Langley before he starts, or I'll be accused of withholding information yet again. What's the fellow's name?' Thornton asked.

'Bunyan,' Marjorie replied.

'Bunyan?' Thripp repeated. 'Splendid.'

Queen Georgiana took a deep breath. 'And in the meantime I will make sure there is no chance the children will be leaving tomorrow.'

Thornton Thripp hurried downstairs, wondering where on earth he'd find Vincent Langley on a day as busy as this. The dining room, he decided, would be his first port of call. The man was meticulous about place settings and, although he had an army of staff to help lay the table, he could often be found with a ruler and polishing cloth, making sure that things were just so.

Thornton poked his head into the state dining room. The enormous table was glittering with crystal and silver and groaning under the weight of candelabras and flowers in anticipation of the evening gala. Several maids were busy doing a final polish and check of the silverware, floating around with feather dusters and cloths.

'Excuse me, Adeline, have you seen Mr Langley?' Thornton asked one of the young women.

'He was here just a few minutes ago, sir, but he was dressed for games and said he was on his way outside,' the woman replied.

Thornton quickly thanked the girl and retreated. He was beginning to think that Vincent Langley had rather a lot on his plate – and the man was no spring chicken. Perhaps the head butler would be grateful for the extra pair of hands.

Thornton Thripp was striding back through the rear foyer when he spotted the man. 'Langley, may I have a word?' he called.

Vincent Langley halted and huffed loudly. 'What now? Can't you see I'm in a hurry?' The man was balancing a huge silver candelabra on a tray and wasn't keen on having to put it down.

'It won't take a minute. I just need to talk to you about a staff member.' Thornton scurried over and met the man by the back doors.

Vincent Langley peered through the middle of the silverware expectantly. 'Well, what is it? I haven't got all day.'

'Her Majesty has employed a new man,' Thornton said.

'Yes.' Vincent lifted his chin. 'I presume he's part of the grounds staff, for which I have no responsibility.'

At that moment Braxton Balfour sped through the back doors. He saw his boss speaking to Mr Thripp, and hesitated. Langley would go off like a firecracker if he realised that Braxton had only just got back.

'Not exactly,' Thornton said. 'He's a butler.'

'A butler!' Vincent exploded, his left eye began to twitch. He almost dropped the candelabra, steadying himself hastily as the silverware wobbled. 'Since when has Her Majesty taken it upon herself to employ butlers?'

Thornton wasn't usually stuck for words. He'd spent more years than he could remember working for Her Majesty's inner circle, but for some reason he didn't quite know what to say. He spotted Braxton Balfour sneaking past, clearly attempting to avoid being seen.

'Her Majesty is concerned by the substandard and unreliable nature of some of your staff and has decided that she wants to give this fellow a trial. His name's Frank Bunyan and he's starting this afternoon.'

Braxton Balfour couldn't help but overhear their conversation. Substandard staff? He hoped Her Majesty wasn't referring to him.

Small flecks of spit began to gather in the corners of Vincent's mouth. 'Who's unreliable? Who is she talking about?' the man demanded, showering Thripp in the process.

Her Majesty's chief advisor wiped the moisture from his cheek and pointed at Balfour slinking away upstairs. 'Well, that one there for starters,' he replied.

'Balfour!' Vincent roared. 'Where have you been?'

Braxton Balfour sighed and turned around.

'And what happened to your face?'

'I . . . I . . . fell in a thicket,' the younger man stuttered.

'What thicket?' Vincent challenged. 'Have you finished setting up for the games?'

Braxton winced. 'Not quite.'

Alice-Miranda and Millie had changed out of their garden-party dresses and were on the way downstairs to meet the others when they heard the commotion below.

Vincent Langley sputtered and frothed. 'Perhaps Her Majesty was right to employ a new butler. You clearly can't be trusted!'

The girls peered over the banister at Mr Balfour, who stood as stiff as a soldier. The man's nose twitched and he looked to be doing his best to stave off a sneeze. He shoved a hand into his trouser pocket and pulled out a handkerchief just in time to catch it. As he did, Alice-Miranda noticed something flutter from his pocket.

'Good grief, Balfour, you'd better not be coming down with something,' Vincent griped. 'Now, get out there and finish what should have been done an hour ago.'

Braxton excused himself and dashed out the back doors.

'Someone's in big trouble,' Millie said.

Alice-Miranda frowned. 'Mr Langley does sound awfully cross,' she agreed.

'Should we wait here until they're finished?' Millie asked.

'No, it will look as if we've been eavesdropping.' Alice-Miranda continued ahead, stomping down the stairs. 'Come on, Millie!' she yelled. 'We don't want to be late.'

Millie looked at her friend, bewildered, then realised that Alice-Miranda wanted the men below to hear her.

Thornton Thripp cleared his throat. 'Thank you, Mr Langley, that will be all for now. We'll see you outside for games in a little while.'

Vincent Langley threw the man one final death stare before he marched away, muttering under his breath.

As the girls waited by the back doors for the rest of their group, Alice-Miranda spotted something on the floor where Mr Balfour had been standing.

She walked over and picked it up, turning the piece of fabric in her hand. It had the loveliest pattern of peacock feathers. 'I think this fell out of Mr Balfour's pocket,' the girl said, holding it up for Millie to see.

'Ready to be whooped, little cousin?' Lucas called from the top of the stairs with Sep, Jacinta and Sloane in tow.

Alice-Miranda looked up and broke into a smile. 'We might be on the same team, you know.'

Lucas frowned. 'I hadn't thought of that.'

Suddenly, the boy mounted the banister and whizzed down the rail.

'Lucas!' Alice-Miranda gasped.

He leapt off at the bottom and gave a bow. 'At your service.'

Jacinta sighed.

'I can't wait to tell Figgy that I slid down the banister at Evesbury Palace. He'll have a fit,' Lucas said, grinning.

'Do it again,' Millie said, 'and this time I'll take a photo.'

'I'll go,' Sep said, throwing his leg over the rail.

Millie held up her camera and snapped away as Sep flew down. He leapt to the floor just as Mr Langley walked back into the room.

'What on earth! Out! All of you! Now!' the old man roared.

'Sorry, Mr Langley,' Sep said sheepishly.

'You certainly will be.' Vincent Langley looked set to erupt like Mount Vesuvius.

The children exchanged grim glances and raced outside.

Chapter 15

Alice-Miranda and her friends ran around to the east lawn, where the guests were gathering outside a large open marquee, which was set up with drinks stations and snacks. Although the tent had no exterior walls, it boasted a silk-lined ceiling and crystal chandelier, and long tables laid with crisp linen cloths and fine china.

'It's a bit better than the tuckshop at our sports days, don't you think?' Millie grinned as she scanned the cupcakes and finger sandwiches on offer.

Alice-Miranda nodded. 'Everything's so beautiful.'

'Hello darling,' Cecelia Highton-Smith called to her daughter, beckoning her and the other children over.

'Hello Mummy. Do you know which team we're on?' Alice-Miranda asked.

Cecelia nodded. 'Aunty Gee has nabbed Jacinta, Lawrence and Lucas, and you're with Daddy, me and Millie. Sloane and Sep are with Ambrosia and Granny. Charlotte's gone back to feed the babies and have a nap before the ball tonight. The poor girl's exhausted.'

'Wow!' Millie exclaimed as she surveyed the badminton courts, the croquet and boules greens and the area that had been set aside for French cricket. 'It does sort of look like the school oval on games day but with way better grass.'

'And a few dozen priceless statues,' Sloane added.

It seemed the palace staff had also undergone a costume change. They were now dressed in white polo shirts, white shorts and tennis shoes, and each had a whistle around their neck.

Alice-Miranda grinned. 'Daddy wasn't kidding when he said that Aunty Gee takes the games seriously.'

Mr Langley was now marching about with a clipboard and loudhailer, directing the partygoers to their first contests. He also had a whistle slung around his neck and looked as if there were a million things he would rather have been doing.

Alice-Miranda smiled at Jacinta. 'I think our teams are playing each other in boules.'

'You'd better be careful, Jacinta,' Millie warned. 'You know what happened last time.'

The child pulled a face. 'Don't remind me – a broken toe and a trip to hospital in Paris.'

'And missing out on gymnastics for six weeks,' Lucas added.

'Where's Aunty Gee?' Alice-Miranda asked as her group assembled.

The competition was a round robin and it appeared that Mr Balfour was in charge of time-keeping. He was standing beside a giant clock, which had been wheeled onto the lawn beside the marquee. But unlike the rest of the staff, he was still dressed in his formal work clothes. He blew a shiny silver whistle to commence the games.

'There she is.' Hugh grinned as he spotted Her Majesty striding towards them wearing long casual pants, a collared shirt and a sunhat with a peacock-patterned scarf tied around its crown.

'Sorry, darlings,' the woman puffed. 'Just some urgent dinner arrangements to attend to.'

Hugh frowned. 'Did someone burn the pudding?'

'I jolly well hope not,' Aunty Gee said. 'I've got Venetia Baldini in charge of the kitchens tonight. It's costing me the annual budget of a small country, so I hope she doesn't mess it up.'

Hugh chuckled. 'The woman's a genius. We hired her for a corporate do recently and I have to say that she produced one of the best menus I've ever tasted.'

'Pity about her daughter,' Millie muttered under her breath.

'I wonder where those grandsons of mine have got to.' The Queen frowned, looking around the park. 'They were supposed to be playing on Freddy and Elsa's team.'

'They ran off into the garden ages ago,' Millie said. 'I don't think they liked us at all. They were trying to start a fight so that Jacinta would have a tantrum.'

Alice-Miranda nudged her friend. 'I'm sure they weren't really going to start a fight.'

'Darling girl, there's no need to shield me from

the truth,' Aunty Gee said with a sigh. 'They are just about the worst-behaved children in the world, and I blame myself for that.'

'But it can't be your fault that the twins are naughty,' Alice-Miranda replied.

'I'm afraid it is. You see, Leopold and I indulged their father, letting him get away with far too much, and now he's utterly hopeless with his own brood. The girls are thoroughly spoilt and the twins are horrid. Of course I still love them, even though they drive me to distraction whenever they're about. I can only hope that they may grow out if it at some stage.'

'Of course they will, Aunty Gee. Freddy didn't turn out too bad, did he?' Hugh said.

Just as the man spoke, a loud shout rang out from the other side of the lawn.

'I need my sunglasses, Elsa,' Freddy spat. 'How am I supposed to play properly without them? The glare is in my eyes.'

Millie thought he sounded like a spoilt five-year-old, not the man who was next in line to the throne.

Queen Georgiana sighed and shook her head. 'What were you saying, Hugh?'

'His heart's in the right place, Gee. He just needs to toughen up a bit and take some more responsibility.'

'Perhaps you're right. I haven't really given him a chance to show what he can do,' Gee replied. 'I probably should think about retiring sometime soon. I don't want to be forgetting things and spilling my tea, like I did all over the American President last time he popped in for a visit. Poor President Grayson was terribly gracious about it, but I felt a right clod. At least if I'm still alive when Freddy becomes King I can have a guiding influence for a while.'

'I don't think you need to give up the reins anytime soon, Aunty Gee. Why don't you try delegating Freddy a project or two?' Hugh suggested.

Aunty Gee nodded. 'You may be onto something, dear. Why don't you do the honours and roll the jack?'

'Don't we have an umpire?' Millie asked, looking around.

'We should have. I wonder who's meant to be with us.' The Queen waved to a bald man standing a little way off.

The man hurried over. 'Yes, Ma'am,' he said uncertainly.

'Right, you can umpire, Mr . . .?' Queen Georgiana wondered if she *was* losing her marbles. She knew all of her staff by name and was horrified to be drawing a blank on this man.

'Bunyan, Ma'am,' the fellow replied quietly. 'Frank Bunyan.'

Her Majesty sighed. 'Oh, that's a relief. Jolly good.'

Alice-Miranda recognised him as the man she'd seen leaving the grotto earlier.

'Okay, teams, this is Bunyan and he's our umpire for the match,' Queen Georgiana hastily introduced the man.

At the mention of the fellow's name Millie began to giggle.

As always, Jacinta was much less subtle. 'Bunyan!' she blurted. 'Is that really your name?'

'Jacinta!' Alice-Miranda admonished.

'Sorry,' Jacinta said, suddenly sheepish. 'It's just that I've never heard anyone called that before and it made me think of Granny's feet.'

Hugh and Lawrence looked at each other and bit back grins.

'Charming,' Frank Bunyan said tightly. The man turned his attention back to Her Majesty and cleared his throat. 'Excuse me, Ma'am, have you decided which team is going first?'

'Hugh was about to roll the jack,' Her Majesty replied.

'And I presume everyone is familiar with the rules,' Bunyan said.

The group nodded.

'Well, may the best team win,' Bunyan said with a twitch of his nose.

Hugh picked up the small red ball and bowled it underarm down the pitch. Jacinta waited until it came to a halt, then lined up with a silver ball and readied herself to roll it towards the little red jack.

No one noticed the twins and Caprice hiding behind a large statue of the Venus de Milo on the edge of the lawn.

'I thought you said we were going to play some games,' Caprice whined.

'Who'd want to play boring old boules?' Edgar said.

'Me!' Caprice retorted.

'We've got something much more fun than that,' Louis said.

'Yeah, watch this,' Edgar said with a grin. He had hold of a remote control unit which looked as if it operated a toy helicopter.

'What are you doing?' Caprice asked, poking her head out and looking across the lawn to where the games were taking place.

The boy waggled his eyebrows. 'You'll see.'

Jacinta lunged forward and rolled the first silver ball. It curved inwards and stopped about a metre from the red jack.

Her Majesty clapped. 'Well done, dear.'

Jacinta spun around and grinned widely.

'Great work,' Lucas and his father both said at the same time. 'Snap!'

The handsome pair smiled and sent hearts fluttering all over the garden.

It was Alice-Miranda's turn next. Her ball headed right for the jack when, all of a sudden, the little red orb seemed to develop a mind of its own and rolled off to the left, away from the target.

Millie squinted. 'I didn't think you hit that.'

Alice-Miranda shrugged. 'I must have.'

Frank Bunyan, who was keeping a close eye on the proceedings, scratched his head.

Lawrence Ridley was up next. 'Aunty Gee, I know you have high expectations but I'm not an expert at this,' the man said as he leaned forward and released the ball.

It wobbled down the pitch and came to rest between Jacinta and Alice-Miranda's balls. Just as Hugh was about to congratulate his brother-in-law on a good first effort, the jack rolled away to the right.

'What?' Hugh frowned. 'How did that happen?'

Lawrence grinned. 'The pitch must have some run on it.'

'I'd be surprised about that. Mr Budd prides himself on his level lawns,' Aunty Gee said.

A loud snort of laughter rang out from some-where close by.

'Aunty Gee, it's your turn,' Alice-Miranda said, but Her Majesty seemed lost in her own thoughts. 'Aunty Gee?'

The old woman jerked back to reality. 'Sorry, dear, what's that?'

'Are you all right, Aunty Gee? You look a bit pale,' Cecelia said with concern. 'Would you like me to organise a cup of tea?'

'Sorry, dear,' the Queen replied. 'There's something I wanted to ask you.'

'Of course, what is it?' Cecelia said.

'I've been thinking it's a little bit . . . stingy of me to invite the children to stay for less than two days. There's so much more to see and do, so if I may, I'd love to keep them for another week. Perhaps longer?'

The girls' eyes grew wide.

'Oh, Aunty Gee, that's terribly kind but we don't want to put you out,' Cecelia said, glancing uncertainly at Hugh. This all seemed rather out of the blue. 'And I'm not sure what everyone has planned for the holidays.'

'Nothing!' Millie piped up. 'Nothing at all. Daddy's busy on the farm and Mummy's got loads of work to do, so I'm sure they wouldn't mind if we stayed another week.'

Alice-Miranda jigged up and down on the spot. 'I'd love to stay if it's all right with Mummy and Daddy.'

'Are you sure, Aunty Gee?' Hugh asked. 'You do realise that you could end up with all six of them here with you?'

'Hugh, look at the place. I wouldn't mind if I

had an extra sixty people here,' Her Majesty replied. 'Besides, we have excellent security and loads of helpers to look out for the children.'

'Security?' Hugh repeated. 'Is there a problem, Aunty Gee?'

'Oh, silly me. I meant to say "staff" – like Bunyan here. I'm afraid I don't know where my brain is today,' Her Majesty said, shaking her head.

Frank Bunyan's lip twitched and he gave Her Majesty the slightest of nods.

'We'll have to call the children's parents,' Cecelia said, 'but I can't imagine they'd say no.'

Alice-Miranda leapt into the air and hugged Millie tightly. 'We'll get to see the hunting tower after all!'

'Well, that's settled.' Queen Georgiana breathed a loud sigh and her cheeks took on a rosy glow. 'Why don't you go and check with Ambrosia and call Sloane and Sep's parents so I can have everything sorted?'

'Would it be all right if we finished the game first?' Cecelia asked. She wondered why Aunty Gee was in such a rush.

'Of course, Cee. Pass me that ball, please, Alice-Miranda.' Her Majesty rubbed her hands together and performed a couple of lunges before sweeping her arms up over her head and stretching from side to side.

Cecelia and Hugh frowned at each other. The woman had perked up remarkably in the past couple of minutes.

Alice-Miranda picked up a shiny silver ball and passed it to Her Majesty, who closed one eye and lined up the jack. With expert precision, Queen Georgiana rolled the ball down the pitch.

Lawrence smiled. 'You're on target, Aunty Gee. I think you've got it.'

He clenched his fists in anticipation while the rest of the group held their breath. They watched the ball roll closer and closer until, just as it was about to touch the jack, the little red sphere veered wildly to the left, then to the right before it shot into the air towards the group.

'What on earth?' Queen Georgiana squawked as she leapt out of the way.

The jack whizzed past her and across the lawn, hitting Lord Tavistock hard on the shin as he was in the middle of a hotly contested game of badminton against Thornton Thripp.

'Ow! Ow! Ow!' The man hopped about on one

foot. 'Who threw that?' he yelled, glaring at Queen Georgiana.

'Don't look at me, Tavistock. It was the best bowl of the game so far,' Her Majesty huffed, folding her arms.

Millie heard someone giggling not far away and turned to scan the grounds. 'Over there!' she yelled, pointing at the statue of the Venus de Milo. A mop of curly hair could be seen poking out from under one of the marble woman's missing arms.

Millie grabbed Alice-Miranda's hand and, together with Lucas and Jacinta, they shot off towards the statue.

'Who's there?' Aunty Gee squinted into the distance. 'Well, don't just stand there, Bunyan. Off you go!'

Frank Bunyan sighed and jogged after the children.

'We know you're up to something,' Millie yelled out as they neared the statue.

The twins tumbled out and made a dash for the edge of the garden, running for the cover of the woodland.

'Hey, don't leave me here!' Caprice called after them, but it was too late. The twins were gone.

Alice-Miranda spotted the girl and stopped while the others charged on ahead, chasing after the twins. 'Caprice? What are you doing here?'

Caprice blinked innocently. 'The twins said we were going to play a game. I promise I had no idea what they were up to.'

Alice-Miranda wondered if the girl was telling the truth. She didn't exactly have a good track record. 'I suppose they did leave you here,' Alice-Miranda conceded. 'That wasn't especially gallant of them.'

'That's what I thought,' Caprice said, emerging from her hiding spot.

'You'd better come with me,' Alice-Miranda said.

Caprice reluctantly followed the girl back towards the games. She stopped dead in her tracks when she realised that Queen Georgiana was standing there with her hands on her hips.

'Who do we have here?' the Queen demanded.

The girl gulped. 'I was playing with your grand-sons. I didn't know what they were doing, I swear. I thought they had a remote-controlled helicopter or something.'

'The speed that jack came at me, I'm surprised I didn't lose a leg. As it is, Tavistock is going to have a bruise the size of Belgium. Wait until I get my hands on those two,' Queen Georgiana harrumphed. 'Anyway, who are you?'

'My mother is in the kitchens,' Caprice began.

'If your mother works in my kitchens, why don't I know you? I pride myself on knowing all the offspring of my staff by name.' Aunty Gee's brow had begun to resemble a furrowed field.

'Her mother is Venetia Baldini,' Alice-Miranda volunteered.

Her Majesty nodded. 'Ah, very clever woman, your mother.' She looked at the girl closely. 'Are you sure I haven't seen you before?'

Caprice glanced at Alice-Miranda, waiting for the girl to remind Her Majesty that they'd met at the children's school camp earlier in the term.

'This is Caprice,' Alice-Miranda said. 'She started at school with us a little while ago.'

Aunty Gee's frown lines disappeared. 'Oh, hello. I suppose I have met rather a lot of children lately.'

'I'd better go and see if my mother needs any more help,' the child said, eager to leave before the Queen's memory sharpened up.

Hugh had retrieved the jack from the middle of the badminton court and brought it back to the group for examination. He gave the red orb a twist and it came apart in two sections, revealing a tiny motor inside.

'You know, this is remarkably clever,' Hugh said. 'If the boys put this together themselves I see a big future in engineering.'

'At the moment the only future I see for them is breaking rocks in the far field,' Her Majesty replied.

'Why don't we get some tea?' Cecelia suggested.

Aunty Gee nodded. 'Yes, I think I could do with a cup.'

'Lawrence and I will give you a hand, Cee,' Hugh said, patting his brother-in-law on the back.

Aunty Gee and Alice-Miranda watched as Millie, Jacinta and Lucas jogged back across the lawn. There was no sign of the twins, or Bunyan for that matter.

'We lost them in the woods and then we thought we were probably going to get lost too,' Millie puffed. 'So we came back.'

'Never mind,' Aunty Gee said. 'They won't get away with it.'

'What happened to you?' Jacinta asked Alice-Miranda.

'Oh, she found a friend of yours from school that my grandsons had been leading astray,' Aunty

Gee said. 'She was a very pretty thing. What was her name again?'

'Caprice,' Alice-Miranda replied.

Millie looked as if she'd just stepped in something particularly unpleasant. 'What's *she* doing here?'

'Her mother is preparing our meal for this evening and she's been helping down in the kitchens,' Aunty Gee explained.

'She was probably the ringleader,' Millie muttered.

'What did you say, dear?' Queen Georgiana asked. Her hearing wasn't what it used to be.

Alice-Miranda looked at her friend and shook her head.

'Nothing, Aunty Gee,' Millie said, forcing a smile.

'Oh, well, I think that's the end of boules for us today.' Queen Georgiana spotted Cecelia balancing two cups of tea and walked over to meet her. Hugh and Lawrence were a little way behind with some plates of food and drinks for the children.

'Is Caprice staying here?' Millie asked.

'The dinner will run late, so I suppose so,' Alice-Miranda said.

Millie made a face. 'She'd better be gone by

tomorrow. We don't need her lurking around and messing things up.'

'That's for sure,' Jacinta chimed in.

'Don't worry about her, Millie,' Lucas said reassuringly. 'She won't try anything. Not after what happened at camp.'

'We probably won't even see her,' Alice-Miranda added. 'It sounds as if her mother is keeping her busy.'

'Good,' Millie said with a nod. She hoped Venetia Baldini would run Caprice ragged.

Chapter 16

'Marjorie,' Queen Georgiana called as she approached the badminton courts, 'may I have a word?'

Marjorie and Lloyd were in the middle of beating the socks off Elsa and Freddy. Freddy was storming around the court while Elsa was doing her best to placate him. At that moment, Marjorie slammed the shuttlecock. It flew over the net and bounced off Freddy's balding crown.

'Ow!' the man whimpered. 'That wasn't very sporting.'

'Sorry, Freddy, you'll just have to learn to move faster.' Marjorie winked at him, then ran over to the sideline.

'Good shot, Marjorie!' Her Majesty exclaimed.

Marjorie grinned. 'Thank you, Ma'am.'

'I just wanted to let you know that I've lined up those ducks,' Queen Georgiana whispered. 'And I've met your man Bunyan too.'

Marjorie gave a small nod. 'Very good, Ma'am.'

'Oh, I think my team is about to make a start at French cricket,' Her Majesty announced loudly. 'Wish us luck. And those grandsons of mine are in huge trouble when I find them, Freddy. Did you know they tampered with our boules jack? Just wait until I get my hands on them for ruining our game. My team was looking good for the win,' Her Majesty blustered before heading on her way.

'What was that about, darling?' Lloyd Lancaster-Brown asked.

'Nothing to worry about,' Marjorie said, patting him on the arm.

'Are we finishing this game or not?' Freddy called tetchily from the other end of the court.

'I'd just as soon not,' Elsa said, her nerves threadbare. 'I should look for the boys and work out what they have to do to make amends with their grandmother.'

'Forget about them, Elsa. Boys will be boys,' Freddy said, not realising his mother had walked back to retrieve her sunhat.

'And perhaps,' Queen Georgiana boomed, 'fathers should be fathers.'

Freddy leapt into the air. 'Yes, Mama,' he said before slinking off the court.

Lloyd looked at Marjorie. 'Why don't you have a rest in the marquee for a few minutes? I've just realised I need to get one of the butlers to press my pants for tonight, so I'd best go and get that organised.'

'I'm sure Balfour could arrange it for you, darling,' Marjorie gestured to Braxton, who was standing beside the giant clock.

'Over my dead body,' Lloyd hissed.

Marjorie frowned.

'It's all right. He's busy playing timekeeper. I'll find someone to do it inside.'

Lloyd kissed Marjorie's cheek and sped off, leaving her wondering what that was all about.

Caprice trudged back towards the palace, annoyed at the twins for leaving her high and dry. The last thing she felt like doing was peeling more potatoes. She bypassed the service entrance and decided to take herself for a wander through the gardens, away from the games.

Evesbury Palace was like nothing she'd ever seen. There was a new surprise around every corner – statues, ponds, a maze or a woodland with hollowed-out trunks, where Caprice almost expected to find real fairies. Apart from the trilling of larks and the rustling of leaves, there was a magical silence about the place.

Caprice followed a stream into a grove of trees but stopped when she heard voices. She couldn't see where they were coming from but they were low and clearly didn't want anyone to hear their conversation. Naturally, she crouched down behind an oak tree to listen.

'So are we still on track?' the first voice asked.

'Yes,' the second replied.

'Good. Timing is everything. We should be ready to make a move by Tuesday at the latest.'

'What about Fiona?'

'She's onside. At least, she will be by tonight.'

'But how?'

'Never mind. Let's just say, it's done.'

Caprice peered around the tree, hoping to catch a glimpse of whoever was speaking. But she could only see their backs through the undergrowth. They were both wearing polo shirts, one white and the other a pale pink. She craned her neck to see who they were when, suddenly, she overbalanced and fell into the clearing with a dull thud. The girl scrambled to her feet and peeked through the hedge, hoping they hadn't noticed her.

'Oh, hello Caprice,' Edgar said as he and Louis traipsed into the glade. 'We've been looking for you everywhere.'

The girl spun around and narrowed her eyes at the pair. 'You left me to take the blame.'

'It's not our fault you didn't follow us,' Edgar scoffed.

'Your grandmother is furious,' Caprice said.

'She'll get over it.' Louis seemed as if he couldn't care less. 'What are you doing?'

'Nothing,' the child replied. 'I just heard some voices. I don't know who they were.' Caprice turned back to see if they were still there but they'd gone.

'What were they talking about?'

'Someone called Fiona,' Caprice said with a shrug. 'It didn't mean anything to me.'

Edgar yawned. 'Sounds boring.'

'Come on, then, what are we going to do now?' Louis asked.

Caprice shook her head. 'I'm not doing anything with you two. I have to go back to the kitchens.'

'That's a shame,' Edgar said. 'I was going to suggest showing you the tower, but if you'd rather help your mummy . . .'

Caprice's eyes lit up. 'Are you kidding? Lead the way!'

Chapter 17

'How much further?' Caprice whined. It felt like they'd been climbing forever. The sun was beginning to dip behind the hill, and she knew that if she didn't get back soon her mother would have a fit.

'You'll see,' one of the boys yelled. They continued to speed along a track through the undergrowth.

Before long, the brambles and thickets thinned out, and it dawned on Caprice that they were on top of the ridge that ran high above the palace. She stopped for a moment to catch her breath and take in the spectacular view. Down below, the residence and gardens were laid out in all their splendour.

'You can see for miles up here,' she exclaimed.

'Hurry up,' Louis called over his shoulder, 'or we'll just have to turn around and go back again!'

Caprice groaned and once again took off up the track. She charged around the corner and almost collided with Louis.

'Whoa! What's that?' she said, looking up at the imposing building in front of them.

'It's the hunting tower,' Louis said.

'It was built by our great-great-great-great-great grandfather for hunting parties,' Edgar said importantly.

Caprice scanned the cream stone building with its strange architecture. There were four turrets, each with its own domed roof capping off four storeys. The building was tall and narrow, and Caprice imagined it was just the sort of thing the Brothers Grimm had in mind when they wrote *Rapunzel*.

'What do they use it for now?' she asked.

'No one uses it anymore,' Louis said. 'Except us.'

'You can't tell anyone about this,' Edgar said sternly.

Caprice rolled her eyes. 'I won't.'

'Come on, I want to get some things for tonight,' Louis said, disappearing around to the back of the tower.

'How do you get in?' Caprice called after them. 'And what do you mean you want some things for tonight? What do you keep up here?'

'You'll see,' Louis shouted as he dashed over to a huge conifer. He ducked in underneath its branches and returned with a milk crate.

Caprice watched as Edgar positioned it under a small window a couple of metres off the ground. He climbed up, prised open the window and heaved himself through.

'Why don't you go through that one?' Caprice asked, pointing to the lowest opening, which looked as if it might drop into a basement.

'Because all the windows except this one have been nailed shut,' the boy replied.

'Why?' Caprice asked.

Edgar shrugged. 'I suppose they don't want anyone up here.'

The windows further up the tower were larger with diamond-shaped leadlight panes and heavy drapes.

'Ladies first,' Louis said, holding out his hand.

Caprice wrinkled her nose. 'Can't you just go and open the front door for me?'

The boy shook his head.

'If I have to, then,' the girl moaned. She pulled herself up and over the windowsill, then leapt down inside a tiny room.

Louis quickly followed.

'Pooh, it stinks in here.' Caprice breathed in the musky scent. Centuries of damp and goodness knows what else had penetrated the thick outer walls.

'It's not that bad,' Edgar said, brushing past her.

Caprice followed the boys through a doorway that led into a central foyer. From here, she could see why they weren't able to open the tower door. Hanging off it were several large locks, all of which looked as if they required equally large keys.

Louis dived through a door to their left and sped up a narrow staircase with a rope banister. The trio bounded their way up, taking two steps at a time, and didn't stop until they reached the second floor, where Caprice found herself in another central vestibule. It was sort of like a sitting room, with three threadbare floral couches and dark furniture lining the walls. A huge circular light fitting made of antlers took up the entire ceiling. There were three other doors leading off the landing, but what lay behind them was a complete mystery. Caprice was taken by the faded grandeur of the building with its timber panelling and assortment of antiques.

Edgar pushed open the door closest to them.

In the centre of the room sat a large table laden with wires and batteries, pliers and dismantled computers. Caprice recognised some camera parts and remote controls. There were blueprints stuck to the walls, with handwritten instructions scrawled all over them. Another bench contained a chemistry set with flasks and beakers, measuring cups and a range of labelled jars.

Caprice's eyes drank it all in as she walked around the room. 'What's all this?'

'Welcome to our workshop,' Louis said with a bow. He plucked a white lab coat from a hook on the wall and pulled it over his clothes.

'Workshop?' Caprice repeated.

'We invent things,' Edgar replied, as if it were the most obvious thing in the world. He pulled on a lab coat too and set to work.

'Does anyone else know about this?' Caprice asked. She leaned in to inspect a set of crude drawings, one of which appeared to be a seating plan, and the other a soup bowl.

'No, and they're not going to either,' Edgar said sharply, giving Caprice a stern look.

'Don't worry, I'm not going to tell anyone,' Caprice sniped. 'So you made the boules jack remote-controlled, then?'

Louis smiled proudly. 'All our own work.'

'Wasn't it magnificent?' Edgar preened.

'Very clever,' Caprice agreed. She pointed at a glass jar with brown goo in it. 'What's that?' she asked, beginning to unscrew the lid.

'Noooo!' Edgar shouted, snatching the jar from her hands.

'Yuck! That's disgusting!' Caprice gagged. 'What is it?'

Edgar quickly wound the lid back on. 'Liver paste.'

'It's rank,' Caprice sputtered, trying not to breathe in the smell. 'What are you going to use that for?'

'Shoes,' Louis said.

Caprice looked at him blankly.

'Well, we've been fermenting it for ages and we've worked out a way to extract the smell so that humans can't detect it,' the boy explained. 'But animals can. Obviously that jar is still in its early stages.'

'This is the finished product,' Edgar said, patting a jar on the other end of the table.

'But what's it for?' Caprice couldn't see any use for the revolting goo except perhaps wild animal traps and, as far as she knew, there weren't any bears or tigers roaming the woods.

'We painted it on the soles of Langley's shoes.' Edgar held up a pair of black brogues and grinned. 'We're taking them back down tonight. He has this thing where he alternates a pair of shoes each day.'

'I still don't get it,' Caprice said. 'Do you want him to get eaten by a lion or something?'

'No, of course not, but can you imagine what fun it will be when Archie and Petunia pick up the scent? They won't leave him alone and he'll never know why.' Louis explained with a mischievous grin.

'That is pretty clever,' Caprice admitted. 'Can we go back now?'

'Why? Are you worried you'll be in trouble with your mummy?' Edgar pouted mockingly.

'No, of course not,' Caprice replied, staring the boy down. 'But don't you have to get ready for the ball?'

'As long as we turn up on time no one will care,' Edgar said. 'We've got to finish something special for tonight, anyway.'

Louis turned to Caprice. 'Actually, you're not coming to the dinner, are you?'

The girl shook her head. 'I'll be downstairs getting bossed about by my mother.'

'That's perfect.' Louis smiled at his brother. 'Edgar and I have a job for you.'

Caprice eyed them suspiciously. 'What do you mean?'

'I think Grandmama needs to see that Little Miss Perfect is not all she's cracked up to be,' Louis said, grinning like a Cheshire cat.

'Do you think it's ready?' Edgar asked. He pressed his finger against a long strip of what looked to be extremely thin blu tack.

His brother nodded. 'I think so. As long as we've got enough strength in it.'

Edgar picked up a silver teaspoon and held it over the strip. Suddenly, the silverware flew out of his hand and slammed onto the table.

'Whoa!' Caprice gasped.

The pull of the strip was so strong, Edgar had to use both hands to yank the spoon from it. He glanced up at Louis and smirked. 'Looks ready to me.'

Louis smiled and turned to Caprice. 'And you're the perfect person to put it in place.'

The girl listened intently as the boys revealed their plan.

Chapter 18

Venetia Baldini wondered if she should have packed a pair of rollerskates, the way she was racing from one section of the kitchen to the next. A cumquat disaster had been averted, largely because one of Her Majesty's chefs kindly took her to the greenhouse, where she located some additional fruit. And while cheese soufflé was admittedly a risky choice for entree, Venetia was determined to make this dinner memorable for all the right reasons. It was just after quarter past five when she glanced at the kitchen clock and realised that Caprice was late.

'Excuse me, ma'am, but would you like me to make you a cup of tea?' a young kitchenhand asked.

'Oh, that would be brilliant,' Venetia replied gratefully. The woman looked down at her splattered apron, which bore evidence of just about every dish she'd worked on that day. 'Gosh, I must look a terrible mess.'

'Not at all,' the young man said. Despite having been on the go for hours, Venetia's hair and make-up were still flawless. 'And if you don't mind me saying so, Ms Baldini, I think you might do well to sit down for a few minutes. I haven't ever seen anyone work at the rate of knots you do, and you've still got hours before the dinner service.'

Venetia smiled at the lad. 'That's awfully kind of you to say . . .'

'I'm Tom,' the young man said, reading Venetia's mind.

'Thank you, Tom,' Venetia replied. 'I suppose I should check my messages, and I would like to know where that daughter of mine has got to.'

Venetia's handbag was sitting on the desk inside the little office she'd been provided by Mr Langley.

She pulled out her phone and was alarmed to find twelve missed calls from a number she didn't recognise. There were five messages too.

She dialled the number to listen to her voicemail and, within seconds, the colour had drained from her face and she had begun to shake all over. Tom walked into the room, balancing a teacup and a plate with a large slice of chocolate cake.

'Ms Baldini, are you all right?' the lad asked with concern. He quickly placed the tea and cake on the table and rushed to the woman's side.

'My father . . . h-he's had a stroke,' Venetia stammered as tears began to flood her face. 'My husband is away with the boys and I can't get in touch with them and my father is in Italy.'

'Everything's under control for tonight,' Tom said soothingly. 'We can take it from here. You should go to your father.'

'I'm so sorry. I need to find my daughter and Mr Langley,' Venetia said.

She picked up her handbag and fled through the kitchens and upstairs to the rear hall, almost crashing into Cecelia Highton-Smith, who was on her way outside to round up the children. Aunty Gee's games had finished an hour earlier and the children had begged to do some more exploring in the gardens. Cecelia had agreed to meet them near the back doors at half past five, allowing the children enough time to have a rest before getting ready for the ball.

'Hello Venetia, Aunty Gee said that you were in charge of dinner tonight,' Cecelia said warmly. 'I must say we're all very excited. That function you did for Highton's was certainly the most fabulous meal I can remember. It was –'

'Have you seen Caprice?' Venetia blurted.

'Yes, I saw her about –' Cecelia stopped as she registered the woman's tear-stained cheeks. 'Whatever's the matter?'

Venetia burst into tears. 'It's my father,' she sobbed.

Cecelia placed her arm around the woman's shoulders and listened to the story between hiccupping gulps.

'I have to find Caprice,' Venetia sniffed.

Cecelia hoped the girl was out playing with Alice-Miranda and the other children. Not a minute later, Alice-Miranda, Millie, Jacinta, Sloane, Sep and Lucas tumbled through the back door, dishevelled and dirty, looking as if they'd had quite the adventure.

'Hello darling, I was just coming to find you,' Cecelia said.

'Sorry, Mummy, we discovered an enormous maze, then we got lost and it took us ages to find our way back,' the child babbled. 'Hello Ms Baldini, we're really looking forward to dinner tonight. I'm starving! But are you all right?' Alice-Miranda had only just noticed the woman's red-rimmed eyes.

Millie and Jacinta looked at each other. 'Has she been crying?' Jacinta whispered.

'Children, have you seen Caprice?' Cecelia asked.

'Only when we were playing boules,' Alice-Miranda volunteered. 'She left us and said that she was coming back inside to help you, Ms Baldini.'

Venetia sighed and dabbed at her eyes.

'What's the matter with her?' Millie mouthed to Jacinta.

'Ms Baldini, is something wrong?' Alice-Miranda asked.

The woman's eyes filled with tears again. 'My father is seriously ill and I need to get to him right away, but I have to find Caprice,' she replied, her voice faltering.

'We can go and look for her,' Sep offered, and Lucas nodded. Though, with the fading light and the size of the palace gardens, neither of the boys was confident that they'd find her very quickly.

'She's probably with Louis and Edgar,' Millie said. 'They could be anywhere.'

'I told her to be back by five o'clock and it's almost quarter to six,' Venetia said. 'I need to get to the airport now or I won't get a flight tonight.'

Alice-Miranda had an idea. 'Why don't you go on ahead, and Daddy can arrange for Cyril to take Caprice to meet you when we find her?' the girl suggested.

Venetia blinked.

'In Birdy, our helicopter,' Alice-Miranda explained.

Venetia hated the thought of leaving not knowing where her daughter was, but she'd never forgive herself if something happened and she didn't get to see her father.

Cecelia nodded. 'That's an excellent idea, darling.'

'Are you sure? I don't want to be a nuisance, and you've got the ball tonight,' Venetia said, trembling like one of the jellies she'd made for the trifle.

'Are you all right to drive, Ms Baldini?' Lucas asked the woman.

Venetia nodded and smiled at the thoughtful lad. 'It will give me something to concentrate on other than Papa.'

'Have you got everything?' Cecelia asked.

'I don't know. I haven't even told the chefs what's happened.' The woman's forehead wrinkled at the thought of everything that had to be done down-stairs.

'Don't worry about a thing,' Cecelia reassured her. 'I'll go and let them know right away, and I'll tell Mr Langley too.'

'You're all so kind.' Venetia held onto Cecelia's hands and squeezed. 'Langley's going to be furious.'

'Just get to your father, and don't worry about Caprice or the dinner. We'll look after her and make sure that she's with you as soon as possible,' Cecelia said, embracing the woman goodbye.

'Thank you, Cee. Thank you so much.' Venetia gave Cecelia an extra squeeze, then raced out the back door.

Chapter 19

Cecelia Highton-Smith headed straight to the kitchens to inform the staff that they would be going it alone for the rest of the evening, while the children set off in search of Caprice in the gardens nearest the palace. They were to divide up and meet back at the rear entrance foyer in half an hour. If Caprice was not to be found, Cecelia planned to notify the palace staff to organise a search party.

Sloane and Jacinta dashed off to the back garden while the boys decided to look around the front of the palace. Alice-Miranda and Millie exited the courtyard where the guests' cars were parked, and ran along the driveway towards the stables.

'I know she's not my favourite person in the world but I am sorry about her grandfather,' Millie said.

Alice-Miranda nodded. 'Yes, it's horrible, and I imagine Caprice she is going to be quite upset.'

'We should break it to her gently,' Millie said. 'I remember when Miss Reedy told me my granny had died. I was a mess. Howie made me hot chocolate and everyone was so kind. It made things much easier.'

'Well, her grandfather hasn't died but it didn't sound good,' Alice-Miranda said. 'I can't imagine not having Granny and Aunty Gee around. There are just some people who you think will be in your life forever, aren't there?'

'Like you and me.' Millie linked arms with her friend and smiled at her.

Alice-Miranda squeezed Millie's arm affectionately. Just as she did, the path lit up as thousands of fairy lights awakened to twinkle in the trees and illuminate the magnificent stable building and its clock tower. The girls gasped with delight.

'Wow, that looks amazing,' Alice-Miranda marvelled, taking the words right out of Millie's mouth.

'Caprice!' Millie called as the girls approached the stable block. On the other side of the wall, a horse whinnied. 'Should we go in?'

'I don't think we have time,' Alice-Miranda said.

Just as the girls turned to head back down the driveway, Millie stopped and squinted into the distance. 'Do you see someone?' she asked, pointing towards a figure standing on the stone bridge that crossed the river a little way from the palace.

Alice-Miranda focused her eyes. 'I think it's a woman.'

'Do you think she's a hunchback or something? Her shoulder looks weird,' Millie said. It was hard to tell in the fading light but the woman seemed to be wearing a long cloak with a hood. Millie took her camera out of her jacket pocket and zoomed in on the mysterious figure. 'It's a bird!' she exclaimed.

'Really?' Alice-Miranda said.

All of a sudden the creature took off and flew towards the girls. It rose higher into the sky, then circled and glided back to the woman.

'It's a raven,' Millie said.

'Goodness, that is unusual.' Alice-Miranda watched as the woman stood on the bridge facing the palace. The bird landed on her shoulder again. 'I wonder who it is.'

Millie pulled a face. 'Some weirdo if you ask me. Who walks around in a hooded cape with a pet raven? We should tell Aunty Gee.'

'Maybe she lives somewhere on the estate,' Alice-Miranda said as the woman disappeared into the woods.

'I should have taken a photograph,' Millie said. 'Do you think Aunty Gee knows who she is?'

'Come on, Millie, we'd better get going.' Alice-Miranda took hold of her friend's hand, and the girls scurried back to the palace. They raced under the archway and into the rear courtyard, where they found the others, having just returned themselves.

'You didn't find her either?' Sloane said.

Millie shook her head. 'No, but we saw a strange woman wearing a long cape and she had a raven on her shoulder.'

'Creepy,' Jacinta said, wrinkling her nose.

'Millie, we don't know anything about her,' Alice-Miranda chided. 'And we certainly don't know that she's strange.'

Sloane shrugged. 'Sounds weird to me. Who'd want to have a raven as a pet? They're so sinister-looking.'

Jacinta nodded. 'Come to think of it, that's what Mr Langley reminds me of – a raven. His hair is that same purple-black colour. Seriously, he must go through a lot of hair d–'

'Look, there's something up there.' Sep pointed to a blinking light on the hillside. It seemed to be heading downwards.

'It could be Caprice and the twins,' Lucas said hopefully.

They followed the light as it got closer and closer then disappeared as whoever it was entered the bottom of the garden. Finally, after another few minutes, three silhouettes came into view.

Alice-Miranda rushed across the courtyard. 'Thank goodness it's you.'

'What's with the welcome party?' Louis said, eyeing them warily.

'We need to talk to Caprice,' Alice-Miranda said quietly, trying to think of the best way to broach the subject.

Caprice rolled her eyes. 'Did my mother send you? She's such a fusspot.'

'It's not that,' Alice-Miranda replied, looking at the others for help.

'It's your grandpa,' Millie said gently.

Caprice looked at her with surprise. 'What about him?' she asked.

'He's very sick and your mother's had to go to him,' Millie explained.

'Go to him? But he's in Italy! What am *I* supposed to do?' Caprice huffed. 'I'm not slaving away in the kitchens until she can be bothered to come and get me.'

'I thought she'd be upset,' Millie whispered to Jacinta and Sloane, who both raised their eyebrows.'

'Mummy is going to organise a helicopter ride to the airport so you can catch the flight with your mother,' Alice-Miranda told the girl.

'Oh,' Caprice said, barely masking her disappointment.

'But that's not going to work.' Edgar glared at Alice-Miranda. 'We –'

Louis elbowed him in the ribs.

'Ow! What did you do that for?' Edgar bellowed.

Cecelia Highton-Smith dashed out the back door and spotted the children huddled in the courtyard. 'Oh, thank heavens!' she exclaimed, and raced towards Caprice to give the girl a hug.

Not knowing quite what to do, Caprice froze on the spot with her arms awkwardly by her sides.

'I'm afraid there's a bit of a problem,' Cecelia began. 'Birdy is being serviced, and your mother just telephoned to say that she's managed to get the last seat on a nine o'clock flight. Caprice, how do you feel about staying here with us tonight? We can arrange to get you to your mother and grandfather first thing in the morning.'

The twins smirked at each other, and Caprice looked visibly relieved.

'Perfect,' Edgar muttered.

Cecelia squeezed the girl's shoulder. 'Your mother said that she's spoken to the hospital again and your grandfather is resting comfortably and his condition is stable.'

Caprice shrugged. 'I don't really know him that well,' she said.

'What do you mean?' Millie asked.

'Mummy and Nonno didn't speak for a long time because he was mad at her for leaving Italy to come and study here, and he was even angrier when she married Daddy and decided to stay. I've only met him a few times and he doesn't speak any English, so it's a bit awkward,' Caprice said. 'He talks with his hands and he gets cross when I can't understand what he's saying.'

'I see.' Cecelia nodded. She thought that explained a bit.

'Mummy, can Caprice come to the ball tonight?' Alice-Miranda asked.

'No!' Edgar stepped in. 'She's not invited. She's got jobs to do downstairs.'

Cecelia eyeballed the lad. 'Edgar, I'm sure that we can find a place for Caprice to join us.'

Louis stared at Caprice, trying to send her telepathic messages that she would ruin their plan if she came, but the girl wasn't paying him the slightest bit of attention. She had just been invited to the Queen's Jubilee Ball and nothing in the world could persuade her to miss it.

'But I haven't got anything to wear,' the girl complained.

'Don't worry, we'll be able to rustle up something for you,' Cecelia said, remembering that she'd packed several extra dresses just in case any of the girls had a last-minute disaster. Ever since the time a waiter collided with Alice-Miranda, turning her white frock into a mango-and-passionfruit mess at a dinner for Prince Shivaji, Cecelia was always prepared for a frock emergency. Caprice was about Jacinta's size, so there would definitely be something.

'I still don't think she should be allowed to come as a guest,' Edgar insisted. 'Grandmama will not be happy.'

'I don't agree with you there,' Cecelia said. 'Your grandmother is one of the most generous people I've ever met, and she would be horrified to learn that we'd left Caprice on her own for the evening.' The woman glanced at her watch. 'Speaking of which, we'd better get a move along.'

As the children followed Cecelia back inside, Edgar and Louis positioned themselves on either side of Caprice.

'We're going to have to change our plan,' Louis hissed.

'All because of you,' Edgar scowled.

'Don't worry, it will be even better now,' Caprice said, careful to keep her voice low. 'This way, I'll get to see exactly what happens.'

'You better not squib out on us,' Edgar threatened.

Caprice rolled her eyes and put her hand into

her jacket pocket, checking that their surprise was still there. 'I won't.'

Alice-Miranda turned around and noticed the twins were being oddly attentive towards Caprice. 'Are you okay?' she asked the girl.

Caprice nodded.

'Try not to worry about your mother and your grandpa,' Alice-Miranda said.

Caprice frowned. 'I'm not.'

'Heartless cow,' Millie whispered under her breath.

'Caprice, come upstairs with the children and we'll find something for you to wear,' Cecelia said. 'And I'll arrange for an extra bed to be moved into Alice-Miranda and Millie's room for the night.'

Caprice grinned. 'This is going to be so much fun!'

As the girl ran to catch up to Jacinta and Sloane, Millie's heart sank like a stone.

Chapter 20

Cecelia Highton-Smith flopped open the lid of the box on Alice-Miranda's bed. 'Caprice, do you want to come and choose a dress?'

The girl was standing by the window and fiddling with something in her pocket. 'Sure,' she said, walking over to the bed.

Cecelia held up a stunning pink gown with a full skirt and beading around the waist. 'What about this one?'

Caprice shook her head and scrunched up her nose. 'It's pink.'

'I gather that's not your favourite colour,' Cecelia said, laying the dress on the bed. Next, she pulled out a long blue dress with a delicate floral pattern.

'Yuck! It looks like Mummy's bedspread.'

'Oh, that's a pity. I thought this one was rather pretty,' Cecelia said, hoping that the third offering might hit the spot. She lifted out a gorgeous white dress with the most intricate gold lace on the bodice and a box-pleated floor-length skirt.

Caprice nodded. 'I like that one,' she said, running her hands along its satin folds.

'Let's see if it fits.' Cecelia unzipped the back and held it out for Caprice to step into. She zipped it back up and the child turned around. Cecelia smiled. 'Oh, Caprice, that's lovely.'

Alice-Miranda walked out of the dressing-room, her cascading chocolate curls bouncing. 'That dress is perfect on you.'

Caprice bounded over to the full-length cheval mirror and admired her reflection, studying the dress from all angles. 'It is, isn't it? But what about shoes?'

'That's not going to be quite as easy, I'm afraid,' Cecelia said. 'What did you wear today?'

Caprice held up a pair of blue plimsolls.

'They won't do,' Cecelia said. She clicked her tongue and thought for a moment. 'What size do you wear?'

'A seven,' the child replied.

'That's much bigger than Millie and me,' Alice-Miranda said.

'I might have something that will do the trick,' Cecelia said, remembering that she had packed some extra ballet flats. She wondered if she could stuff the toes with tissue paper. 'I'll be back in a little while, girls. I need to get dressed, and I'll see what I can find.'

'Caprice might be the same size as Sloane or Jacinta. Do you want me to go and ask them, Mummy?' Alice-Miranda suggested.

'You'll have to put your dress on first,' Cecelia said. 'You don't want to be caught walking the palace hallways in your underwear, darling.'

'It's okay, Mummy, we have a secret passage.' The child smiled and disappeared into the dressing-room.

'See you soon, girls,' Cecelia called as she left the room.

Alice-Miranda knocked on the tiny door before pulling it open. 'Hello?'

'Hello back,' Jacinta shouted. 'I'm just putting my dress on.'

Alice-Miranda vanished through the doorway and reappeared a minute later with some silver ballet flats. She held them out to Caprice. 'I think we have a problem,' she said.

'Yes, they're the wrong colour,' Caprice replied, pulling a face.

'It's not that –'

'I can't wear a dress with gold accents and have silver shoes,' Caprice scoffed. 'It will look stupid.'

Before Alice-Miranda could set the girl straight, there was a knock on the door.

'I forgot that I had these too, and I didn't want to come through the little door just in case my dress got caught,' Jacinta said, barging into the room. She was about to hand over a pair of beige ballet slippers when she caught sight of Caprice. 'What are you wearing?' she demanded. 'Why have you got the same dress as me?'

'Sorry, Caprice, you'll just have to wear one of the others,' Alice-Miranda said, lifting the pink gown off the bed.

'No! I like this one and your mother said it was perfect,' Caprice snapped.

'But Mummy bought me this dress especially for tonight,' Jacinta said. 'And we were *properly* invited. You're just last-minute.'

Millie walked out of the bathroom with a towel wrapped around her head. 'Whoa – twins,' she blurted, looking at the pair.

'Don't worry, she's getting changed,' Jacinta said.

'No, I'm not,' Caprice retorted.

'Caprice, please be reasonable,' Alice-Miranda said, trying to prevent an all-out war. 'Mummy didn't know that Jacinta had that dress. She wouldn't have offered it to you if she had.'

'But I don't like the others. I like this one and it looks way better on me than it does on her.' Caprice stamped her foot so hard the vase of daffodils on the dressing table rattled.

'Caprice, that's not very kind,' Alice-Miranda chided.

Jacinta's eyes began to fill with tears. 'I can't believe you!' she spat.

Caprice's eyes filled with tears too. 'Why are you being so mean? My nonno is in hospital and he might die and I won't even get to see him.' Her bottom lip trembled.

'You didn't seem that worried before,' Millie muttered.

'I was just trying to be brave and keep my mind off everything, and now I can't even wear the dress that I want.' Caprice blinked her long eyelashes and fat tears fell onto the tops of her rosy cheeks.

'You're disgusting.' Jacinta stormed over to the bed and looked at the other dresses. She picked up the pink one and indicated for Alice-Miranda to undo her zipper. The girl quickly slipped out of her dress and tried on the new one.

'That looks beautiful,' Alice-Miranda said, and Millie quickly agreed.

Jacinta walked to the mirror to see for herself. She didn't like it nearly as much as the other one but there was no point arguing.

Alice-Miranda walked over to stand behind Jacinta. 'That was really kind of you,' she whispered, giving her friend a hug.

'It looks nice,' Caprice said, having apparently made a miraculous recovery. She walked over to take the beige ballet slippers.

'Oh, no you don't.' Jacinta sniffed and snatched them off the bed.

Caprice's jaw dropped. 'But the silver ones won't look any good at all.'

'Deal with it,' Jacinta said. With that, she turned around and stalked out the door.

Chapter 21

After spending forever in the bathroom fixing her hair, Caprice disappeared to collect the belongings she'd left in her mother's office. By the time the girl returned with bag in hand, there was a foldaway bed complete with matching daffodil-patterned sheets and white duvet waiting for her.

'We should get going,' Alice-Miranda called to Caprice, who was busy preening herself for the second time.

The girl wandered out of the bathroom, sighing.

'I wish I didn't have to sleep on the foldaway bed,' she whined.

'And I wish you weren't sleeping here at all,' Millie grumbled.

Alice-Miranda smiled and led the way. 'It's just for one night,' she whispered, trying to console her friend.

Lawrence, Hugh, Sep and Lucas were all waiting at the top of the landing. Jacinta and Sloane exited their room at almost the same time and joined Millie, Alice-Miranda and Caprice.

'Don't you all look gorgeous?' Lawrence Ridley said as the girls paraded down the hallway, showing off their beautiful gowns. 'Not that you lads aren't looking pretty dapper yourselves,' he said, grinning at Sep and Lucas in their tuxedos.

Alice-Miranda wore a striking blue satin dress which sparkled with crystals, while Millie had chosen a teal frock with a full organza skirt and fitted bodice. Sloane loved the way her coffee-coloured dress swished as she walked and Caprice just couldn't help herself, striking a model-like pose as she reached the gentlemen, who all remarked on how stunning she looked. Jacinta was still furious about what had happened earlier and stood at the back of the group.

'I wish your mothers were as snappy at getting ready as you girls are,' Hugh said.

The man pushed back his left sleeve and glanced at his watch.

Ambrosia Headlington-Bear emerged from her room wearing an exquisite gold gown with her glossy brunette locks pulled back into a high ponytail. A glittering choker of diamonds adorned her neck.

'Ambrosia, you look amazing,' Sloane complimented the woman.

'Thank you, sweetheart. The dress is on loan from Christian Fontaine,' Ambrosia replied. 'I can no longer afford to buy anything like this, but at least the jewels are mine – a certain someone wasn't getting these back in the divorce settlement.'

Ambrosia studied the girls and quickly realised that something wasn't right.

'Jacinta, why aren't you wearing your dress?' she asked, confused as to why Caprice was wearing it instead. She had specifically chosen the frock to complement her own.

Seeing Jacinta's face fall, Alice-Miranda decided it was best to step in. 'Mummy had the exact same dress as a spare and offered it to Caprice without knowing what Jacinta was wearing,' the child explained. 'And Jacinta was kind enough to choose another gown for the ball.'

'Well, after the shock you've had this afternoon, Caprice, I'm very glad that my daughter has been so thoughtful,' Ambrosia said graciously, giving Jacinta a nod and a wink.

But Jacinta was still fuming. She hated that Caprice looked incredible in *her* dress. The girl's copper-coloured hair matched the gold accents perfectly, and Caprice's already luminous skin looked even more flawless than usual. Jacinta kept her mouth clamped shut in case she was tempted to say something she might regret.

Lucas leaned in close to Jacinta. 'I think you look beautiful.'

'Thanks,' the girl replied, immediately feeling better.

Cecelia and Charlotte walked into the hallway at the same time. Cecelia was in a black sequinned off-the-shoulder floor-length gown while Charlotte wore a blush-toned lace frock with a plunging back. Both women had diamond-encrusted tiaras and matching earrings.

'Check out the supermodels,' Lawrence said with a grin.

'Lawrence Ridley, you are incorrigible,' Cecelia said with a giggle.

'He's right, though, darling,' Hugh agreed. 'You both look smashing.'

'Where are the twins?' Alice-Miranda asked.

'Aunty Gee arranged for one of the lovely young housemaids to watch them,' Charlotte replied.

'Well, come on, I don't know about the rest of you, but I'm dying to see what your mother has in store for our dining pleasure,' Lawrence Ridley said, winking at Caprice.

'Oh, yes, I'm sure there are lots of interesting surprises,' the girl replied sweetly.

The guests gathered in the rear foyer as a convoy of palace staff, dressed in black tail coats, accompanied them through to the front entrance hall.

'Good evening, ladies and gentlemen, children.' Braxton Balfour smiled as the group reached the bottom of the stairs.

'Hello Mr Balfour,' Alice-Miranda said. 'Where are we having dinner?'

'I'll take you through to meet everyone in the

front hall for drinks first, then it's off to the dining room and finally to the ballroom for some dancing,' the man replied.

Alice-Miranda's eyes lit up.

'Good evening, everyone,' Elsa said as she and Freddy entered the room.

'Well, well, well, Braxton Balfour,' Freddy said, archin an eyebrow.

The under butler lowered his eyes.

'Never thought I'd see you back here, but Mummy tells me you're a fine specimen . . . for a butler.' Freddy smirked. 'I only realised it was you this afternoon. The years haven't been kind, have they, old chap?'

'No, Sir,' Braxton mumbled.

'Well, carry on,' Freddy said, waving a hand. 'I'm sure you've got people to serve and all that sort of thing.'

Alice-Miranda wondered what Freddy was talking about. Poor Mr Balfour's face had flushed a dark shade of red.

'Good grief, what's Elsa wearing?' Sloane whispered to Jacinta, who worked hard to smother a grin.

The woman was enveloped by a long yellow satin gown that seemed to have more tucks and pleats than all the palace curtains put together. Her hair was piled high into a beehive with a diamond tiara perched on top. Her neck and her wrists twinkled as if she'd ransacked the entire collection of crown jewels just for the occasion.

Hugh grinned at the girls, a cheeky glint in his eye. 'Yes, it's lovely to see our future queen looking so understated, as always.'

The girls snickered and Cecelia gave her husband a playful nudge. 'Behave yourselves,' she said, suppressing a laugh.

'Please go ahead.' Braxton Balfour swept his arm forward, gesturing for the group to move on.

The children and adults walked through a gallery lined with priceless artworks and into a salon housing Her Majesty's favourite collection of marble statues. Two enormous lions guarded the entrance while, at the other end of the room, a naked man and woman cast in stone reclined on granite couches. Marble busts were arranged on tall plinths, and dotted about were ancient urns easily big enough for the children to climb inside should they have wanted to.

'Here, let me take a photo of you next to that head,' Millie said.

Alice-Miranda giggled. 'That's Julius Caesar.'

'I like his curls,' Millie said with a nod. She took her camera out of her little purse and snapped a couple of shots.

'Why don't we get a photograph of everyone together?' Alice-Miranda suggested, but the group had already spilled out all over the room.

'Would you like me to round them up for you, miss?' Mr Bunyan asked.

Millie recoiled at the sight of his head poking out from around the other side of a large statue of David. 'Were you spying on us?' the child asked.

'I was merely offering to help,' the man huffed.

Alice-Miranda wondered how long he'd been watching them. 'Thank you, Mr Bunyan,' she said, and watched as the man proceeded to gather the group of family and friends together in front of the lions.

'There's something really weird about that guy,' Millie said. 'And I think he shaves his legs.'

Alice-Miranda looked at her friend and laughed. 'What are you talking about?'

'Didn't you notice at the games this afternoon? He was standing next to your dad, who has quite a decent set of spidery pins on him, and I noticed that Mr Bunyan didn't have any hair on his legs at all. Aren't all men supposed to be hairy?'

'Maybe not,' Alice-Miranda said. 'Perhaps he cycles in his spare time. Sometimes cyclists shave their legs for greater speed.'

Millie glanced over at the bald man. 'Seriously, do you think he's about to enter the Tour de France? Not likely.'

'Excuse me, girls, everyone's ready,' Bunyan called.

'Coming,' Millie said.

'Would you like me to take the photograph, Miss Millie?' Braxton offered.

Millie smiled and nodded.

'But I could take it for you,' Bunyan said tetchily, hurrying over.

'It's all right, Bunyan, I'm perfectly capable of taking a photograph,' Braxton said through gritted teeth as Millie passed him the camera. 'I'm sure you have other things to do.'

Having only been formally introduced to the man after the games, Braxton hadn't yet had time to form an opinion on Frank Bunyan. But he was suspicious of the man's motives and, after what had happened earlier with Mr Langley, Braxton didn't need the added pressure of a potential rival.

The children and adults smiled as Braxton took

their picture. 'Lovely,' he commented before handing Millie her camera. 'If you're ready, I'll take you all through to the entrance foyer.'

Bunyan hovered in the background as the group proceeded through another set of grand doors to the front entrance hall with a magnificent central staircase and black-and-white marble chequerboard floor. A gallery with ornate gold balustrading sat above huge French doors, while the hand-painted ceiling and giant fresco above the marble fireplace rivalled the best works of Michelangelo.

'Here we are. I'll leave you to enjoy the party.' Braxton Balfour gave a bow and retreated. He was desperate for the evening to be over so he could have some time to himself. He couldn't stop thinking about what had happened earlier at the cottage and now it seemed he had Bunyan to worry about as well.

Meanwhile, Millie's eyes were the size of dinner plates as she struggled to take it all in. 'This place just gets more and more incredible,' she breathed. 'Imagine how long it would have taken to do that painting.'

Alice-Miranda turned to her friends with a gleam in her eye. 'Do you want to go up onto the gallery level?'

Jacinta and Sloane nodded. 'Yes, please,' they said at exactly the same time. The two girls looked at each other and giggled. 'Snap!'

'Could you two get any more cheesy?' Caprice scoffed.

'Cheesy beats being mean any day of the week,' Sloane retorted. 'And, speaking of mean, could we avoid those two?' She pointed at the twins, who were standing at the top of the stairs.

One wore a black waistcoat while the other had opted for grey, which Alice-Miranda noted would come in handy when trying to tell them apart.

'They're not that bad, you know,' Caprice piped up.

The children were about to move off when a waiter stopped in front of them, holding a tray laden with canapés.

'Yum, these are delicious,' Sep said as he shovelled a small pastry into his mouth.

Caprice shuddered. 'Revolting.'

'Why? What was it?' the boy asked, his mouth full.

'Snail puffs.' Caprice widened her eyes in disgust.

Jacinta and Sloane looked at one another uncertainly, wondering if she was joking or not. Lucas reached out to take a different hors d'oeuvre.

'That's minced boar's tongue,' Caprice commented, 'and that one there is pickled quail livers, just so you know.'

Lucas hesitated, his hand wavering above the plate. He smiled apologetically at the waiter and shook his head. 'No, thank you.'

'Oh, Lucas, you simply must try these,' Aunty Gee gushed, approaching the waiter from the other side. 'The quail is to die for.'

Her Majesty popped the tasty morsel into her mouth, chewed with lightning speed and swallowed. The children all looked at Caprice, who smiled like the cat with the cream. The girl certainly wasn't going to tell them that the quail was actually breast meat and the other dish was pork belly – it was much more fun watching them squirm.

'Aunty Gee, you look beautiful,' Alice-Miranda said, admiring the Queen's pale pink dress. Unlike her daughter-in-law, Her Majesty opted for a classic style with a lace bodice and long chiffon skirt. She wore a sparkling diamond-and-pearl tiara and matching pearl drop earrings.

'Thank you, darling girl. You all look a treat yourselves.' The Queen's eyes came to rest upon Caprice, who was trying to make herself invisible lest Her Majesty's memory of the camp presentation ceremony kicked in.

'You remember Caprice, Aunty Gee,' Alice-Miranda prompted. 'Her mother is Ms Baldini.'

'Yes, of course. I am sorry to hear about your grandfather, dear. You're most welcome to stay here for as long as necessary,' Queen Georgiana said sympathetically.

Caprice was positively glowing as she smiled and gave a curtsy. 'Thank you, Your Majesty.'

Millie, Sloane and Jacinta looked at each other in horror.

'I'm sure that Caprice will want to go to her mother as soon as she can,' Alice-Miranda said, 'but that's very kind of you to offer, Aunty Gee.'

'It's probably going to be hard to get to where Nonno lives,' Caprice began. 'It's a very long drive from the airport, and I'd hate for Mummy to have to leave his side. I think it's important to be with friends at a time like this.'

'Yes, it does make things easier,' the Queen said, nodding. 'And by the way, Caprice, that dress is certainly one of the prettiest I've seen in a very long time. Stunning. Absolutely stunning.'

Caprice smiled. Behind her, Jacinta felt as if she

might throw up. The girl had a hide thicker than a rhinoceros.

'Enjoy the party, children,' Aunty Gee said, taking another quail tart to go. 'I can't wait to tell you about the things I've got planned. We're going to have such a wonderful time.'

The children grinned and nodded. Exploring Evesbury Palace for the whole week was going to be buckets of fun.

'That's worked out well,' Caprice said happily. 'I'll call Mummy later and let her know that I've been invited to stay and she doesn't have to worry about me at all. She can concentrate on making sure that Nonno gets better.'

'You didn't get invited, Caprice,' Millie said. 'You invited yourself. I'm sure that if we mentioned something about camp Aunty Gee will un-invite you.'

'How can you say that, Millie, knowing that my nonno is on death's door and I don't want to be a burden to my mother?' The girl batted her eyelashes. 'You're so mean!'

'And you're unbelievable,' Millie said, and stalked off across the room.

Chapter 22

Marjorie Plunkett sat at the dressing table and checked her reflection in the mirror. She sprayed her wrists and neck with perfume before straightening her glittering headband. She was pleased with the way the diamonds and emeralds highlighted her eyes and matched her green dress perfectly. She hadn't realised that Lloyd's dear departed mother had left him such an enviable collection of jewels until she'd persuaded him to give her a peek in the family vault the week before. She was just borrowing the headband for now but, soon enough, the entire Lancaster-Brown collection would be hers.

'Are you ready, Marjorie?' Lloyd called from the sitting room. 'We're late. Although, if you'd prefer not to go, I can be out of this monkey suit in minutes and we can watch the Saturday movie.'

'Oh, Lloyd,' Marjorie huffed. He was going to have to learn to love these occasions. As she reached for a tissue she noticed the face on her watch light up. 'What now?' she muttered.

'What was that, darling?' Lloyd said, standing in the doorway.

Marjorie spun around in her seat. 'There's a problem with Her Majesty's hat for tomorrow's picnic,' she said, trying not to look flustered. She smiled and stood up, smoothing her dress with her hands. 'I need to pop up and make a couple of alterations.'

'Really? Are you sure it can't wait?' Lloyd asked. He walked towards her and gently kissed her cheek. 'Or I could come and help you. You never let me see you work.'

'I've told you before that I don't fare well with an audience,' Marjorie said. She linked arms with him and led him to the door. 'Why don't you go ahead, and I'll meet you there? Dinner isn't until eight.'

Lloyd pouted and gave a nod. 'If I have to, but don't be too long. Aunty Gee surely has a whole cupboard full of hats she could wear instead. And it's only a picnic, for heaven's sake. You know I won't enjoy a second of it until you're by my side.'

'I'll be there as quickly as I can. Remember, it is Her Majesty's special weekend and she could wear ten different hats if she wanted to,' Marjorie tutted. She accompanied him to the end of the hall and waited until he'd disappeared downstairs before racing back to their suite and locking the door behind her. Marjorie pressed the winder on the side of her watch and waited.

'Good evening, Chief,' Fiona answered.

'Hello Fi. What is it?'

'There's been a security breach at the cottage, ma'am, but I cannot determine the extent of the intrusion.'

'When?' Marjorie asked.

'Earlier this afternoon,' Fiona replied, 'but I have only just received the information. I think some-thing is interfering with our reception.'

Marjorie listened as Fiona explained the situation. 'Is she all right?' Marjorie asked.

'I believe so, ma'am.'

Marjorie paced the room, her mind racing. 'Is she in danger?'

There was a long pause.

Marjorie stopped pacing. 'Fi, is she in danger?'

'No, ma'am, but depending on what he saw, you may have been compromised.'

'We need to find out what he knows as soon as possible,' Marjorie said.

'Yes, ma'am. I've already generated a new assignment for one of our operatives on the ground,' Fiona replied.

'Well done, Fi. Let me know as soon as you have anything,' Marjorie said.

As Head of SPLOD, the Secret Protection League of Defence – the most secure and powerful spy unit in the country, Marjorie's cover was paramount.

'And what about the footage from the camera?' she asked. 'Is there anything coming through?'

'Yes, ma'am. The owner of the camera seems to take it everywhere with her and she rarely leaves Alice-Miranda's side.'

'Transmit the photographs to Bunyan – I mean, Treadwell,' Marjorie directed. 'I'd like her to review them and make sure there's nothing unusual.'

'Of course, Chief,' Fiona replied.

'Thank you, Fi,' Marjorie said.

Alice-Miranda followed Millie upstairs with Jacinta and Sloane, and Caprice slunk along behind them. The boys had been cornered by Lord Tavistock, who was teaching them the finer points of clay-pigeon shooting in anticipation of tomorrow's picnic by the river.

'Having fun, girls?' Edgar asked as he and his brother stepped out to block the girls' path.

Millie nodded. 'Yes, it's a lovely party. We were just going to look at the paintings.'

'Boring,' the twins said in unison.

'There are loads more interesting things to see around here,' Louis said.

'Like what?' Jacinta challenged, folding her arms.

Edgar looked at his brother with a sly grin. 'Well, there are the dungeons and the torture chambers.'

'There's a rack where our relatives used to take their enemies and stretch them until their arms and legs popped off,' Louis added.

200

'What do you mean our relatives *used* to take their enemies there?' Edgar said. 'Grandmama still does.'

'No, she doesn't,' Alice-Miranda said, shaking her head. 'Daddy said Evesbury was built as a beautiful home, not as a castle or a fort, so I'm sure there aren't any torture chambers or dungeons here.'

The twins looked at one another. 'So cute, isn't she?' Louis said.

'Yes, always thinking the best of everyone,' Edgar replied. 'She has no idea what Grandmama is really like. Just wait until bedtime when the palace is quiet and you can hear the wailing of all those lost souls on the shadows of the wind.'

'You should be a poet, Edgar,' Alice-Miranda said. 'You've got a wonderful imagination and a rather good way with words.'

'A poet! What stupid romantic nonsense,' Edgar scoffed. '*I'm* going to be an inventor.'

Louis stared fiercely at his brother.

'What would you invent?' Millie asked.

'I can tell you,' Caprice chimed in.

The twins looked as if they wanted to throw her off the balcony. But just as the girl was about to spill

201

the beans on the boys' secret hideaway, a loud gong reverberated throughout the hall.

The crowd hushed and a man dressed in red-and-white livery appeared in the middle of the upstairs gallery. Alice-Miranda recognised him as the young footman she'd spoken to when they'd arrived that morning. She smiled and waved at him.

He caught her eye and gave her a wink, then took a deep breath as he unfurled a short scroll. 'Your Majesty, My Lords, ladies and gentleman, boys and girls, dinner is served.'

'I jolly well hope not or it will be cold by the time we get there,' Freddy grumbled.

Queen Georgiana rolled her eyes. 'Must you always make such banal comments? You know exactly what he means,' she whispered. 'You'd better up your game, or you'll be the laughing stock of the country – when and if I hand over the reins.'

Freddy flushed. He'd been hoping his mother would announce her retirement at her jubilee celebrations, but that hardly seemed likely now. Elsa, meanwhile, stood beside her husband with her mouth gaping open.

Her Majesty grinned sweetly at her daughter-in-law. 'Close your mouth, dear. Gawping like a stunned carp is hardly becoming of the woman who would like to one day call herself Queen.'

She quickly turned her attention to the handsome man beside her.

'Robert, darling, would you mind escorting an old woman to dinner?' She smiled at Lord Adams, whose wife, Lady Sarah, was chatting animatedly with Charlotte Highton-Smith.

'It would be my pleasure, Your Majesty,' the man replied with a bow.

From the other side of the room, Thornton Thripp had been watching the exchange. Whatever had just happened, the look on Freddy and Elsa's faces was priceless. Thornton shook his head. How on earth a woman with as much grace and dignity as Her Majesty possessed had managed to produce such a gormless worm of a son was anyone's guess.

Chapter 23

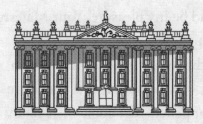

Millie gasped as the children were swept along on a tide of fabulously dressed guests into the state dining room.

'I wonder where we're sitting,' Jacinta said, surveying the long table dotted with beautifully written place cards.

A footman intercepted the group and guided them to their seats.

'You're here, Alice-Miranda,' Sep said, pointing to a spot at the table. He looked at the names to the right and left of her place setting. 'Oh, that's strange. I thought Millie would be next to you but it says Caprice is.'

Caprice smirked at Millie. 'You must be on the other side.'

Alice-Miranda had Caprice and Lucas on either side of her, with Sep next to Lucas, while Jacinta, Sloane and Millie were sitting opposite. Edgar and Louis sat across from each other, with one of them next to Caprice and the other beside Millie.

Sloane went to pull out her chair and sit down when a footman swooped in behind her and pushed it back in towards the table, almost jamming her arm in the process.

'*Excuse* me!' Sloane glared at the man.

'Wouldn't you prefer to wait for Her Majesty like everyone else?' The man's syrupy voice was sickly sweet.

Sloane looked around and realised that everyone was standing behind their chair, waiting, as Queen Georgiana proceeded to the head of the table on Lord Adams's arm. 'Oops,' she said sheepishly.

'Peasant,' Louis said under his breath.

Millie turned and looked at the lad. 'If you had

any manners you'd teach us the right things to do instead of being so hoity-toity.'

'Why would I want to teach you anything?' Louis hissed. 'You don't belong here.'

Millie glared at the boy and wrinkled her lip.

'Oooh, you're so scary,' Louis scoffed.

Millie huffed and turned her back to the insufferable lad.

Alice-Miranda's parents were further along the table, sitting opposite Charlotte and Lawrence, and Ambrosia Headlington-Bear was quite a way down, beside a gentleman with just about the most frightful comb-over the children had ever seen.

Queen Georgiana took her place at the head of the table and waited until Lord Adams found his seat halfway down the room, next to his wife. Once everyone was in place, Her Majesty gave a nod and, suddenly, what seemed like an army of attendants stepped forward to help everyone into their seats.

Millie noticed Bunyan staring at them from his spot behind Marjorie Plunkett. She nudged Jacinta. 'Why is he looking at us?' she asked.

Jacinta looked over at the man, who quickly turned away.

Alice-Miranda glanced up from the other side of the table, where she had been counting the cutlery and wondering just how many courses there were going to be at dinner. 'What are you looking so worried about, Millie?' she asked quietly.

Millie nodded her head towards Bunyan, who was staring in their direction again. 'He gives me the creeps.'

'He works here – it's his job to be attentive,' Alice-Miranda reasoned. Though, the child had a strange feeling about Mr Bunyan too. She couldn't say exactly what, but there was something odd about him and the way he kept popping up all over the place. His bald head and youthful face didn't seem to tally either. Alice-Miranda wondered if perhaps he was a fan of extreme wrinkle treatments, given the smoothness of his complexion.

A flourish of trumpets silenced the chatting guests. Thornton Thripp, who was sitting at the end of the table to Queen Georgiana's right, stood up. 'Good evening, Your Majesty and honoured guests. Before we begin our first course I would like to propose a toast.' He raised his glass. 'Long live the Queen.'

The rest of the guests were on their feet in a flash, raising their glasses towards Aunty Gee. 'Long live the Queen!' they chorused.

Alice-Miranda noticed that Freddy, who was sitting directly to the Queen's left, had barely moved his lips.

Millie had seen it too. 'Doesn't look like Freddy's that keen for his mother to live quite so long,' she whispered, a little louder than she'd anticipated as the diners sat back down.

'That's our father you're talking about,' Louis snapped.

Millie turned and glared at the boy. 'Well, he could be a bit more enthusiastic about celebrating his mother's achievement.'

'Why? Grandmama should stop hogging the throne and let Daddy have a turn. If she doesn't do it soon, he won't have that long until it will be one of us,' Louis said.

Braxton Balfour noticed Frank Bunyan lingering behind the children. 'For heaven's sake, make yourself useful,' Braxton hissed.

Startled, Bunyan looked around and snatched up a silver pitcher from the sideboard behind him.

'Don't just stand there with it!' Braxton wondered where on earth the man had done his training. He didn't seem to have a clue. Braxton watched for a moment as the new butler leaned in to refill the children's glasses.

'What do you mean "one of you"?' Millie asked. 'Don't you have five older sisters?'

'The boys are first in line,' Louis said. 'Everyone knows that.'

'Wow, I thought we'd come out of the Dark Ages,' Millie said. 'Aunty Gee should –'

'What are you doing, you numbskull?' Louis squawked. Bunyan had just overfilled the lad's glass and poured water all over the table.

'I am terribly sorry, Sir.' Bunyan grabbed a napkin and began to mop up the mess.

Braxton Balfour had heard the commotion from further down the table and charged back to see what the matter was. He glared at the man.

'Here, Master Louis, let me clear that up,' Braxton said. 'Go,' he barked at Bunyan. Braxton cleared the spill as quickly as he could, aware that he was long overdue to be back downstairs.

Meanwhile, in the kitchens, Her Majesty's head chef wiped his brow and cursed Venetia Baldini's selection of cheese soufflés for entree. He knew they would have to be timed to perfection and he'd been counting on Venetia to oversee that particularly tricky part of the evening meal. It was just an added complication as they were serving wild mushroom soup first for the appetiser.

Vincent Langley looked at his watch, his right eyelid twitching madly. 'Are we ready?' he yelled.

'Almost, sir,' the head chef shouted from the other side of the kitchen.

'Hurry up, man. Thripp's already made a toast.' Langley pressed the earpiece further into his ear. A useful addition to the palace gadgetry, the earpiece and microphone were to enable him to keep track of what was happening upstairs and down during large dinners like the one they were hosting tonight. Trouble was, he still hadn't decided who to trust as his man on the ground in the dining room.

At the last function they had held, Braxton Balfour had done a near-perfect job and it had been noted by Her Majesty. Vincent couldn't risk having him feted in that way again. Tonight Vincent had given the duty to the new chap, Bunyan, who he hoped would live up to the task.

Braxton Balfour ran into the room and quickly

slipped into line, hoping that Langley hadn't noticed his absence. In an operation requiring military precision, a long line of waiters (which included footmen, butlers and just about anyone else who worked in the house) stood at attention as the chefs plated up wild mushroom soup. Her Majesty had long ago made the decision that, while her staff could have principal roles, they had to possess skills across a range of activities. The royal budget needed trimming and she wasn't about to put her countrymen offside with unnecessary extravagances.

The head chef gave the nod of approval. 'That's it, Langley!'

'Right, off you go,' Vincent Langley barked. The waiters dived in and each filled their tray with bowls. 'And I shouldn't have to tell you how important it is that you to stay in order. I don't want Mrs Marmalade complaining about getting Lady Luttrell's gluten-free, taste-free, low-fat alternative again, do I?'

There was a mumbling of 'no, sir' along the line as the young men marched towards the dining room. After a fiasco at the last dinner, none of the staff wanted to be on the sharp end of Mrs Marmalade's tongue.

The production line of waiters made their way through the vast network of kitchens, towards a door positioned right below the end of the state dining room. Guests often marvelled at the swiftness with which meals were served. Most never realised it was due to the extraordinary planning of previous monarchs. Some said that the kitchens had been extended back in Queen Georgiana's great-great-great grandfather's time because he couldn't abide cold peas.

Just as the group was about to enter the dining room, the line came to an abrupt halt.

'What's going on up there?' Vincent Langley hissed into his earpiece. He was poised to serve Her Majesty's own soup and Thornton Thripp's as well.

'Fly, sir,' a voice called back.

'What fly? Where?' Vincent Langley sputtered.

'Kamikaze pilot, sir,' the young man replied.

'Oh, good heavens.' Vincent Langley stepped out of the line and charged as quickly as he dared to the young waiter, trying not to slop any of the soup as he went.

The fellow lowered the dish so that his boss could see. 'I think he's doing backstroke, sir.'

'How on earth do we have a fly down here? In all the years I've been at Evesbury I don't ever remember having flies in the palace kitchens,' Langley fumed. 'Well, you can't serve that, can you?'

The young waiter suppressed a cough. 'It's for Prince Freddy, sir.'

Braxton Balfour, who was standing a little further down the line, had to stop himself from shaking with laughter and spilling soup all over the place.

'I don't care who it's for! You will not be serving fly-infested soup on my watch!' Langley roared so loudly Balfour felt his hair ruffle. 'Now, get back there and replace those bowls!'

'Yes, sir.' The young waiter scurried away like a mouse on the balls of his feet.

Unfortunately, Frank Bunyan, who was in charge of the invisible door at the end of the dining room, hadn't realised there was a problem down below. He opened the panel, having heard something of a commotion on the other side. He could see that Queen Georgiana had already devoured her first bread roll and was beginning to look quite impatient. 'Hurry up, Her Majesty is getting a bit tetchy,' he whispered to the first lad in the line.

The young man hesitated, then charged through the door towards his assigned area.

Vincent Langley realised all too late that the group was on the move. 'No, no, no, you'll be out of order!' he squealed.

He frantically did the calculations in his head, trying to work out how he could rescue the impending soup disaster. Little did he know that things were about to go from bad to much, much worse.

Chapter 24

'Oh, look, our first course is here,' Millie announced, grateful for the distraction.

Suddenly, all one hundred guests had steaming-hot bowls of soup in front of them. Jacinta marvelled at the efficiency of Her Majesty's wait staff and wondered how on earth the chefs managed to serve up that many plates all at the same time.

'Hello Mr Balfour.' Alice-Miranda turned and smiled at the butler after he set a bowl of soup down in front of her and another in front of Caprice.

'Hello Miss Highton-Smith-Kennington-Jones,' the man whispered, keeping an eye on Langley. He knew the man would disapprove of his fraternising with the guests.

'What's this slop?' Edgar demanded.

'It looks like mushroom soup to me,' Millie said, staring at the creamy brown liquid in front of her.

Edgar dropped his napkin on the floor. Just as he leaned down, Braxton Balfour swooped in to pick it up. 'Leave it!' the boy barked. 'I can do it.'

Braxton Balfour looked as if he'd almost had his fingers taken off by a terrier. 'Sorry, Sir,' the man mumbled, stepping back.

Edgar tugged on Caprice's arm. She ducked her head down, pretending to search for Edgar's napkin. 'Did you do it?' the lad asked.

Caprice smirked. 'Of course I did.'

'How did you know which one was hers?' the boy asked.

'I checked the plan that was on the wall in the kitchen. That Langley is really obsessive-compulsive,' Caprice whispered. She sat up and passed Edgar his napkin.

'This soup smells delicious,' Alice-Miranda said, smiling at Caprice.

'It's just mushrooms,' Caprice replied. She promptly turned to continue talking to Edgar.

All around the table, diners were delicately dipping their spoons into their soup bowls in the proper fashion, pushing the spoon from the front to the back. Except, not everyone was finding it as easy as they should have.

'Gosh, this soup is thick,' Millie said as she tried to push her spoon through the bowl.

Jacinta looked over at Millie. 'What's wrong?'

Millie frowned. 'My spoon's stuck.'

'Well, that's ridiculous.' Jacinta leaned over to take a closer look.

It seemed that Millie wasn't the only one having trouble.

'Freddy, what on earth are you doing?' Elsa whispered to her husband.

'There's something wrong with my soup,' Freddy whispered back while trying to force his spoon through the bowl.

'Yum, this is delicious.' Alice-Miranda took a spoonful of soup and smiled at Caprice. 'Your mother is a whiz.'

Edgar's jaw dropped and he elbowed Caprice sharply in the ribs.

'Ow!' the girl protested.

'I thought you had this all worked out,' the boy said through gritted teeth.

'I did!' Caprice snapped. 'Those idiots must have got the bowls out of order.'

Several guests were having similar troubles.

'I say, this soup is awfully stodgy,' Lord Luttrell commented as he attempted to dig his way through it.

'What's wrong with it?' Sloane asked as Millie wrestled with her spoon.

'I don't know.' Millie battled on, determined to get a taste. She gave it one last push until the spoon released without warning. A huge brown splodge flew across the table and smacked Caprice right on the nose.

'Ahhh!' the girl shrieked like a banshee. Caprice picked up her own spoon, poised to launch a counterattack.

Alice-Miranda flung her arm out to stop her. 'No!'

A little further down the table Lord Luttrell had also finally managed to free his spoon, flinging a glob of soup at Lord Adams.

'Steady on, Luttrell!' Lord Adams exclaimed, wiping at his forehead with his napkin.

Queen Georgiana looked up and was stunned to see soup catapulting from one side of the table to the other. 'Good heavens! This is not the dining room at Fayle, for Lord's sake.' Her Majesty shouted. 'Langley!'

The butler's eyes were almost popping out of his head.

Edgar and Louis both glared at Caprice, who was mopping at her face and snivelling.

'You were supposed to only put one strip on *her* bowl,' Edgar hissed, pointing to Alice-Miranda.

Caprice wrinkled her nose. 'Well, there was some left over and I wanted to be sure.'

'Caprice, I'm so sorry!' Millie exclaimed. 'My spoon was stuck and I couldn't get it out. I don't know what happened.'

Suddenly, a huge dollop of soup flew into the air and landed with a splash on the front of Alice-Miranda's dress. She had no idea where it had come from but the look on Freddy's face said it all. The man's jaw just about hit the table.

'Oops.' Alice-Miranda picked up her napkin and dabbed at the runny mess.

Queen Georgiana leapt to her feet. 'Stop! Stop this at once!' she commanded.

The chinking of cutlery silenced and the guests stared at one another, wondering what on earth had just happened.

'What's the matter?' Lawrence glanced to his right and realised that several of the diners including his niece were covered in soup. 'Oh dear, what a mess!'

Further down the table, Marjorie Plunkett twitched nervously. She wondered if whoever was sending those notes had created the soup fiasco as some sort of diversion, though it did just seem like a childish prank.

'Freddy, pick up your bowl, please,' the Queen directed.

The man balanced the dish while his mother felt around underneath it.

'Aha! There's something here.' She picked at the thin strip on the underside of the crockery.

Millie held up her bowl and Jacinta did the same, nimbly releasing the offending magnetic gunk and holding it up for all to see.

'What's that?' Sep asked.

All of a sudden Jacinta's salad fork flew up from the table and attached itself to the strip.

'How curious,' Marjorie marvelled at the hovering cutlery.

'It's magnetic,' Lord Adams said, examining his strip. 'Must be terribly strong.'

Queen Georgiana had managed to prise the strip from her son's bowl and now had a jangling row of silverware hanging off it too.

'My dear guests, I do apologise for this dreadful trick,' she said. 'Rest assured that I will arrange to have your clothes cleaned and the expenses taken from the allowance of the two boys whom I suspect are responsible.' The Queen glanced from one side of the table to the other, staring down her grandsons. Louis and Edgar sank in their seats. 'If anyone needs to freshen up, we'll hold off the next course until you return.'

Freddy glared at his sons. 'It's all right, Mama. I'll deal with those two after dinner. And I promise you – losing their pocket money will be just the start.'

Queen Georgiana felt the tickle of a grin on her lips. While she was utterly horrified by her grandsons' behaviour, hearing their father step up to the mark was a very pleasant surprise.

Several of the diners began to make a move.

Alice-Miranda looked at Caprice. 'Do you want to go upstairs and get changed?' she asked.

Caprice wiped her tear-stained face and nodded.

Millie watched from the other side of the table. She had a nagging suspicion the girl had something to do with the debacle. But she had no proof and there was no point accusing Caprice without it.

Chapter 25

Braxton Balfour finally retired to his room just after 2 am. The band had played until well after midnight, when the last guests left the ballroom. Fortunately, the rest of the evening had run smoothly after the soup fiasco. But there was work to be done before he and the household staff could get to bed. Vincent Langley would allow no evidence of the party to remain and there were preparations for the picnic brunch in the morning too. Although he was dead on his feet, there was something Braxton needed to find before he'd be able to sleep. He pulled the old trunk from under his narrow bed and unclipped its rusted latches.

When Braxton had left home at twenty years of age to work for Her Majesty at Brackenhurst Castle, he'd gathered every precious possession he owned and placed them into that trunk. His father and mother had stayed on the farm at Evesbury for another fifteen years before they moved into a retirement home. After they left, their old house was converted to rental accommodation for people who fancied a holiday on a royal estate, and the surrounding acreage was leased to another tenant farmer.

Having spent eighteen happy years of service as a footman at Brackenhurst, Braxton was promoted to the position of under butler at Evesbury just a couple of months ago. More than anything, he desired to be head butler. It had been a dream of his since he was a small boy, when Her Majesty's father had visited their home to thank Braxton's father for catching his treasured stallion, who had escaped from the Evesbury stables. The King had joined the family at the kitchen table for a cup of tea and some of Mrs Balfour's home-made scones.

During Braxton's time at Brackenhurst, his father had passed away and his mother had succumbed to the darkness of dementia. She was now seventy-five, and he feared she would not be with them much longer. Braxton had considered whether returning to Evesbury would open old wounds, but there was never any thought of turning down the position.

He pulled out the crocheted rug his mother had made for him years before and laid it on the bed. Next, there was a schoolbook filled with his attempts at fancy script, and his one and only cricket trophy. There were treasured magazines from his boyhood and an old cricket cap. Tucked in at the very bottom, Braxton found a small envelope of photographs. He wondered if the one he was searching for was still there.

He shuffled through the black-and-white pictures. There were several shots of him as a baby, then as a toddler with his faithful dog Nuff. There were some school photographs evidencing terrible haircuts, and a couple of shots of a camping trip he took with his friends. Braxton's heart sank as he reached the end of the pile. He tried to picture her in his mind but the image was hazy.

He returned the stack to the envelope and was about to put them away when he noticed an outline of something under the newspaper that lined the bottom of the trunk. And then he remembered. He'd hidden the picture under the layer of ancient news.

Braxton gulped. He pulled back the pages and picked up the photograph.

It had been a perfect day. She looked back at him, her eyes sparkling and every bit as lovely as he remembered. He was standing beside her, holding her hand. Braxton felt an ache in his chest and wondered how, all these years later, he could still feel so happy and so sad at the same time. There had never been anyone else. It was as if his heart had been torn in two and no woman, no matter how perfect, could mend it.

Braxton searched her face. Was it really her? Tomorrow he would take that picture with him and find out for sure.

Chapter 26

'Good morning, sleepyheads.' Cecelia Highton-Smith breezed into the girls' bedroom just after nine.

Alice-Miranda had been awake for a little while, reading. In the bed beside her, Millie stretched her arms and yawned. Caprice was still fast asleep in the foldaway under the windows, her breaths punctuated by gentle snores.

'Hello Mummy.' Alice-Miranda sat up as her mother perched beside her. 'Wasn't the party wonderful?'

Cecelia smiled and stroked the top of her daughter's head. 'Yes, it was. Although, I think your father pulled a muscle from all that dancing.'

Millie rolled over and sat up too. 'Aunty Gee was hilarious! Who would've thought that she and Mrs Marmalade would have that funny dance all choreographed? I could hardly believe it when the rest of the palace staff joined in. I should have taken more photographs.'

'Aunty Gee knows how to have fun, that's for sure,' Cecelia agreed.

'And even Freddy got up and danced, but Elsa looked as if she'd swallowed a fly,' Millie said with a giggle.

'Yes, it was good to see Freddy and his mother getting on,' Cecelia said. 'I don't think that's been the case for quite some time. Anyway, girls, why don't you get up and have a shower? Then we'll head out to brunch.'

Alice-Miranda pushed back the covers and scurried off to the bathroom.

Caprice's eyes fluttered before she yawned and pushed herself up onto her pillows.

'Good morning, Caprice,' Cecelia said as she pulled back the curtains and the sunshine streamed through. She took a seat on the end of the girl's bed. 'I spoke to your mother a little while ago and she said she'd like you to join her today.'

Caprice's bottom lip began to tremble. 'But I don't want to see Nonno when he's sick, and Aunty Gee said I could stay.' Fat tears threatened to spill.

Millie was watching from her bed, wondering when the girl was going to win her first Academy Award.

'Why don't I phone your mother again?' Cecelia suggested, surprised at the girl's reaction. 'Perhaps you can stay another day and then we can reassess.'

Caprice nodded. Her long wet lashes framed her sparkling sapphire-blue eyes.

Millie rolled her eyes. It was so unfair that the brat looked beautiful even when she cried.

'All right, we'll be leaving for the picnic brunch in about twenty minutes,' Cecelia said as she got up and walked to the door. 'It's a bit of a trek across the field to get there but it's a gorgeous day.'

'You should go to your mother,' Millie said after Cecelia had left.

'Why should you get to have all the fun?' Caprice retorted. 'Besides, I don't want to be near anyone who's dying.'

'Your grandpa might not die, you know, Caprice,' Millie said.

'Then I'll see him when he gets better,' the girl sniffed. 'Bags having the next shower.'

Caprice gathered up her things and ran off to the bathroom, leaving Millie shaking her head.

Aunty Gee's brunch was never going to be your average family picnic. A huge blue-and-white striped marquee had sprung up by the stream and there were pretty folding chairs and small tables dotted across a stretch of freshly mown grass.

Inside the tent, a long oak table heaved under the weight of breakfast treats. There were all manner of pastries, cereals, fruit and yoghurt, and a row of silver chafing dishes with little lamps burning beneath them to keep the bacon, eggs, sausages, hash browns, tomatoes and pancakes warm. Over in one corner stood a counter with three chefs making eggs to order.

'Good morning, my darlings,' Granny Valentina greeted Alice-Miranda and her friends as they gambolled across the field to join the festivities. Lucas and Sep had taken charge of the twins in their buggy while Jacinta couldn't resist doing some tumble turns in the long grass. Caprice hovered behind the boys walking beside Sloane, who was doing her best to ignore the girl.

'Hello Granny.' Alice-Miranda ran towards the woman and gave her a tight squeeze around the middle. 'Have you already had your breakfast?'

Millie skipped in beside her friend and Valentina gave her a hug too.

'Yes, Gee and I came down a little while ago. Good thing too, because she's been called back to the palace to sort out some official business. I tell you, that woman works far too hard. She was supposed to be taking it easy this weekend,' Valentina Highton-Smith tutted.

'Aunty Gee is amazing,' Millie said. The girl checked herself and shook her head.

'What's wrong, Millie?' Alice-Miranda asked.

'I still can't believe I get to call Her Majesty "Aunty Gee" and that I'm here at the palace and now I'll be staying for a whole week. If someone had told me a year ago that this would happen, I'd have said that they were completely bonkers.'

Alice-Miranda and her grandmother smiled at the girl.

'Well, Millie, I've known Gee since we were toddlers and I have to say that the woman hasn't changed a bit. She's still the same generous, kind-hearted girl I've always known,' Valentina said. 'So you make sure that you enjoy every minute and don't be afraid to tell everyone exactly what she's like. I think far too many people form views about someone when they don't know the person at all.'

'What do you mean, Granny?' Alice-Miranda asked.

Valentina sighed. 'There are certain members of society who'd be very happy to see Gee give up the crown. In fact, there are plenty of people who'd be happy to see the whole monarchy crumble,' she explained.

Alice-Miranda's brow creased. 'I thought everyone loved Aunty Gee.'

'Lots do, of course. It's just that there are individuals who would love to see her gone. But not in my lifetime if I have anything to say about it,' Valentina said.

Lloyd Lancaster-Brown had been standing nearby drinking his tea when he overheard their conversation. 'What are you talking about, Valentina?' he asked.

'I was just telling the girls that there are people who'd like to see Gee give up the throne,' the woman explained.

'Surely not.' Lloyd frowned. 'The woman's a brick. Her son, on the other hand . . .'

Valentina playfully smacked him on the arm. 'I'm sure that Freddy will do a fine job when his turn comes.'

'I can't imagine Aunty Gee not being the Queen,' Alice-Miranda said.

'Me either,' Millie said. 'She's like the stars, really.'

Alice-Miranda and her grandmother looked at the child quizzically.

'You might not see them every night but you know they'll always be there,' Millie explained.

'What a lovely way to look at it,' Valentina said with a nod.

'That buffet looks amazing.' Millie had been eyeing the plump croissants ever since they'd arrived in the marquee.

'Off you go, girls.' Valentina smiled at the children and waved them off. 'Get in there while there's still something left. I can see Edgar and Louis coming now, and you know what teenage boys are like when it comes to food!'

Chapter 27

The morning passed in the blink of an eye. Lord Tavistock showed off his expert skills at clay-pigeon shooting, barely letting anyone else take a turn, much to the disappointment of Sep and Lucas. After having listened to the man blather on about it the night before, the two boys had been keen to give it a go, but soon they had great fun careering around in one of Her Majesty's buggies instead.

The head horseman and several stablehands brought down a variety of traps and drays and organised rides along the river. Millie and Alice-Miranda had hoped they might go riding later in the day but in the meantime Millie, Jacinta and Caprice were learning the art of fly fishing. Millie hooked a very impressive trout, which jumped all over the river before leaping right off the hook. Soon after that, Caprice boasted that she'd caught an even bigger fish. With her rod bending and curving under the strain of the catch, she was determined to reel in the monster. Sadly for her it turned out to be just a snag in the river.

Alice-Miranda spent much of the time cuddling Marcus and Imogen, who she decided were the world's best sleepers. And, to everyone's surprise, Sloane was proving to be a very helpful babysitter.

'Darling, Daddy and I need to get going,' Cecelia called as the girls climbed down from the buggy they'd just ridden around the field.

Alice-Miranda raced towards her mother and gave her a hug. 'Already? What about Aunt Charlotte and Uncle Lawrence and the babies?'

'They're off too, I'm afraid,' Cecelia replied. 'Lawrence has some red-carpet commitments back in Los Angeles, and Granny is going home with them to help Charlotte with the twins.'

Cecelia knelt down and brushed the hair from her daughter's face.

'You know you can come home with us if you'd like to,' she said. 'I'm sure Aunty Gee wouldn't be upset if you changed your mind.'

Millie, Jacinta and Sloane's faces fell at the suggestion they might not be staying. Caprice huffed loudly.

'No, no, no, that won't do at all,' Queen Georgiana said, walking up with Valentina Highton-Smith. 'I've already made arrangements and I've promised this for ages. The children will have a lovely time.'

'It's all right, Aunty Gee,' Alice-Miranda said. 'I still want to stay if you'll have us.'

'Well, thank heavens for that.' The old woman grabbed Alice-Miranda around the shoulders and hugged her tight.

'Is everything all right, Aunty Gee?' Cecelia asked. The woman wasn't renowned for her outward displays of affection, yet Alice-Miranda had been receiving hugs on a regular basis all weekend.

'Yes, of course. I'm just thrilled to have the children staying. It will put a bit of life back into the old place.' Queen Georgiana released Alice-Miranda and smiled at the group. 'Anyway, Mrs Marmalade will help me.'

Marian Marmalade, having just joined the group, wondered what she'd been volunteered for this time. 'What am I doing?' she asked.

'I said that you'd help me look after the children for the week,' Aunty Gee said.

'Wonderful,' Mrs Marmalade muttered, horrified at the thought.

Millie, Jacinta and Sloane all clenched their fists and exchanged grins. 'Yes!' A collective hiss went up between them, while Caprice wore a smarmy grin.

Alice-Miranda smiled. 'Don't worry, Mummy. I'll be home on Sunday and then I'll have two more weeks to drive you quite mad. You'll be glad I'm going back to school.'

'Darling, I am never glad when you go back to school. Daddy and I miss you like crazy.' Cecelia leaned down and kissed the top of her daughter's head. 'Now, I want you all to look after each other and do everything Aunty Gee asks.'

The girls nodded.

'And, Caprice,' Cecelia looked over Millie's shoulder at the girl standing a few steps away, 'I've asked Mr Langley to telephone your mother again tomorrow and see what she wants you to do, but I suspect she's happy for you to stay. She says, though your grandfather is much better, she wants to organise for him to move into a retirement village so there's someone to keep an eye on him.'

'I'm so glad that Nonno is going to be all right.' Caprice smiled, a tear forming in the corner of her eye. 'And it sounds like Mummy has a lot to deal with, so if you don't mind me staying, I'm sure it will make things much easier for her.'

Queen Georgiana nodded. 'Of course, dear. You're welcome to stay as long as you like.'

Millie, Jacinta and Sloane traded glances.

Caprice smiled. 'Thank you, Aunty Gee.'

Millie looked at the girl and thought she might throw up.

Chapter 28

By Monday morning the palace had taken on a completely different feel. Most of the guests had left the previous afternoon, except for Alice-Miranda, her friends and Edgar and Louis. Though the boys only lived a couple of miles away, they preferred to stay at their grandmother's because Evesbury Palace was much closer to the tower.

The children had enjoyed a simple supper in the casual sitting room the night before. They'd played board games until Caprice was caught cheating and stormed off to bed in a huff. Aunty Gee had been called away on some official palace business, leaving Mrs Marmalade to make sure they all got to bed at a reasonable hour. It had been arranged for the children to meet Aunty Gee for breakfast in the small dining room at half past seven, and one of the butlers was to escort them downstairs.

At exactly twenty-five past the hour there was a sharp knock on Alice-Miranda's bedroom door. Millie raced to open it.

'Good morning, Miss Millicent.' Frank Bunyan bowed his head slightly. 'I've come to collect you all for breakfast.'

Millie frowned, wondering why he had to come.

'Hello Mr Bunyan,' Alice-Miranda bounded over to the door. 'How are you today?'

'Fine, thank you,' the man said with a nod. 'Are you ready to go?'

'Caprice is still in the bathroom,' Millie said. She turned and yelled for the girl to hurry up.

'I'm coming,' Caprice called back. 'If *someone* hadn't taken all day in the shower I'd be ready by now.'

A smile tickled Millie's lips. She hadn't been that long in the shower but she'd purposely kept busy in the bathroom, grooming herself within an inch of her life. Her nails were neatly filed and scrubbed clean, her ears were completely wax-free and she'd even had time to blow-dry her hair.

Millie looked at the butler. 'Mr Bunyan, is there something the matter with your face?' she asked. The skin on the man's jaw seemed to be hanging loose.

'What?' Mr Bunyan squeaked.

'Your face – it's coming apart,' Millie said.

'Millie!' Alice-Miranda chided from where she had gone to collect her cardigan. When she rejoined the pair, the girl quickly realised that her friend was right. 'Oh, there *is* something unusual.'

Mr Bunyan stalked across to the dressing-table mirror, and the girls watched as he pulled a small tube from his pocket. He squeezed a tiny amount of liquid onto his fingers and rubbed at his jawline.

'What are you doing?' Millie asked.

'It's just some chafing,' Mr Bunyan replied.

Millie grinned. 'I get that all the time from riding, but not on my face.'

Bunyan sniffed. 'How utterly unpleasant.'

'It's not that bad,' Millie said with a shrug. 'You get used to it.'

Alice-Miranda studied the man's face. There was

something that just didn't add up. She wished she could work out what it was.

'I'll go and get the others, shall I?' Bunyan said and hurried out the door.

Within a couple of minutes the group was gathered on the landing. As instructed, the children all wore casual clothes, suitable for running about and exploring.

'Come along, everyone.' Bunyan turned to lead the way downstairs. 'You don't want to keep Her Majesty waiting.'

The breakfast room was a bright and pretty space with lemon-coloured curtains covered in floral sprays, and comfy wicker chairs with matching cushions. Archie and Petunia were dozing in two baskets on the floor, bathed in the morning sunshine. They raised their heads and began to growl as Mr Bunyan and the children walked into the room.

'Good morning, my darlings.' Queen Georgiana trilled from where she was sitting at the head of a long white dining table.

'Hello Aunty Gee.' Alice-Miranda greeted the woman with a hug, then bounced to the other end of the table and greeted Mrs Marmalade in a similar fashion.

'Oh, good morning to you too,' Mrs Marmalade reeled.

Queen Georgiana raised her eyebrows at the woman. 'Marian, the child gave you a hug, she didn't thwack you with a cattle prod.'

Marian allowed herself a small smile.

The other children greeted Her Majesty and Mrs Marmalade with a cacophony of good mornings.

The two little beagles scampered out of their baskets and made a beeline for Bunyan, sniffing the man's legs and barking.

'Stop that nonsense, Archie, Petunia,' Her Majesty scolded. She waved the children to sit down. 'I haven't a clue what they're upset about. They never properly bark at anyone.'

'Except that wretched woman who managed to get into your bedroom the last time we opened the palace for tours,' Mrs Marmalade said. 'It was lucky Archie took a nip out of her, or we'd never have found your watch in her pocket.'

'That's horrid,' Alice-Miranda said.

'Well done, Archie!' Jacinta said, patting the dog on the head.

'My mummy says that dogs have an excellent

radar for people,' Millie chimed in. 'They can always tell if someone's up to no good.'

Frank Bunyan jumped and began to retreat from the room when Thornton Thripp walked through the door with a newspaper tucked under his arm.

'Bunyan, I'll have a white tea.'

The butler hesitated.

Thripp looked at him. 'Is there a problem?'

'No, sir.' Bunyan walked over to the sideboard and picked up the teapot.

'What's the matter with the dogs?' Thornton asked as he sat down.

'Archie, Petunia, heel,' Her Majesty commanded, but the beagles seemed intent on investigating Mr Bunyan.

The butler walked over to the table and poured Thornton's tea, with Archie and Petunia relentlessly sniffing about his heels.

Caprice giggled. She wondered if Louis and Edgar had been painting the soles of the new butler's shoes too.

Braxton Balfour walked into the room, carrying a large silver tray which he placed in the middle of the table. 'Scrambled eggs, Ma'am,' he said.

'Thank you, Balfour,' Her Majesty replied.

'Perhaps Bunyan can help you bring the rest of the food before it's stone-cold.'

'Yes, Ma'am.' Braxton gave a small bow.

Frank Bunyan shook his leg and tried to prise himself free of Petunia, who had latched on to the bottom of his trouser leg.

'Petunia, stop that at once,' Queen Georgiana called sharply. The little dog let go and she and Archie scampered back to their baskets.

Frank Bunyan walked out of the room as quickly as he dared and was almost barrelled over by Edgar and Louis. The boys each kissed their grandmother on the cheek and quickly found a place to sit.

'Goodness me, look at the pair of you,' Her Majesty tutted. 'Before you go outside, please attempt to run a comb through those birds' nests you call hair.'

Louis scratched at the side of his head, making his dark locks even more unruly.

'The palace feels strange today,' Jacinta said as she buttered a piece of toast.

'What do you mean, dear?' Queen Georgiana asked.

'Well, sort of empty,' the girl replied. 'I suppose

now that everyone has gone home, the palace just seems so big.'

'Oh, yes, that's exactly why I wanted you all to stay,' Aunty Gee said before taking a sip of tea. 'I hate rattling around here on my own. It's always much nicer when there are children. Well, some children.'

The Queen looked at each of her grandsons and waggled her eyebrows.

'We're not that bad, Grandmama,' Edgar said.

'No, not always,' she said with a frown, 'except yesterday afternoon and last night when you were positively deplorable. But I'll leave your father to deal with you both.'

The boys looked sheepish.

'Now, how about we start off with a tour of the palace this morning?' Queen Georgiana suggested.

'Yes, please!' Millie clapped her hands together and there was murmur of agreement around the table.

'Excellent,' Her Majesty replied.

'Would we be able to go riding later?' Alice-Miranda asked.

Jacinta and Sloane both wrinkled their noses. Neither of the girls were big fans of horses.

Queen Georgiana looked at Thornton Thripp,

who glanced up from his newspaper and gave a slight shrug. 'I don't see why not. Perhaps I can come with you,' Her Majesty replied.

'I'd like to see the library,' Sep suggested. 'I've heard that there are lots of first editions.'

'Oh, yes!' Aunty Gee nodded. 'We have a fabulous collection, and I'm thrilled that someone as young as yourself would want to see it, Sep.'

'Boring,' Caprice muttered under her breath.

'What was that, dear?' the Queen asked.

'I said I'd love to see the library too,' the child said sweetly.

'What about you, Lucas? Is there anything special that you'd like to do?' Queen Georgiana asked.

'I've been dying to visit that tower up on the ridge,' the boy said.

There was a chorus of yesses from the girls and Sep. Edgar and Louis glanced at each other and then at Caprice, who looked as if she was about to say something. Louis ran his finger across his throat and glared at the girl.

'I haven't been up there for a long time. I'm not even sure what condition the place is in,' Her Majesty replied.

'I think it's locked up tighter than Fort Knox,'

Thornton Thripp said. 'Last time I asked Mr Budd about it he said that they'd lost the keys, so it might prove difficult.'

Edgar and Louis smirked at one another.

'That's a pity,' Queen Georgiana said.

'I would love to have seen it too,' Alice-Miranda said, slightly disappointed.

As the group munched on their breakfast, Vincent Langley appeared at the door with Marjorie Plunkett close behind.

'Miss Plunkett to see you, Ma'am.' The man nodded. 'And the twins' mother telephoned to say that she will be here shortly to take them to have their hair cut.'

Langley then retreated from the room.

'Nooo!' the boys wailed in unison.

Caprice leaned over towards Edgar. 'Are you sure you took Langley's shoes?' she asked.

'Yes,' the boy whispered. 'But maybe Bunyan's wearing them instead.'

'I thought that too,' Caprice replied with a giggle.

Marjorie smiled nervously. 'Excuse me, Your Majesty, but I was wondering if I might have a word. It's rather urgent.'

Queen Georgiana pushed back her chair and stood up.

'Miss Plunkett, I loved that hat Aunty Gee was wearing at the garden party,' Alice-Miranda piped up.

Marjorie stared blankly at the child.

'The hat you made?' Alice-Miranda said.

'Oh, yes, of course,' Marjorie replied quickly. 'It was very pretty.'

'I found a little piece of peacock fabric in the back hall yesterday afternoon too. I only realised when I looked at it again this morning that it was just like the band from Aunty Gee's sunhat. I think it fell out of Mr Balfour's pocket.'

'Really?' Marjorie inhaled sharply. She needed to find out exactly what Braxton Balfour knew.

'Mummy said that you only make hats for Aunty Gee,' the child continued. 'You must be so clever. I can't imagine how hard it must be to make a hat.'

Thornton Thripp stood up and excused himself from the table. As he brushed past Marjorie, he whispered something in her ear. She nodded and waited for Queen Georgiana to stand up.

'Mrs Marmalade, perhaps you could take the children on the tour of the house until Marjorie and

I have finished our business. I'll come and find you as soon as I can.'

Her Majesty gave the woman a meaningful look, then followed Thornton out the door with Marjorie right behind her. Archie and Petunia scrambled out of their baskets and scampered after them.

Chapter 29

'Right, where shall we go first?' Mrs Marmalade asked as the children finished their breakfasts.

'Why don't we just wander along the corridor and see where we end up?' Alice-Miranda suggested.

The rest of the children nodded.

Marian Marmalade pinched her nose. 'That sounds a little . . . haphazard,' she said.

'Oh, Mrs Marmalade –' Lucas walked up to the woman and offered her his arm – 'half the fun is not knowing where you might end up.'

The old woman felt a tickly buzz in the corner of her lips. 'Well, if you say so.'

Lucas turned and winked at his friends behind him.

Jacinta rolled her eyes and the girls giggled.

Marjorie Plunkett sat down opposite Thornton Thripp in Her Majesty's private study. 'We've received another letter,' she said, holding up a plastic sleeve.

'Are you any closer to finding out who's responsible?' Her Majesty asked as she pulled a pair of white gloves from the top of her desk drawer and put them on.

'We may have a DNA sample from one of the envelopes,' Marjorie replied.

'What?' Thornton raised his eyebrows.

Marjorie shook her head. 'I'd rather not say more until we've had time to run some further tests.'

'I don't believe there's any reason to withhold information from Her Majesty,' Thornton bristled.

'Quite honestly, I would prefer not to speculate,'

Marjorie replied with a sharp edge to her voice. 'It's not helpful.'

'Agreed.' Queen Georgiana pulled the letter from the sleeve, laying it on the table. She looked at the note. A deep furrow of lines crisscrossed her forehead. 'What's this nonsense?'

Silver will never be gold.
Time to hand over the reigns.

Her Majesty frowned. 'Well, for one thing, they can't spell, and thank heavens they've stopped that ridiculous rhyming nonsense.'

'Yes,' Marjorie said, pursing her lips. 'At least there's no reference to Alice-Miranda this time.'

'What do you think, Thripp?' The Queen looked at her chief advisor.

'Perhaps it's Freddy.' The man's eyes widened. 'He's keen to get rid of you, isn't he? "Time to hand over the reigns" sounds like a play on words. Silver could be a reference to your silver jubilee.'

'That's preposterous,' Marjorie retorted.

Queen Georgiana glared. 'I know my son is a lot of things, Thripp, but I doubt he would go to these lengths to get me to relinquish the crown. He may be a buffoon but he's a good-hearted one. And, despite my misgivings, I know he will make a suitable king one day.'

Thripp's eye twitched. 'Yes, of course, Ma'am.'

Marjorie Plunkett clasped her hands together. 'I'm confident we'll find the perpetrator very soon.'

'Really?' Thornton said. His eye seemed even twitchier.

'Everyone makes mistakes, and I'm sure whoever is responsible for the letters will trip up sooner or later,' Marjorie said.

Thornton nodded. 'We can only hope.'

'On a related topic, what are you doing today, Thripp?' Queen Georgiana asked. 'I thought you could help me entertain the children for a while.'

Thornton hesitated. 'I really don't have time . . .' he began.

The Queen arched an eyebrow. 'We've just had the jubilee, and as far as I know there's nothing too pressing on your plate at the moment.'

Thornton's shoulders slumped. He knew when he was defeated.

'Wonderful! Let's find Mrs Marmalade and the children.' Her Majesty pushed her chair out and stood up. The others were quickly on their feet too. 'Goodbye, Marjorie, and thank you for taking the lead on this – I wouldn't want anyone other than the Chief of SPLOD in charge of the investigation. Come along, Thornton.'

The man followed Her Majesty out of the room.

Marjorie Plunkett returned the letter to its plastic sleeve and slipped it down the side of her oversized handbag. She noticed the face of her watch light up and pressed the button on the side to answer. 'What do you have for me, Fi?'

'Good morning, ma'am. I've run those tests you asked for,' Fiona replied.

'And?' Marjorie hoped this was the breakthrough they were looking for. Fi had been confident that there were traces of saliva on the last envelope.

'Nothing, ma'am,' Fi replied.

'Nothing! Are you sure?' Marjorie's earpiece exploded with the harsh crackling of static. The woman's eyes crossed and she almost leapt out of her skin. 'What on earth was that?' Marjorie demanded.

The line went dead.

Marjorie frowned. Nothing like that had ever happened before, and she didn't have a good feeling about it. She needed to get back to headquarters as quickly as she could.

Chapter 30

The children and Mrs Marmalade wound their way through several rooms, ogling the incredible architecture and opulent furnishings. To Sep's great delight, the boy had located a first edition of Charles Dickens's *A Christmas Carol* in the library, and Mrs Marmalade had found the lad a pair of gloves so that he could examine the book more closely. The rest of the children had taken turns pushing each other on the giant ladder that snaked around the bookshelves on rails.

Upon leaving the library, the group found themselves in an enormous gallery that showcased the best artists of every generation. There was barely a space between each painting.

'How many artworks does Her Majesty own?' Lucas asked as he admired a stunning Monet.

'I believe there are about one hundred and fifty thousand pieces in the royal collection. Paintings, sculptures and the like,' Mrs Marmalade replied. She was quite enjoying her role as tour guide. 'Not just here, of course.'

'That's amazing,' Sloane gasped.

'Greedy, more like it,' Caprice muttered.

Sloane glared at the girl.

The children followed Mrs Marmalade through the gallery and into a vast sitting room where there were at least four separate areas laid out with couches as well as funny little love seats, a grand piano and a sideboard that took up the length of one wall. The rich gold wallpaper lit up the room and a glittering chandelier dominated the panelled ceiling.

'Everything is so gorgeous,' Jacinta said as she twirled into the room. 'Does Aunty Gee own any ugly furniture?'

Mrs Marmalade thought for a moment then smiled. 'Yes, there have been more than a few pieces relegated to the attics over the years.'

'Attics!' Millie's eyes bulged. 'Can we go up there?'

There was a murmur of agreement from all of the children. Suddenly, claws skittered on the floor-boards as Archie and Petunia raced into the room ahead of their mistress.

'Did I hear you ask whether you can see the attics, Millie?' Her Majesty asked.

The child nodded.

'I don't see why not.' Queen Georgiana bustled over to the children with Thornton Thripp behind her.

The man stiffened. 'There are far more interesting things to look at than those dusty rooms full of household detritus,' Thornton said.

'Come now, Thripp, I haven't been up there in years – and they were one of my favourite places to explore as a child. There's a whole room full of clothes too! I'd almost forgotten about them but I used to love trying things on and parading around the palace.'

'Could we play dress-ups, Aunty Gee?' Alice-Miranda asked excitedly.

The woman reached out and took Alice-Miranda by the hand. 'Yes, let's!' she said with a grin.

The children followed Alice-Miranda and Queen Georgiana out of the sitting room and down a long corridor. They soon arrived in the front entrance hall, where they climbed the stairs and Aunty Gee led the children to the right, down another long hall.

'Here we are,' Queen Georgiana announced, coming to a stop in front of an ornate wall. There were birds of all descriptions carved into the timber, from tiny blue jays and wrens, to owls and other birds of prey.

'Is it a secret passage?' Jacinta whispered to Alice-Miranda, her eyes wide.

Aunty Gee reached out and poked a peacock in the eye. There was a loud click and the wall pivoted.

'Cool!' Millie exclaimed.

Even Caprice seemed impressed.

Queen Georgiana reached inside and flicked a switch. A dim glow lit the space. The group followed Her Majesty up a narrow staircase to another landing, where there was a narrow passageway with doors leading off on either side.

'In the early days, before the servants' quarters were extended and incorporated downstairs, these rooms used to be bedrooms,' the Queen explained. 'But they've been receptacles for all manner of cast-offs since I was a girl.'

Her Majesty pushed open the first door on the left and poked her head inside.

'Come and have a look,' she said, beckoning the children to join her.

'What's all this?' Jacinta breathed. Her eyes tried to take in all the shelves weighed down by ancient relics.

Lucas picked up a metal helmet and jammed it on his head. 'Ow! That's uncomfortable.'

'There's some chain mail and armour in the dress-up room, Lucas. Would you like to see yourself as a knight?' Aunty Gee asked.

'A knight in shining armour.' The words were out of Jacinta's mouth before she had time to stop them. The girl's cheeks lit up in embarrassment.

Caprice rolled her eyes. 'Gross.'

The other kids giggled and so did Aunty Gee.

'Jacinta,' Her Majesty whispered, 'I knew I was

going to marry my Leopold when we were children. I suppose you just have to hope that Lucas feels the same way when you're old enough.'

From the other side of the room, the boy turned and smiled, and Jacinta's heart fluttered.

In one corner, a full suit of armour stood guard over a horde of weaponry. There were swords and axes and several long chains with spiky metal balls on the end.

Millie pointed at the instrument of torture. 'What's that horrible thing called?'

'It's a flail,' Aunty Gee replied. 'Said to be the most ghastly ancient weapon of war.'

Millie picked it up and struggled under its weight. 'I can see why. Imagine getting this stuck in your head.'

'Be careful, dear. You don't want to catch yourself on one of those spikes,' Mrs Marmalade warned.

'Where did it all come from?' Sep asked.

'It's been here for as long as I can remember,' Her Majesty replied, running her hands along a row of handmade arrows. 'My father told me that it was dug up on a battlefield not far from here. The best preserved pieces went to the museum but there was so much of it a whole stack ended up at the palace.

There's never enough room to display everything, and I suspect that the country might be a little bit cross with me if I just had a jumble sale to get rid of it all. It belongs to everyone, really.'

The children spent a few more minutes investigating the gruesome cache before Queen Georgiana suggested they move on and have a look in some of the other rooms.

'Where's Thripp?' Her Majesty asked as they walked back into the hallway.

'He dashed off a few moments ago saying something about an urgent phone call,' Mrs Marmalade replied.

Her Majesty shook her head. 'That man really does need to learn to loosen up a bit.'

Chapter 31

Braxton Balfour had been desperate to return to the cottage since Sunday morning, and now it was Monday with no hope of being able to get away. Each time he thought he had a window of opportunity, Vincent Langley would swoop in to find something else for him to do. The aftermath of any large event at the palace always required days of sorting and packing away.

'Did you organise for the marquee to be washed before Mr Budd and his men dismantled it?' Vincent Langley curled his lip at Braxton.

Braxton sighed. 'No, sir, I wasn't aware that was my responsibility.'

'Well, you arranged for them to put it up,' Vincent blustered. 'One would assume you would need to arrange for them to take it down.'

'I'll have them do it tomorrow,' Braxton replied patiently.

Vincent's eyes narrowed. 'You'll have them do it *today*. If the tent isn't cleaned and dried properly, it will grow mould and I won't be the one scrubbing it off before the next event.'

'What about Bunyan?' Braxton said. He could feel his temperature rising. 'Where is he? He hasn't been very helpful as far as I can tell.'

'He's clearing the breakfast room, and what he does is none of your business,' Vincent replied archly. He would never admit it but he had wondered the same thing himself when he couldn't locate the man on numerous occasions. Vincent had already decided that they would not be keeping him.

Braxton put his hand over his coat pocket. He could feel the photograph inside.

'Off you go, Balfour. You'll need to round up some of the men to put the marquee back up again,' Vincent instructed.

Braxton did his best to keep calm. Right at that moment all he wanted to do was to tell Vincent he could put the jolly thing up himself but the man was still his boss and any recommendations he made to Her Majesty would be taken as gospel. Besides, Vincent and Thornton Thripp were as thick as thieves and Her Majesty's chief advisor cut enormous sway with Queen Georgiana too.

Braxton stormed out of the kitchen wondering where on earth he'd find Mr Budd.

'Come along, everyone, the costume cupboard is through here.'

Queen Georgiana led the way along the hall which dog-legged to the right before straightening up again. After the group had left the armoury, they'd stopped to admire some ghastly furniture made of seashells that had once adorned the palace sitting room and had been all the rage a century ago. This was followed by a room bursting with ancient toys and pedal cars that had belonged to Aunty Gee as a child. There were rooms full of fine china, others with architectural cast-offs in the form of doors and fireplace surrounds, and another with cupboards and cupboards of luxurious linens and fabrics.

'You should have an attic sale and donate the money to one of your charities, Aunty Gee,' Jacinta said. 'That way, no one could be annoyed.'

'You know, Jacinta, that's a very good idea,' Her Majesty replied. 'Anyway, I think I've saved the best for last.'

Queen Georgiana pushed open the doors to a room that was at least four times the size of any of the others. Heavy timber wardrobes ran the length of one wall while, in the middle, chests of drawers sat back to back with enough space that you could walk right around them. Hatboxes by the dozen were piled up at the far end of the room and, just as Aunty Gee had promised, there were two suits of armour standing near the entrance.

The woman walked along opening the wardrobe doors while Mrs Marmalade pulled out several of the top drawers.

'Whoa!' Millie's jaw dropped. 'This is the best dress-up cupboard in the whole world!' She took a long mint-coloured satin gown from the hanging rail.

'Ah, that was a favourite of mine,' Aunty Gee

said. 'I wore it to a State dinner once, while on tour in Africa. There were long gloves too, if I recall correctly. I think they should be attached to the coathanger.'

Millie lifted the dress and found the gloves.

'Shall we dress up?' Mrs Marmalade asked, admiring a floral frock in her size. She hadn't felt this young in years.

'Absolutely!' Queen Georgiana said, surprised to see her lady-in-waiting so enthusiastic.

'We'll wait in the hall,' Lucas said.

'You don't have to do that,' Aunty Gee said. She walked over to the middle of the wall and pulled a heavy curtain right across the centre of the room. 'You can wrestle yourselves into that armour while us girls find something pretty to wear.'

Her Majesty then ducked around the other side of the curtain to join in the fun.

'Excuse me, Aunty Gee,' Millie said as she'd just completed her outfit, which consisted of the mint-green satin dress, matching elbow-length gloves and a feathered headpiece.

'Yes, dear?' Her Majesty was helping Jacinta into a cream lace gown that looked as if it hailed from at least one hundred years ago.

'Is there a toilet close by?'

Queen Georgiana nodded. 'There's an ensuite in one of the rooms just down the hall to the left. I think it's the fourth door. I apologise in advance for the state of it. It might not have been attended to in a while.'

'I'll come too,' Alice-Miranda offered. She had just finished pulling on a pair of enormous pantaloons beneath her white cotton pinafore.

'Are you dressed yet, boys?' Millie called before she opened the curtain.

'We've done our best,' Sep replied.

The girls could hear the clanking of metal and poked their heads around.

Millie giggled and snapped a photo of them. 'You look like the Tin Man from *The Wizard of Oz*,' she said.

'I feel like him too,' Lucas said, trying to walk. 'This stuff weighs a tonne. I don't know how they ever fought anyone wearing this. I couldn't pick up a fork right now, let alone swing a sword.'

'Imagine trying to get up on a horse,' Sep added. He attempted to lift his leg as if mounting a steed and failed dismally. 'There must have been a lot of animals with sway-backs in the old days.'

'You both look amazing,' Alice-Miranda said.

'You look like someone from one of those old black-and-white photographs where no one ever smiles,' Sep said.

'Like this?' Alice-Miranda set her face in stone and stared at the boys as if she were sitting for a portrait.

Sep nodded his approval. 'Yeah, that's perfect.'

'I'll take some more pictures once we get back from the loo,' Millie said, jigging about on the spot. She grabbed Alice-Miranda's hand and the two of them raced out the door. They ran to the left along the corridor, as Aunty Gee had instructed.

'I think Aunty Gee mentioned it was the fourth door,' Alice-Miranda said, pushing it open.

Inside, there was a dressing table and a chair and several chests of drawers of varying sizes. Alice-Miranda spotted another door at the back of the room and wondered if the bathroom was through there. Millie rushed past her, thinking the exact same thing.

'Found it!' the girl called out a second later. 'That feels better,' Millie said loudly over the sound of the toilet flushing. 'Do you need to go?'

But Alice-Miranda didn't reply. She had found something too.

'Are you there?' Millie asked as she walked back into the room.

'Sorry, Millie, what did you say?' Alice-Miranda looked up from where she was sitting, in front of an old dressing table.

'I asked if you need to go to the loo,' the girl replied, rubbing her hands dry. 'What's all that?'

'Some sort of make-up kit,' Alice-Miranda said. There was a tray of powders and a row of make-up brushes among bottles of creams and lotions. Alice-Miranda inspected a small tube then set it back down again.

'We could use it with our dress-ups,' Millie said, dipping her finger into a pot of red powder and rubbing it on her cheeks. 'What's that?' She pointed at a crumpled mess of flesh-toned latex.

Alice-Miranda picked it up.

'It's a mask,' Millie said with a shudder. 'Gross.'

'I wonder who it belongs to,' Alice-Miranda said.

'The twins, probably. They're always playing tricks on people,' Millie said. 'I can imagine this would be one of their hangouts. I'd play up here all the time if I could.'

Alice-Miranda put it back down again, with the face staring up towards her. For a split second it reminded her of someone. 'That's ridiculous,' the child said, shaking the thought from her mind.

'What's ridiculous?' Millie asked.

'I was just thinking the face looks a lot like Mr Langley,' Alice-Miranda said.

Millie stared at it. 'You're right. That's so weird. Who'd want to look like old cranky-pants?'

'I'm sure it's just a coincidence,' Alice-Miranda said, but she had a strange feeling about the whole thing.

The girls were about to leave when they heard the echoing of voices. Millie glanced around the room. On one wall there was a cupboard. It was too small to be a wardrobe as it sat about a metre from the ground and was only about a metre wide. 'It sounds like they're in there,' she said, walking over to it.

Alice-Miranda followed her and slid the doors apart. Two ropes dangled from above, attached to a pulley system.

Millie frowned. 'What's that?'

'A dumb waiter,' Alice-Miranda replied. 'We have a couple at our house. They're sort of like mini elevators for food.'

'I wonder if we could fit in there,' Millie said.

The two girls poked their heads inside and looked down. They couldn't even see all the way to the bottom.

'How does it work?' Millie asked.

'You just turn this handle.' Alice-Miranda pointed to a crank to the left of the open door.

Millie grabbed it and began to wind. As the box drew closer, the voices got louder as if the noise was travelling up beneath it.

'We need to make it happen quickly,' a man said. 'Tomorrow or, even better, this afternoon. We don't want to wait until the end of the week.'

'Yes,' a woman replied.

'Is everything ready?'

'It's all in place,' the woman said, 'and Fiona is now completely on board.'

'That is good news. I was worried things were about to go south.'

'No, we're almost there. I'm ready to take up my new posting immediately, and those two are going to be perfect. With her looks, the magazines will be clamouring and the royals will once again be the flavour of the month.'

'Ah, it's been very satisfying, really – like playing chess. Move a queen, gain a king, checkmate,' the man said. 'And that idiot Freddy won't even see it coming.'

'That sounds like Mr Thripp.' Alice-Miranda could almost hear a smile in the man's voice.

Millie nodded. 'But why are they talking about playing chess?'

'That wasn't very nice calling Freddy an idiot,' Alice-Miranda said. 'And I wonder who Fiona is, and why they are talking about the royals being back in favour again?' Alice-Miranda didn't like the sound of it at all.

'Come on, we should head back,' Millie said. She gave the handle one last turn and the box drew level with the opening.

'What's that?' Alice-Miranda peered into the cabinet. An official-looking document sat inside a plastic sleeve. She picked it up and read it. 'That's odd. I wonder what it's doing in there.'

Millie scanned it too. 'Seems a pretty strange place to store important papers, don't you think?'

'We'd better put it back.' Alice-Miranda returned the sleeve and closed the dumb waiter. Then she and Millie scurried back down the hallway to the dress-up room.

Aunty Gee greeted them at the door in a flowing rainbow kaftan and a turban which she explained she'd once worn to a barbecue in India. Mrs Marmalade was in a beautiful burnt-orange brocade gown, which looked as if it belonged in the early 1800s. Jacinta, meanwhile, had opted for a 1920s flapper outfit with a gorgeous sparkling headband. Sloane had selected a 1950s powder-blue organza dress with a tiny waist and wide skirt, while Caprice looked like she'd just stepped from the pages of a Jane Austen novel in an empire-line dress, boots and a bonnet. The boys clanked about in their armour. Together, they resembled a fashion spread through the centuries.

Alice-Miranda grinned. 'You all look amazing.'

'Did you find the loo all right?' Aunty Gee asked.

'Yes, thank you,' Alice-Miranda replied.

'We found a dumb waiter too,' Millie added. 'And we could hear Mr Thripp talking to someone.'

Aunty Gee looked at Mrs Marmalade, and the two women frowned.

'What's the matter Aunty Gee?' Alice-Miranda asked.

'For a start, Thripp is supposed to be up here with us. Secondly, I was just trying to remember which dumb waiter you were speaking of and the rooms that are underneath it. What in the blazes is the man doing down there?'

'Perhaps he has a surprise planned,' Millie said. 'He was talking to a woman and they said that they had to have something done by tomorrow or, even better, this afternoon. And then he mentioned chess and a woman called Fiona.'

'Do you know anything about this, Marian?' Her Majesty asked, turning to Mrs Marmalade.

The woman shook her head. 'No, but Thripp mentioned something about renovations a while ago and there are always tradespeople coming and going. I met a designer called Fiona once but I wouldn't know what he was up to. 'That man never really tells me anything – except for when I can't take holidays.'

'Maybe he's done something special to commemorate the jubilee,' Alice-Miranda suggested.

'Oh.' Queen Georgiana grinned. 'Perhaps I shouldn't be so cross with him. I hadn't thought of that at all.'

'Well, he certainly hasn't shared anything with me about it,' Mrs Marmalade griped. 'I'd have helped if I'd known.'

'Don't get yourself in a lather, Marian. Thripp

prides himself on being a little mysterious. Besides, you could have organised your own surprise.' Her Majesty adjusted her turban.

'Can I take some more photographs, Aunty Gee?' Millie asked, retrieving her camera from where she'd left it sitting on a chair.

'What a wonderful idea,' the woman said. 'And why don't we stay in costume for the rest of the day?'

The children giggled.

'Really?' Jacinta smiled.

'I think we might have to abandon the armour,' Lucas said. 'We'd never make it downstairs.'

'That's for sure,' Sep sighed.

'After we take the photographs, you boys can find something else to wear.' Her Majesty suggested. 'There are plenty of old suits.'

'We found a huge make-up kit in the other room too,' Millie babbled, fiddling with her camera settings.

'Oh, really?' Aunty Gee said, turning to look at the child. 'It must have been up here for years.'

'There were a whole lot of powders and lotions and a latex mask,' Alice-Miranda added, 'like the ones they use in Hollywood movies.'

'Cool,' Lucas said. 'Dad wore a fake nose in the

last movie he did. It was so realistic, even though it was pretty gross.'

'Come along, children, shall we take these pictures? Her Majesty needs a cup of tea and something to eat soon,' Marian Marmalade said.

Millie held up her camera while Caprice took charge and bossed everyone into position. The children had a marvellous time snapping photographs in all manner of poses. Of course, there was one of Lucas on bended knee holding Jacinta's hand.

'Stop pretending to be embarrassed, Jacinta,' Sloane teased. 'We all know you love it.'

Jacinta blushed and smiled. Lucas was smiling too but his face was hidden under his metal helmet.

Meanwhile, back at SPLOD HQ, Marjorie Plunkett stared at the pictures on the screen in front of her. She giggled as Queen Georgiana struck a dramatic pose, looking as if she were about to faint, the two knights poised to catch her. Marjorie breathed a sigh of relief. Her plan to keep Alice-Miranda out of harm's way was working perfectly, although she was disappointed that the saliva sample had led nowhere.

When she'd returned to HQ, Fiona seemed fine. She'd have to do some checking but the interference seemed to have dissipated. Anyway, whoever was behind the plot would slip up soon. In Marjorie's experience, they always did.

Chapter 32

'Well, that was fun,' Aunty Gee said as the group, still resplendent in their dress-up clothes, descended the stairs into the front entrance foyer. She and Mrs Marmalade had been most impressed with the way the children tidied the room, particularly Caprice, who wouldn't allow them to leave until every last article of clothing that they'd taken out was back in its rightful spot.

Even Millie had to admit that the girl was being far better behaved than usual. Although, it was only their first day alone without the rest of the guests.

'Now, shall we have some lunch and decide what we'll do next?' Aunty Gee asked.

The group nodded.

Suddenly, Thornton Thripp rushed through from the back hall. 'Excuse m– what on earth are you wearing?' The words were out of his mouth before he had time to stop them.

'Where have you been, Thripp? I thought you were going to play dress-ups with us, but I gather you have more pressing business on your mind.' Her Majesty gave him a quizzical look. 'You missed out on all the fun.'

Thornton wondered what she was talking about. 'Actually, we have guests.'

'Guests? I don't recall that we were expecting anyone.' Her Majesty glanced at Mrs Marmalade, who shrugged.

'I'm afraid it's the Prime Minister of Samoa.'

'What's *he* doing here?' Her Majesty demanded. 'He's not due until next month!'

'Yes, unfortunately someone sent the incorrect date on his invitation. I've just seen it now,' Thornton said.

'The wrong date!' Her Majesty glared at the man. 'Whose job was that?'

'I believe it was Mrs Marmalade who was responsible.' The man looked at Marian and pursed his lips. 'But it doesn't matter now. We need to get you changed and ready for a meet-and-greet and then some official photographs.'

Mrs Marmalade looked as if she'd been pricked by a pin. In all her years as Her Majesty's lady-in-waiting, she'd never once made such an error. There had to be a mistake. It wasn't like her at all.

'Good heavens, Marian, should I be looking for your replacement?' Queen Georgiana snapped.

Mrs Marmalade blushed a deep shade of red.

Aunty Gee turned to the children. 'I can't believe this has happened. It's just awful.'

'I'm sure that the Prime Minister is very excited to meet you, Aunty Gee,' Alice-Miranda said reassuringly. 'And we've got you for the rest of the week, so please don't feel bad because of us.'

Her Majesty smiled. 'Darling girl, you are ever so understanding. I'll organise for someone to take you on a tour of the grounds, shall I?'

Mrs Marmalade was about to offer when

Thornton Thripp talked straight over the top of her. 'Bunyan is proving most reliable,' he said.

'Yes, of course. That's perfect,' Her Majesty declared. 'Have you told Langley that we have a State visitor? The man will be apoplectic. We'll need rooms made up and a dinner this evening. Good heavens, what a muddle.'

'It's all right, Aunty Gee.' Alice-Miranda grinned at the woman. 'We're very good at entertaining ourselves.'

'We don't need anyone to take us, you know,' Caprice said, taking a sip of her lemonade.

'For once I actually agree with you,' Millie said, her mouth full of apple.

'And for once you're right,' Caprice said sweetly, popping a grape into her mouth.

'Aunty Gee said that Mr Bunyan would take us,' Alice-Miranda reminded the group.

Millie pulled a face. 'Bunyan's weird.'

'Well, I know a really cool place we can go,' Caprice said, showing off.

'Where?' Jacinta asked sceptically.

'The hunting tower,' Caprice said with a glint in her eye.

'But Mr Thripp said that it's all locked up and they can't find the keys,' Lucas said.

'That's not true at all,' Caprice said smugly.

Sloane eyeballed the girl. 'And how would you know that?'

'Because I've been there,' Caprice replied.

Outside in the hallway, Frank Bunyan was listening to their every word. The children's plan couldn't have been more perfect. He'd let them go on their own – except that he wouldn't, of course.

Sep shrugged. 'I'm up for it.'

The rest of the group agreed. 'But we have to make sure that it's all right with Mr Bunyan,' Alice-Miranda said. 'We don't want him to worry.'

Just as Alice-Miranda finished speaking, the butler appeared in the doorway.

'What shouldn't I be worried about?' the man said. He looked around to check that Archie and Petunia weren't around before he proceeded into the room.

'We were just discussing whether to go exploring on our own, seeing as you're so busy,' Alice-Miranda explained.

Frank Bunyan frowned. 'Well, if you're sure,' he said.

'Yes, we're perfectly capable of looking after ourselves. Perhaps we can take something for afternoon tea?' the child said.

'I'll arrange that for you now.' Bunyan nodded and walked out the door.

Chapter 33

Braxton Balfour had been beavering away in the silver room for hours. He glanced up at the clock and gave the last of the dinner forks a vigorous rub, then placed it back into the red-velvet-lined canteen. It seemed he might finally get his chance to see Lydie again. Vincent Langley had blustered into the room half an hour beforehand sputtering and frothing about an unexpected entourage of prime-ministerial guests.

At the time, Braxton's heart sank as he waited for another long inventory of palace-bound duties, but Vincent had instead handed him a shopping list. Braxton was to pick up an order at the farm shop once he'd finished polishing and had organised to have the small dining room set for Her Majesty's evening meal.

He picked up the dirty cloths and was on his way to the utility room when Frank Bunyan walked downstairs.

'Hello,' Braxton said.

'Afternoon,' Bunyan replied stiffly.

'Langley's not here.'

'I was just after some supplies for a picnic,' Bunyan said, looking lost.

Braxton nodded his head towards the main kitchen. 'One of the chefs should be able to help you find what you need.'

Bunyan began to walk past when Braxton couldn't help himself.

'So where is it that you've come from?' he asked. Although the man was utterly useless, he was still a potential threat and Braxton wanted to know exactly who he was dealing with.

Bunyan hesitated, itching the back of his neck. 'Sorry, I don't have time to chat. The children are keen to get going,' he mumbled before scurrying away.

Braxton rolled his eyes. If the fellow couldn't even hold a civilised conversation about his work experience, perhaps he had nothing to worry about at all.

✷

'Is everyone ready to go?' Alice-Miranda asked as the group gathered in the rear entrance foyer. The children had agreed to change back into their play clothes and keep the dress-ups in their rooms for later on. Perhaps they would wear them to dinner instead.

Frank Bunyan walked towards the children with three bulging daypacks.

'Oh, thank you, Mr Bunyan,' Alice-Miranda enthused.

Lucas, Jacinta and Millie took the bags from him.

'This feels like enough food for a week,' Lucas remarked. He slung the heavy pack onto his shoulders.

'Chef thought you might get hungry, and there are drink bottles too,' Bunyan replied. He hadn't actually been able to locate any of the chefs but there was a basket of food that looked just perfect with sandwiches, quiches, cakes, scones and the like.

'Have you got your camera, Millie?' Jacinta asked.

Millie reached into her jacket pocket and felt around but it wasn't there. 'That's strange,' she said. 'I must have left it when we were having lunch. I'll be back in a minute.'

'No!' Bunyan cried, grabbing hold of the girl's sleeve.

'What are you doing?' Millie demanded, wrangling her arm free of his grasp.

Bunyan softened. 'I'll get your camera, miss. You can stay here with your friends.'

'Okay,' Millie said. 'Keep your hair on.' She didn't see why he had to be so pushy about it.

'There is something weird about that guy,' Sloane said as she watched the butler disappear down the hallway.

Alice-Miranda couldn't help thinking the same thing.

A few minutes later he reappeared and handed Millie the camera.

'Thank you,' the girl said.

Bunyan gave a bow. 'My pleasure.'

Just at that moment, Marian Marmalade walked through from the front hall.

'Hello Mrs Marmalade. Is the visit going well?' Alice-Miranda asked.

'Oh, quite,' the woman replied. 'Her Majesty and the Prime Minister seem to have bonded over a mutual love of dogs. The man is besotted with Archie and Petunia.'

Bunyan was glad to hear it. He wasn't keen to see the pesky beagles anytime soon.

'We're going exploring,' Alice-Miranda informed the woman.

Mrs Marmalade nodded. 'Enjoy yourselves, and make sure you're back before dark.'

'You know, she's not as crusty as I thought she was,' Millie whispered. 'Maybe she's better at home, in her own surroundings.'

Jacinta grinned. 'Most people usually are.'

Mrs Marmalade turned and shot the girls a stare. 'I heard that,' she said.

Jacinta and Millie grimaced at one another. Alice-Miranda giggled.

'Come on. Let's go,' Caprice said, impatient to show off her knowledge of the hunting tower.

The children scurried out the back doors with Frank Bunyan behind them.

'You're not coming,' Caprice snapped when she realised that the man was still part of their group.

'Of course not,' he replied amiably. 'I'll just see you to the edge of the garden.' He looked back at the palace windows to see if anyone was watching.

'We're not babies, you know,' Caprice said.

'No, clearly not,' Bunyan replied dryly. 'You seem to know just about everything.'

'Thank you,' Caprice said with a smarmy smile.

Jacinta and Sloane stifled grins. For someone allegedly as smart as Caprice, she wasn't very good at picking up on sarcasm.

Alice-Miranda dropped back to walk beside the man. 'Mr Bunyan, just so you know, we're going to explore the hunting tower,' she said. 'Caprice says that she knows how to get in.'

Frank Bunyan exhaled through gritted teeth. 'Thank you so much for telling me.'

But that's not what he was thinking at all.

Chapter 34

The children followed Caprice across the lawn and down a long wisteria-covered walkway. At the end there was a gate that led into the woodland.

'Is this really the way?' Sloane asked loudly.

'Of course it is,' Caprice snipped, charging ahead.

As promised, Bunyan had remained behind once the children reached the edge of the garden.

'Bye, Mr Bunyan,' Alice-Miranda called. 'We'll see you later.' She turned to wave but the man had already disappeared.

The children trekked along the dappled path which wound its way up and up until they emerged on top of the ridge.

'Whoa,' Lucas said. 'The tower's even more impressive up close.'

Caprice led the way until the boys ran to overtake her and sprinted to the front door. Sep grabbed the handle and turned, but it was locked, just as Mr Thripp had warned it would be.

Caprice smirked. 'You won't get in that way.'

'Okay, smartypants, where's the entrance?' Millie said.

Caprice took off around to the other side of the building and the group followed. She pointed at one of the windows. 'Give me a leg-up,' she commanded Lucas.

He and Sep both knelt down so she could hoist herself up to the window and prise it open. She wiggled her way through, then disappeared from view. 'Well, are you coming or not?' Caprice called from inside.

Within a couple of minutes, the children had hefted and heaved each other into the tower. Sep scrambled up the wall on his own and Lucas helped pull him through.

'This is so cool,' Lucas breathed as he looked around.

Sloane scrunched her nose. 'It smells awful – like someone's stomped kippers into the carpet or something,' she remarked.

'Did the twins bring you here?' Millie asked, looking at Caprice.

The girl nodded.

'Did they say you could bring us?'

'I don't care what they say. They're not here now and they can't stop us,' Caprice said defiantly.

'What's in here, anyway?' Sep asked.

'Follow me and I'll show you,' the girl said, then flounced off towards the stairwell.

Edgar turned around from where he was mixing a sludgy paste in a beaker which sat on a tripod over an open flame.

'Hey, what's Langley doing up here?' he said, dropping the wooden spoon and rushing to the window. In the daylight the twins weren't afraid to draw the curtains, but when it got dark they made sure that the drapes were always fully closed. They didn't want to risk anyone seeing lights on in the tower.

Louis stood up from the table, where he had been fiddling with a circuit board.

'He hardly ever leaves the palace.' Edgar frowned. 'And why is he carrying a hammer?'

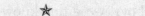

Caprice and the children climbed the spiral staircase while holding onto the rope banister.

'This place is incredible,' Sep said.

'These stairs were built for midgets,' Sloane grumbled after almost tripping on the tiny treads.

Edgar and Louis watched as Vincent Langley approached the building and disappeared around the other side.

'Come on, let's go and see what he's up to.' Edgar turned and raced towards the door. He wrenched it open and charged through to the landing, just as Caprice's head appeared at the top of the staircase.

'You! What are you doing here?' the boy blustered.

Caprice's mouth fell open and for a minute she gasped like a fish out of water.

'I can't believe you,' Louis said, coming up behind his brother.

Alice-Miranda popped up next to the girl. 'Oh, hello boys, we didn't know you were going to be here too. I thought you were getting your hair cut.'

'What's she doing here?' Louis pointed at Alice-Miranda.

'It's not just me,' Alice-Miranda said. 'We all came to look at the tower.'

A few seconds later, the seven children were standing on top of the landing.

'You can't be trusted one little bit, Caprice,' Edgar accused the girl. 'You promised not to tell.'

'Sorry,' the girl huffed. 'Lucas really wanted to see the tower, and it isn't fair to keep this place all to yourselves.'

From somewhere outside, the children heard a loud banging.

'What's that noise?' Sep said.

Edgar and Louis looked at each other and pushed

past the children. 'Langley!' they shouted in unison and took off.

'What about Mr Langley?' Alice-Miranda wondered aloud before turning to follow them. The rest of the group stampeded downstairs behind her.

As they reached the ground floor, the hammering stopped.

The twins ran over to the window. Louis leapt onto the small stool they had positioned beneath it.

'Can you see him?' Edgar demanded.

Louis shook his head. 'I'll go and have a look outside. He tried to push the window but it wouldn't budge. Did you close this?' He turned and asked the group.

'I was last through,' Sep said, unsure if he should be apologising. 'But I think I left it open.'

Louis pushed against the frame but it was stuck fast. 'It won't budge,' he said, shoving harder.

'What do you mean it's stuck?' Sloane asked with alarm.

'It's stuck – it won't open,' the boy replied sarcastically.

'There has to be some other way out of this place,' Millie said. She turned and looked across the hallway at the front doors.

'There is no other way in or out. Trust us on that one,' Edgar said. 'All of the windows are nailed shut and now it looks like this one is too.'

'Do you think Mr Langley locked us in?' Lucas asked.

'But why would he do that?' Jacinta frowned. She didn't like the idea of spending the night in the spooky old tower.

'Well, it's pretty obvious he doesn't like either of you very much,' Millie said to the twins. 'But we haven't really done anything to offend him – except for the boys sliding down the banisters.'

'There's something very strange going on,' Alice-Miranda said. 'Is there a telephone up here somewhere?'

The boys shook their heads.

'Did anyone bring a phone with them?' Millie asked.

There was a cacophony of 'no's.

'Mr Bunyan knows we're here. If we don't get back before dark someone will come and look for us, I'm sure of it,' Alice-Miranda said.

'How does he know?' Caprice scoffed. 'None of us told him.'

'Actually, I did because I didn't want him to

worry about us, especially when Mr Thripp and Aunty Gee were so keen for him to accompany us,' Alice-Miranda said.

Caprice rolled her eyes. 'You're such a goody-goody.'

'You should thank her, Caprice. When it gets late, Mr Bunyan will come looking for us and we won't be stuck here overnight,' Sep said.

Caprice rolled her eyes.

'Then there's nothing to worry about,' Jacinta said, trying to be cheerful.

'Except that we're trapped here with you lot for the rest of the day,' Edgar griped.

'I'm starving,' Sloane declared. 'Can we have something to eat?'

'There's nothing much up here,' one of the twins said. 'Maybe a muesli bar or two, but you're not having those.'

'It's fine,' the girl snipped, remembering the daypacks Bunyan had given them. 'We have our own picnic.'

'Good, you can share it with us then.' Louis grabbed Millie's backpack and took off upstairs.

'Hey!' The flame-haired girl yelled, racing after him.

Chapter 35

Braxton Balfour sped along the lane. By his calculations he had just over ninety minutes to get to the cottage and back, including the time it would take to pick up the supplies from the farm shop. He had no idea if Lydie would be there, let alone if she'd be receptive to his questions, but he had to try.

Braxton parked the car in the usual spot and charged through the undergrowth to the cottage. He couldn't believe his eyes when he spotted her kneeling down beside a flowerbed by the side of the house. 'Lydie!' he called.

She looked towards him, then stood up and started to run away.

Braxton took off after her. 'Stop! I just want to talk to you.' He reached the back door and blocked her path.

'Please leave me alone,' she whispered, catching her breath. Her head felt as if it were stuffed full of cotton wool.

'I don't want to hurt you. I just have to know why,' Braxton pleaded. 'Why did you go away?'

Out of the corner of his eye Braxton spotted the raven. It was flying straight for him.

Lydie must have seen the terror in his eyes. She turned and held out her hand. 'Away, Lucien!' she called.

The beast swooped low, then circled back and landed on the roof of a small outbuilding.

She turned back to Braxton, a look of utter confusion on her face.

He reached into his coat pocket and pulled out the photograph, then held it out for her to see.

Lydie frowned as she took it and traced her

forefinger over the outline of the couple. For several minutes she seemed completely lost.

'Please, Lydie, I don't care if you didn't want to marry me. I just want to know why you ran away,' Braxton began. His heart was pounding so hard he thought it might burst right through his chest. There were so many questions.

'Braxton . . .?' she whispered, looking up at him. 'Braxton Balfour?'

'Yes, it's me, Lydie.' A wave of relief washed over him. He wasn't imagining things, after all.

Lydie's face crumpled. 'Oh my goodness, we were going to get married.'

Braxton nodded sadly. 'We were. And then there was the accident and you wouldn't see me anymore. You left and I had no idea where you'd gone. Please, Lydie, I have to know why.'

Her eyes filled with tears. 'I don't remember.'

'What do you mean you don't remember?' Braxton reached out and held her hands in his.

'I couldn't remember any of it – you, what happened to me, who I was . . .'

'Your brother told me you didn't want to see me ever again,' Braxton said.

Lydie shook her head. 'I didn't know who anyone

was – not even my own mother or father. The doctors all said it would get better and that I'd be okay, but I wasn't. That's why I went away. I needed to discover who I was and hope that one day it would all come back to me.'

'And has it?' Braxton asked.

'No . . . I mean, not properly. For a long time there were scratchy memories here and there, then one day I was walking across a field near the village where I was living in France and I saw an old woman in the distance. I don't know why it happened but something sharpened in my mind, and all of a sudden I remembered my Aunt Marian and I had an overwhelming urge to come home. Except that I didn't really know if I still had a home.'

'Aunt Marian?' Braxton frowned.

'Marian Marmalade – my godmother,' Lydie said. 'I'm told that she was a good friend of my father's when they were young. I wrote to her and asked if she could help me.'

'Do you remember the Queen?' Braxton asked.

'No, not really, other than things I've read about her or seen in the newspapers. I know we were second cousins because Aunt Marian told me but I can't recall anything about being at the palace or things we used to do with her when we were children.'

'You poor darling,' Braxton said. 'I can't imagine losing my memory like that.'

Lydie shrugged. 'Sometimes it feels like a seamstress is picking at a part of my brain, just trying to catch the right stitch so that everything will unravel. When I saw you the other day, I knew there was something more. I've been thinking and thinking.'

'How long have you been here?' Braxton asked.

'Three years,' she replied.

'Three years!' Braxton sighed. 'I can't believe you've been so close. Who knows you're here?'

'Only Aunt Marian, and I suppose Her Majesty must too. I'm not really sure. Aunt Marian arranged for me to live in the cottage. She said that my timing was perfect and so was my trade. I trained as a milliner in France, you see, although I was something of a hermit there too. Her Majesty's milliner had just retired and they needed someone to take up the position. I just couldn't tell anyone and, up until now, that's suited me very well.'

'Hats? That's what I pick up in the boxes?' Braxton asked, remembering the piece of fabric he'd picked up off the sitting-room floor.

Lydie nodded.

'What about your brother? Does he know you're here?' the man asked. He knew that both her parents had died some years ago.

Lydie shook her head. 'Aunt Marian has told me about him and shown me photographs, but I can't remember him at all.'

'Don't you think seeing him might have helped?' Braxton frowned.

'I didn't want to. There was something that just didn't feel right.'

Braxton's heart skipped. 'My dear girl, out here on your own all this time.'

'I thought coming back would help but it didn't. Apparently I'm doing something important for Her Majesty, and Aunt Marian visits when she can. I take walks in the evenings and I've got my animal friends for company,' Lydie said calmly. 'Please don't feel sorry for me.'

'The raven?' Braxton's brow creased.

'Yes, his name's Lucien and he's rather protective, as you learned the other day. There are others too – a rabbit and a wren. I raised them by hand when they were left for dead.' A small smile perched on Lydie's lips.

'You did always love animals,' Braxton said tenderly.

'They don't judge, do they? They just love you for who you are.'

Braxton thought for a moment. 'Have you been to the tower?'

'No,' Lydie replied. 'But I've thought about it a lot lately. I've had small flashes – of arguments, then everything goes black. I don't know what it all means but I think I want to. I'm tired of not knowing.'

Braxton glanced at his watch. He'd already been away for much longer than he should have been.

'Would you take me there?' Lydie asked. 'I don't think I can do it on my own.'

Braxton nodded and drew her close. 'Of course.'

Chapter 36

Queen Georgiana had spent a surprisingly delightful afternoon with the Prime Minister of Samoa. The man told completely inappropriate jokes that she found hilariously funny and he adored Archie and Petunia, who almost licked him to death. He was also a serious follower of rugby – a sport Her Majesty was keen on as well.

'If you'll excuse me, Prime Minister, I'd like to check on my young guests and give you time to freshen up before dinner,' the woman said.

'Your Majesty, you have been so utterly generous with your time. I will take my leave and allow you to get on with far more important things than entertaining a silly old man.'

Queen Georgiana chortled. 'Oh, you do make me laugh, Tuitua. I'm looking forward to our evening.'

The Prime Minister exited the room through the main doors. Queen Georgiana waited a few moments before she left through a side door that directly accessed her study. She almost walked straight into Thornton Thripp. Marjorie Plunkett was standing by the window with a face as pale as a pint of milk.

'What's the matter?' Her Majesty demanded, dread filling her stomach. 'Where are the children?'

'Gone,' Marjorie whispered. She handed Her Majesty a piece of paper in a plastic sleeve.

'What do you mean they're gone? Isn't Bunyan with them? And what's this?' Queen Georgiana's hand began to tremble.

'Bunyan accompanied them on their way to the tower but the children raced ahead, and when he arrived there was no sign of them,' Marjorie explained. 'The place is locked up tight and all of the windows are nailed shut. He's searched everywhere.'

'Well, that doesn't mean anything,' Her Majesty said. 'They could be playing hide-and-seek for all we know . . . right?'

'We hoped that was the case but I think you'll agree that this confirms our worst fears.' Marjorie handed over a grainy photograph of the children standing together in a bare room. There was no furniture and scrawled on the wall behind them in large letters was the word 'help'.

'Oh, good heavens! Where are they?' Queen Georgiana's breath caught in her throat. 'How do we even know that this photograph is real? It could have been tampered with.'

'I'm afraid not, Ma'am,' Marjorie said, shaking her head.

'Do we know what they want? I'll pay whatever they're asking.' The Queen wrung her hands together.

'Would you give up your crown?' Thripp asked, his voice wavering.

'My crown? Is this a joke?' Queen Georgiana demanded.

Marjorie shook her head. She pulled out a page with the same cut-out letters as the ones they'd received before.

With an unsteady hand, Queen Georgiana took the ransom note and read it aloud.

Ring-a-ding-ding, no Freddy the King!
Your line is a lie, now's time to fly,
A Lancaster-Brown should be wearing the crown,
But he must take a bride, for family pride.
The papers are clear – do the right thing, old dear.
Abdicate tonight, and all will be right;
Stay in your place, and I'll show them no grace.

'What's all this rubbish?' Georgiana asked, confused. 'Of course we're the rightful heirs – Lloyd's grandfather abdicated. And why does Lloyd have to be married now?' Her Majesty stared at Marjorie.

'I knew you were ambitious, Marjorie, but this is a little extreme, don't you think?' Thornton glared at her from under his bushy eyebrows.

Marjorie Plunkett recoiled. 'You can't think I had anything to do with this?' she protested.

Queen Georgiana had been wondering the same thing. 'Well, the whole thing is ludicrous.'

Thornton Thripp handed Her Majesty another document. 'This came with the letter.'

Queen Georgiana scanned the piece of paper and huffed loudly. 'What does this prove? It's the abdication document. It's all there in black and white.'

Marjorie shook her head. 'Take a look where the second signature should be, Ma'am.'

'It was probably just an early draft,' the Queen said.

'I'm afraid not, Your Majesty. Fiona has authenticated it,' Marjorie confirmed.

The woman stumbled backwards. 'Good heavens, my whole life has been based on a lie.'

'Your Majesty, please sit down.' Marjorie rushed around and pulled out a chair. 'I'm sorry to say it but there's more.'

'More! Could it get any worse?'

'It depends which way you look at it,' Thripp said, his lip curling in Marjorie's direction. He pulled out another sheet of paper. This time it was as if the perpetrators didn't have time to think up more of their silly rhymes.

PS. You have until nine o'clock tonight. Call a press conference to make the announcement and I will set the children free. If not, you won't see them anytime soon.

'Are you behind all this, Marjorie?' Her Majesty searched the woman's face. 'I knew you were keen to be part of the family but I didn't think you'd take things this far. Lloyd has never expressed any interest whatsoever in being King.'

'Your Majesty, how could you even suggest such a thing? I don't want this to happen any more than you do. I'm not cut out to be Queen.'

The Queen sighed and put her head in her hands. 'What am I talking about? I'm sorry, Marjorie. I don't know why I said that. You've been a loyal servant of the Crown for many years and that was a dreadful slight. I'm just dumbfounded.'

'Ma'am, you can't really be considering this,' Marjorie said, suddenly afraid.

Queen Georgiana swallowed hard. 'I don't see what other choice we have. I'm not letting these monsters harm one hair on any of those children's heads. We need to get Lloyd over here immediately.'

'What about Freddy, Ma'am?' Thripp asked.

'What about Freddy? I think the less he knows the better, don't you? I can't let him stop me, so let's leave it at that, shall we?'

★

'Don't you think it's strange that Bunyan hasn't come to find us yet?' Millie said to Alice-Miranda and Sloane. The three girls had taken up residence in what was once a sitting room. At least there were some armchairs, even if they were threadbare.

Alice-Miranda frowned. 'I wonder if something's happened to him.'

Back in their workshop, Louis was showing Sep, Jacinta, Caprice and Lucas some electromagnets.

'Is there a cellar?' Sep asked, wondering if perhaps there might be a way out from there. 'Sometimes there are tunnels in old places like this. We found one not so long ago when we were on camp at Pelham Park.'

Louis shook his head. 'There's a cellar but we've never found any tunnels.'

'I'm bored!' Caprice huffed. 'Surely there's a way out of this dump. I'll look in the cellar.'

'I'll come with you,' Jacinta said, jumping at the chance to do something other than sitting around. 'But I think we'll need a torch.'

Fortunately, the twins had several of them. 'You can take this,' Edgar said, offering her one.

'Whatever.' Caprice grabbed it and charged off.

Alice-Miranda, Millie and Sloane heard the thumping footsteps and went to investigate.

'Where are you going?' Millie called out to Jacinta, who was heading down the spiral staircase.

'Caprice says we should try to find a way out through the cellar,' Jacinta replied.

'We'll come.' Millie rushed after her, with Alice-Miranda and Sloane on her heels.

Caprice opened a small door on the ground floor and the children scrambled down a small set of steps to what seemed more like a half-height storeroom than a proper cellar.

'What are we looking for, exactly?' Jacinta asked.

'You know – trapdoors, sliding walls, the usual stuff you'd find in scary old buildings like this,' Caprice said.

'Sometimes there are bodies buried in cellars,' Millie whispered.

Sloane shuddered.

Alice-Miranda noticed the girl's discomfort and took her friend's hand, giving it a reassuring squeeze. 'Millie, I'm sure that's not the case,' she said, though truthfully she couldn't be sure at all. Especially not at a palace where there might even have been a battle or two over the centuries.

The girls spent the next half an hour scouring the walls and floors, looking for anything that might lead them outside. But there was nothing – not even a loose flagstone.

Upstairs, Sep and Lucas left the twins to their fiddling and went to explore the sitting room where Alice-Miranda and the girls had been earlier.

'What do you make of this beast?' Sep asked. The boy walked over and stood inside the hearth of the enormous fireplace.

Lucas looked at the stone surrounds. 'What do you mean?'

'Do you remember seeing any chimneys?' Sep asked.

'Mmm, no, just those four turrets,' Lucas replied.

Sep looked up. 'That's weird. It seems the fire-place is just for decoration.'

'Maybe the chimney's been blocked up to keep animals out,' Lucas suggested.

'Who knows? These buildings have probably been changed a zillion times over the years.' Sep kicked his foot against a loose stone. A horrible grating sound of stone on stone assaulted the boys' ears.

'What's that?' Lucas rushed forward. The entire

side of the fireplace had disappeared, revealing the narrowest of staircases. 'How . . .?'

'Quick,' Sep said. 'Get the others. There may be a way out of here after all.'

Chapter 37

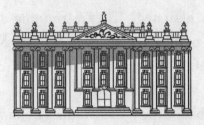

Back at the palace Vincent Langley was about to blow a fuse. He'd searched high and low for Braxton Balfour and couldn't find the man anywhere. Mrs McGill had telephoned from the farm shop to say that they were about to close and no one had come to collect the order. Vincent was furious. He would have to do it himself, or there would be nothing for the Prime Minister's dinner.

He picked up the telephone and dialled Marian Marmalade's extension, tapping his foot impatiently as it rang for what seemed like an age before the woman answered.

'What time should I arrange for the children to have their supper?' Vincent barked down the line. The arrival of the Samoan Prime Minister had thrown his entire evening schedule into disarray, and to top it off, he'd received no word about the children's supper all afternoon.

Marian hesitated. 'They're running a little late from their outing.' Truth be told, Mrs Marmalade had just left Her Majesty's chambers, completely shocked by what she'd learned.

'Don't blame me if the children don't want to eat the congealed mess that will await them if they ever come back,' Langley blustered.

'What is that supposed to mean?' Mrs Marmalade didn't like the tone of the man's voice one little bit.

'Exactly what I said,' Langley spat, then slammed down the handset.

Marian Marmalade sat for a moment, thinking about the children and where they could be. All of a sudden she felt a strange prickling sensation in the backs of her eyes. Without warning, a tear sprang, then another and another. She quickly retrieved a handkerchief from her sleeve and dabbed them away, then hurried from her office into the hallway, where she almost charged straight into the man she'd just been speaking to.

Mrs Marmalade flinched. 'Oh, I thought you were in your office.'

It would usually take a good ten minutes to walk from Langley's office to the kitchens.

The man said nothing.

'What's the matter with you?' Marian demanded. 'You had a lot to say just a moment ago.'

Langley cleared his throat and mumbled something indecipherable.

'Well, seeing as though you're here,' Marian continued, 'I forgot to mention that the Prime Minister would like to have a bath before dinner. You need to go and draw it immediately.'

Langley glared at her.

'What are you waiting for? Go on!' Mrs Marmalade snapped, waving the butler away.

The man couldn't believe his bad luck. He'd been on his way to get changed at least four times when various palace staff had intercepted him and insisted there were urgent jobs he had to do right there and then. He wondered where on earth the real Vincent Langley had got to.

Meanwhile, downstairs, the real Vincent Langley snatched up his car keys and raced out the back door, bubbling and hissing about what he'd do the next time he saw Braxton Balfour.

'What are you shouting about?' Caprice yelled as she stomped back upstairs, annoyed at having wasted another hour. 'Whoa!' the girl gasped as she entered the sitting room and realised what all the fuss was about. 'Where do *they* go?'

Sep shrugged. 'I don't know but they must be inside the external wall. Imagine how thick it is.'

'How come we never knew about this?' Louis's eyes were on stalks.

'Come on, then.' Edgar just about bowled Sep out of the way to reach the top step.

'Edgar, do you think just a few of us should go down? Those stairs are so narrow,' Alice-Miranda said. 'It would be silly for all of us to get stuck and make it impossible for Mr Bunyan to find us.'

'Alice-Miranda's right,' Sloane said.

'But I want to see what's down there,' Caprice bleated.

'*We're* going. It's *our* tower,' Edgar spoke for himself and Louis.

'Well, Millie and Alice-Miranda are the smallest,' Jacinta reasoned. 'They should go first.'

It was true. The girls stood a much better chance of negotiating the tiny stairwell than the rest of them.

'That's not fair,' Caprice whined. 'I want to go.'

'Oh, be quiet, Caprice!' Lucas had heard enough of the girl's whining to last him all week.

The girl looked as if she'd been slapped with a wet fish. 'I don't care what you say, Lucas. I'm going with them,' Caprice retorted.

Edgar passed Alice-Miranda a torch. 'You'd better take this if you're going first.'

'Thanks.' She smiled gratefully, then stepped carefully onto the widest part of each narrow tread.

Millie was right behind her, and Caprice had barged her way in between Millie and the twins.

'Can you see anything yet?' Jacinta called out.

'The stairs seem to go on forever . . . ever . . . ever,' Alice-Miranda's voice echoed back.

'Can't you go any faster?' Caprice grumbled.

Alice-Miranda ducked as the ceiling sank even lower. 'Watch your heads!' she said just as Louis cracked his forehead on a stone.

'Ow!' the boy complained.

'She told you to watch out,' Millie said with a grin. Served him right, she thought.

The staircase wound around the building at least three times before Alice-Miranda spotted a small door up ahead. The dark wood was intricately carved with what looked like hundreds of tiny birds and there was a tarnished brass nameplate in the centre.

'Fiona?' Alice-Miranda said with a frown. The rest of the children huddled around behind her.

'Do you think someone lives in here?' Millie said.

'As if,' Edgar snapped. 'We'd know if they did.'

Millie turned and looked at the lad. 'You didn't know about the secret staircase.'

Edgar shot Millie an evil stare.

'Didn't you say something about those men in the woods talking about someone called Fiona the other day, Caprice?' Louis asked the girl.

Caprice nodded.

'That's strange,' Alice-Miranda said. 'When we were playing dress-ups and Millie and I had to go to the toilet, we heard Mr Thripp talking about a Fiona too.'

'Go on, then. Open the door,' Louis said to Alice-Miranda.

She reached out and tried to turn the handle but it wouldn't budge. 'It's locked.'

'Well, that's disappointing.' Millie turned to go back upstairs.

But Alice-Miranda wasn't ready to give up yet. She shone her torch on the door, taking in all of the tiny creatures. There were wrens and blue jays, and a slightly bigger owl was perched in the bottom corner. The panel was so busy it was hard to make out each bird.

'What is it?' Millie asked.

'There!' Alice-Miranda pointed. 'Can you see it?'

The children peered up, wondering exactly what they were supposed to be looking at.

Alice-Miranda jigged about excitedly. 'It's a peacock.'

'So what?' Caprice said. 'How's that going to help?'

Millie bit her lip. 'Do you really think it could work?'

'Louis, can you help me?' Alice-Miranda asked. 'I need a leg-up.'

'Okay. I have no idea what you're doing but I suppose there's no harm trying.' The boy leaned down and clasped his hands together.

Alice-Miranda climbed up and Edgar helped to steady her. She reached as high as she could and poked the peacock in the eye.

All of a sudden, there was a whirring sound and clanking followed by a whoosh of air.

'Wow,' Millie breathed as the door creaked open.

'How did you know to do that?' Louis asked, his eyes almost popping out of his head.

Alice-Miranda shrugged.

'We saw your grandmother do it when she took us up to the attics,' Millie said.

'That's so unfair! Grandmama never takes us up there,' Louis sulked as he and the girls followed Edgar into the room.

'What is this place?' Alice-Miranda asked.

Rusted metal cabinets lined the walls and in the centre sat a vast machine. It had discs and dials and looked like something you might have seen on television during an early NASA space mission.

'It's a computer,' Edgar said. 'It looks like one of those ancient mainframes from when computers took up whole rooms.'

'What's it doing here?' Millie said. 'And who does it belong to?'

Alice-Miranda shone her torch onto what looked like the control panel. Spelled out in bold letters were the words 'Forensic Investigations Overseeing National Alliances'.

Millie frowned. 'What does that mean?'

Caprice walked over to take a look as well.

Alice-Miranda traced her fingers over the letters. She stopped and looked at the first letter of each word. Caprice did too. At that extact moment, both girls came to the same realisation. 'Fiona!' they cried out.

'What did you say?' Millie asked.

'Fiona – she's not a person, she's a computer.' Alice-Miranda thought for a moment. 'I wonder what Mr Thripp is really up to.'

'Does it still work?' Caprice said. 'It looks pretty dead to me.'

'There's one way to find out,' Edgar said. He reached out and pressed a big green button in the centre of the console. The machine zipped and buzzed and within a few seconds the panel lit up.

'Good evening, Chief, how may I be of help?' a cheery voice said.

Caprice almost leapt out of her skin. The children looked at each other.

'It thinks we're its boss,' Millie whispered.

'Who are you?' Edgar asked tentatively.

'My name is Fiona,' the machine replied.

'Fiona, who owns you?' Louis asked.

'SPLOD,' the machine said.

'What's SPLOD?' Caprice blurted.

'The Secret Protection League of Defence,' Fiona replied.

'What's that?' Millie asked.

This time Louis answered. 'It's the most important spy organisation in the country. It protects our family from any threats. We don't know very much about it, but Father has told us a little bit. Gee, I wish we'd known this was here before. We could have had heaps of fun.'

'This computer looks so old and it had to be turned on,' Alice-Miranda said. 'Don't you think that it would be more modern if it were still in use? Maybe there's another one somewhere else.'

'Ask her?' Edgar suggested, motioning to the control panel.

'Fiona, are you still in use?' Alice-Miranda asked.

'I am officially retired. Fiona 2.0 is now in charge.'

'Where is Fiona 2.0?' Edgar asked.

'She is located at headquarters.'

'Fiona, who's the boss of SPLOD?' Alice-Miranda asked.

'Marjorie Plunkett,' Fiona replied.

Alice-Miranda gasped.

'I knew she wasn't a milliner!' Millie exclaimed. 'She didn't even know what Alice-Miranda was talking about when she complimented her on the hat Aunty Gee wore to the garden party.'

'Do you think she was the person Mr Thripp was talking to when we were in the attic?' Alice-Miranda asked. 'Do you remember what he said about chess and moving kings and queens?'

'What are you talking about?' Louis and Edgar said in unison.

'Millie and I found a copy of King George's abdication document from years ago but it only had one signature and the space where it should have been witnessed was blank, then we overheard Mr Thripp saying something about Fiona being under their control and that things would soon be right,' Alice-Miranda explained. The girl's eyes suddenly lit up as something dawned on her. 'I think he wants to get rid of Aunty Gee!'

'But then father would be King,' Edgar said.

'No, if King George never signed the abdication

document properly, Lloyd Lancaster-Brown would become King, and Marjorie would be Queen when she marries him. We heard Mr Thripp say that he couldn't stand your father. He wants to put someone else on the throne,' Alice-Miranda said. She left out the part about them being young and beautiful. It was obvious that Mr Thripp wasn't talking about Freddy and Elsa. 'Come on, we need to find a way out of here and get back to the palace before it's too late.'

While the rest of the children had been focusing on Fiona, Caprice had been huffing and blowing about being bored and hungry. She'd begun investigating the contents of the drawers that lined the circular room.

'Caprice, are you coming?' Alice-Miranda turned and called to the girl.

'What is she looking at now?' Millie said impatiently.

'I think you're going to want to see this.' Caprice held up an official-looking document. She had found it in a file containing papers bearing the royal seal.

Alice-Miranda rushed over to take a look. 'Is this what I think it is?' She pointed at the two signatures at the bottom.

'Move it!' Edgar shouted. 'Marjorie Plunkett gets to be Queen over my dead body!'

'What's taking them so long?' Jacinta asked.

She walked over to the window and peered out at the sparkling lights of the palace in the distance. Then she scanned the grounds closer to the tower. The dull glow of torchlight flickered in the trees.

'There's someone coming!' she yelled. 'Here, help me get their attention,' she said, and flicked the torch on and off.

'We could use morse code,' Sep said. 'SOS.'

He and Lucas had been studying the form of communication as part of the next level of the Queen's colours award.

Sep flicked his torch on and off with three quick flashes, then three long ones followed by another three short ones. He repeated the sequence over and over.

'What's that?' Braxton looked towards the tower. 'There's someone up there.'

Lydie pulled back the hood of her cape and glanced at the building. Her body stiffened.

'Do you want to turn back?' Braxton asked her.

The woman stood resolute. 'No.'

'What if someone sees you?' Braxton asked.

'Maybe it's time they did,' Lydie replied.

Braxton looked back at the tower. 'It's probably those horrid grandsons of Her Majesty's,' he said. 'They're always disappearing somewhere and no one can find them.'

Lydie stared at the blinking lights. 'No, it's morse code,' she said.

'Morse code?' Braxton repeated. 'What are they saying?'

Lydie watched again to be sure. 'SOS,' she said. 'Whoever it is, is asking for help.'

Chapter 38

'Sloane! Jacinta!' Alice-Miranda shouted as the children ran up the stairs. They were puffing and blowing as they reached the fireplace.

'Where is everyone?' Edgar said, surprised to find the room empty. He ran out into the hallway, calling out to the other kids.

'We're down here,' Lucas yelled back. 'Mr Balfour's outside and he's going to try to open the window.'

Alice-Miranda led Millie, Caprice and Louis out into the hallway and followed Edgar down the stairs.

'We've got to get back to the palace,' she said.

'Where did those other stairs go?' Jacinta asked.

'There's a secret room with this big old computer and it's called Fiona,' Millie blurted.

'Why do we have to get back to the palace in such a hurry?' Sloane asked, bewildered.

'Because we think Mr Thripp is going to make Aunty Gee abdicate,' Alice-Miranda explained.

'How do you know that?' Sloane asked.

'It's complicated,' Millie said and started to explain.

The children could see Braxton's face at the window.

'Hello Mr Balfour,' Alice-Miranda called out. 'Thank you for coming. Did something happen to Mr Bunyan? We thought he'd be here ages ago. Anyway, there's no time to lose. We need to get back. Aunty Gee is in danger of losing her crown.'

Braxton frowned and wondered what the girl was talking about. 'Quickly, move away from the window,' he instructed. 'I'm going to have to smash the glass. Go back into the stairwell until I call you again.'

The children scattered. There was a loud smash followed by the sound of glass shattering onto the flagstone floor.

Alice-Miranda peered into the room.

'Can you get me a towel or something?' Braxton called. 'And be careful when you come out again.'

Edgar raced upstairs and quickly returned with an old sheet and a blanket.

The children followed him, picking their way through the glass that littered the floor.

Braxton poked his head through the window. 'What happened to you lot?'

'Mr Langley nailed the window shut,' Lucas informed the man.

'Langley? What would he do that for?'

'We don't know, Mr Balfour, but we need to get back to the palace immediately,' Alice-Miranda urged.

'Hang on a tick and I'll just make sure that there's no glass sticking out of the frame. May I have that blanket please, Master Edgar?'

The boy stood on an old chair and handed it to the man, who used it to prise loose some small shards of glass, which he dropped outside. He then used it to line the inside of the window frame. 'All right, then, out you come.'

One by one the children clambered out of the window. As they gathered outside the tower, Millie noticed a woman standing just a little way off. She nudged Alice-Miranda.

'Is that the lady we saw with the raven?' Millie whispered.

The child peered into the darkness. 'I don't know. It could be.'

'Now, what's all this about Her Majesty being in danger?' Braxton Balfour asked.

Alice-Miranda quickly explained about Fiona and Mr Thripp.

'And there's someone else involved too – a woman,' Millie said. 'We think it might be Marjorie Plunkett.'

'And don't forget about Langley. He locked us in here,' Edgar snapped.

'I'm sure Her Majesty must be worried sick about all of you.' Braxton shone his torch on his watch. 'It's after eight o'clock.'

'No wonder I'm starving,' Sloane said.

'Who's that?' Caprice pointed at the cloaked woman.

'This is Lydie,' Braxton said, 'but I don't have time to explain about her now.'

Chapter 39

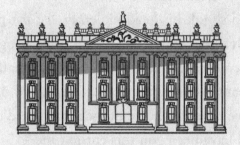

Lloyd Lancaster-Brown raced through the rear entrance foyer at the palace and shot straight upstairs, where he was met by Marjorie. 'Darling, what's going on?' he asked, grabbing the woman's arms.

'Quickly, Lloyd, we need to get to Her Majesty and she can explain everything.'

The pair rushed to Queen Georgiana's study.

'Gee, what's happening?' Lloyd greeted the woman with a hug, then looked at the array of official documents that were spread across the table.

'Lloyd, I know this is going to come as a huge shock, but please don't interrupt me until I've explained the situation,' Her Majesty began. Within a minute Queen Georgiana had blurted the entire sorry tale. 'We need to get downstairs to the throne room,' the woman said.

Lloyd shook his head violently. 'I can't possibly do this. It's not right. I don't want to be King.'

Queen Georgiana drew in a deep breath. 'And I don't particularly want that either, Lloyd, but you can see we have no choice in the matter, and besides, it should have been you this entire time.'

'But Marjorie and I need to be married first,' Lloyd said. 'We don't know anyone who could do that at such short notice, do we?'

Marjorie flinched. She hadn't mentioned that part yet and neither had Her Majesty.

'Well, Thripp has just surprised me with the news that he's an ordained minister and a marriage celebrant; apparently he's completed both qualifications quite recently – so that won't be a problem.' Queen Georgiana placed a hand on Marjorie's arm. 'I realise this is probably not the way you imagined your wedding, but let's just get the formalities sorted now so the children get back home safe and sound. I can make an announcement to the country that I'm stepping down and we can go through the proper pomp and ceremony at a later date.'

'Are you sure about this, Your Majesty?' Marjorie was feeling dizzy and short of breath.

'We have no choice,' Queen Georgiana replied, looking at the clock on the mantelpiece.

'Excuse me, Mrs Marmalade,' Alice-Miranda called as she skidded into the back entrance hall with the rest of the children, Mr Balfour and Lydie behind her.

'Alice-Miranda!' the old woman exclaimed. 'Thank heavens you're safe.'

Marian Marmalade wrapped her arms tightly around the child and wept tears of sheer relief. After a lingering moment she released the girl and reached into her pocket for a handkerchief. Marian looked up and, through hazy eyes, noticed the rest of the party standing behind the girl.

'Lydie, darling, what on earth are you doing

here?' She raced over to her goddaughter and embraced her too.

'I'm sorry, Aunt Marian,' Lydie said quietly.

'Please, Mrs Marmalade, we need to find Aunty Gee and Mr Langley immediately,' Alice-Miranda said. 'Have you seen them?'

'But I don't understand. Where have you been?' Marian took a step back and looked at the group.

Alice-Miranda shook her head. 'We haven't got time to explain.'

'I sent Mr Langley to run the Prime Minister's bath a while ago but I haven't seen Her Majesty since –'

'Excuse me, miss,' the young footman who had announced dinner at the ball had been attending to some pot plants in the rear hall and overheard their conversation.

Mrs Marmalade gave the fellow a blistering look but he pressed on.

'I just passed Her Majesty with Miss Plunkett and Mr Lancaster-Brown. They were heading along the downstairs corridor past the ballroom,' he replied.

'They're going to the throne room!' Braxton exclaimed.

'Is there anything I can do?' the young man said.

'No, but thank you for offering,' Alice-Miranda said. The footman gave a small bow and walked up the back stairs. 'Right,' the child said, 'we need to split up.'

'You can't go after Langley,' Braxton said. 'He locked you all in the tower. We don't know what part he's playing in this, but the man might be dangerous. What about if I round him up?'

'Langley? Locked the children in the tower?' Marian Marmalade was incredulous. 'Just wait until I get my hands on him.'

Braxton looked at Lydie, who seemed terribly out of breath and shaky. 'Lydie, perhaps you should wait in the small sitting room,' he suggested.

Marian nodded. 'I think that's best. I'll take you, dear.'

'It's all right,' Lydie said. 'I know the way.' The corners of her eyes wrinkled into a smile. 'I can't believe it. I'm starting to remember.'

'Lydie, that's wonderful,' Braxton said, squeezing her hard. 'Now, go to the sitting room and rest. I'll come for you as soon as I can.'

'Don't worry, Balfour, I'll look after her,' Marian said, taking Lydie by the hand. 'You go and do whatever you need to – you can tell us all about it later. I'm just glad you're all back.'

Marian Marmalade and Lydie hurried away.

Braxton turned his attention to Alice-Miranda and her friends. 'I'll go and find Langley. You lot get to the throne room and make sure that Her Majesty hasn't done anything silly,' he instructed.

The children took off along the corridor while Braxton ran downstairs into the labyrinth of kitchens and storerooms. He hoped Mr Langley would be in his office, but at that time of night the man could have been anywhere.

'Where have *you* been?' Vincent growled. Braxton turned around to face the man. Langley's shoes were filthy and the bottoms of his trousers were covered in mud.

'What happened to you?' Braxton asked.

'The better question is, what happened to *you*? Where have you been? I had to go over to the shop myself and then the car got a flat just as I was crossing the causeway. I had to push it through the mud to be able to change the tyre. I'll be telling Her Majesty that you can't be trusted. She needs to send you back to Brackenhurst and as far as I'm concerned you'll be demoted back to footman, if you retain your job at all.'

Braxton took a deep breath and drew himself up to his full height. 'I don't think that will happen.

Not after Her Majesty hears what you did to the children.'

'The children? What are you talking about?' Langley exploded. 'I haven't seen them since this morning, and they'd jolly well better be back by now or they won't be getting any supper at all.'

Braxton Balfour flinched. 'But you knew exactly where they were. You locked them in the tower.'

'I did no such thing,' Langley sputtered.

'But they saw you,' Braxton said. 'You followed them to the tower and nailed the window shut.'

'I never!' Langley shouted.

'Well, if you didn't do it, who did?' Braxton looked at the man. 'Come on, we need to get to the throne room before it's too late.'

'Too late for what?' Langley demanded.

'Never mind, I'll explain on the way,' Braxton said as he charged upstairs with Langley hot on his heels.

Chapter 40

`All right, I'll just sign this and then we can get on with the wedding.' Her Majesty read over the abdication document, which was sitting on a large mahogany desk to the right of two matching red velvet thrones. Archie and Petunia had followed the group into the room and were lying beneath Her Majesty's feet while Thornton Thripp hovered behind her. Lloyd Lancaster-Brown and Marjorie Plunkett were there too, standing to the side.

'Are you sure, Your Majesty?' Thripp asked.

'Yes.' Queen Georgiana picked up the fountain pen and placed its tip on the page. 'And we'll make sure that this one is witnessed properly, won't we?'

Just as Her Majesty was about to sign, the doors to the room burst open.

'Aunty Gee!' Alice-Miranda called out as the rest of the children tumbled in behind her.

'Oh my heavens! Darling girl, you're safe!' Queen Georgiana dropped the pen and charged across the ruby-coloured carpet, embracing the child in her arms. 'However did you get away from those monsters?'

'Oh, thank goodness,' Marjorie Plunkett sighed.

Thornton Thripp's eye began to twitch uncontrollably.

'What monsters?' Alice-Miranda frowned.

'The kidnappers,' Aunty Gee said.

'We weren't kidnapped, Grandmama,' Edgar said, 'but we *were* locked in the tower.'

A hidden door in the middle of the timber panelling flung open and Braxton Balfour raced through with Vincent Langley behind him.

'By him.' Edgar pointed at Langley.

'Why are you pointing at me?' Vincent Langley protested, shaking his head.

'Aunty Gee, you haven't signed any papers, have you?' Alice-Miranda asked.

'Not completely, but how do you know about that?' the Queen replied.

'Because it's all a lie. Someone doesn't want Freddy to be King, and the only way to make that happen is for you to think that your line shouldn't be on the throne in the first place.'

'Who'd want to do such a thing?' Her Majesty demanded.

'Mr Thripp. But he's working with two others – a man and a woman,' Alice-Miranda explained.

Marjorie Plunkett's eyes were like dinner plates. 'How do you know all this?'

Queen Georgiana turned around just in time to see her chief advisor ducking off behind the thrones. 'Thripp!' she roared.

'Get him!' Sep yelled.

The four lads charged after him. Sep dived and tackled Thripp around the ankles, bringing him crashing to the ground.

'Well done, Sep!' Queen Georgiana cried out, thinking the boy must be a great asset to his rugby team.

'Quick, take this.' Lucas snatched a tassled rope

from the velvet curtains and threw it to Louis and Edgar, who quickly bound Thripp's arms behind his back.

The boys helped him to his feet and marched him over to Her Majesty.

'What do you have to say for yourself?' Her Majesty demanded.

Thripp gulped.

'He's in on it too!' Caprice said, pointing at Vincent Langley.

'I most certainly am not! I won't have you accusing me of things I know nothing about,' the man frothed.

'Marjorie, I think you'd better call for reinforcements,' Queen Georgiana looked at the woman.

'Yes, Ma'am.'

'No, don't let her get away!' Millie said. 'It might be her, for all we know.'

'Oh, goodness,' Queen Georgiana said. 'Marjorie, don't move.'

At that moment Marian Marmalade charged through the door with another Vincent Langley behind her. There was a collective intake of breaths.

Mrs Marmalade's jaw dropped when she saw Thripp with his arms bound. 'I spotted Langley when

I was going to fetch some tea,' she explained. 'I told him to come up here, but I thought I'd better accompany him just in case. What on earth is going on?'

'And why are there two Mr Langleys?' Caprice demanded.

The two men faced each other.

'It's clear, he's an imposter,' the man who'd just walked in with Mrs Marmalade shouted.

'I beg your pardon,' the other Langley said. 'How dare you?'

Suddenly, Archie and Petunia leapt to their feet, growling. Archie charged towards the man beside Mrs Marmalade and started nipping at his feet while Petunia raced over to the man beside Mr Balfour and began licking his shoes.

'Archie and Petunia don't seem to like either of them,' Mrs Marmalade said.

'There's an easy way to tell,' Alice-Miranda said. 'Remember when Millie and I found a latex mask upstairs in the attic and we thought it must have belonged to the twins?'

'Don't look at us,' Louis retorted.

Caprice raced over to the man standing next to Braxton Balfour while Millie headed for the man beside Mrs Marmalade.

'Ready?' Millie looked at Caprice. 'On three. One, two, three!' At exactly the same time, the girls reached up and yanked the men's noses.

'Ow! Stop that at once.' The man beside Braxton pushed Caprice away.

Millie's jaw dropped as the other man's nose flew off his face and sprang back with a solid slap. 'You're not Mr Langley! Who are you?'

The man swallowed hard.

Archie was growling much louder now and biting the man's trousers.

'Well, whoever *that* is, he locked us in the tower. And whatever's going on, he's definitely in on it,' Alice-Miranda declared.

The man turned to run but was intercepted at the door by a cavalry of footmen. No one had seen Jacinta slink out to go and find them. She thought they might need some back-up.

'Oh, no you don't.' The first footman pushed the man back inside the room. There was no escape. He was surrounded.

'Reveal yourself!' Queen Georgiana commanded.

The crowd watched as the man dug his fingernails under the skin of his neck and began to peel back his face, right up over his hairline.

Caprice scrunched up her nose. 'Eww, that's disgusting!'

'Who is it?' Lucas said.

Marjorie Plunkett's jaw dropped.

'Miss Broadfoot!' Millie declared. 'I knew there was something weird about you.'

'Actually, my name's Treadwell,' the woman spat. Her voice had changed too, as her voice-modifying device had been removed along with her mask.

'And I thought she was one of your most trusted agents, Marjorie,' Queen Georgiana remarked.

'So did I,' the woman replied. 'Rowena, what were you thinking?'

Agent Treadwell glared at her. 'That I should have been Chief, not you. I've always been smarter and stronger yet, somehow, you got the job and I was relegated to undercover fieldwork, having to use ridiculous names like Bunyan. What were *you* thinking, Marjorie?' she hissed.

'Miss Plunkett, you're not really Her Majesty's milliner, are you?' Alice-Miranda said.

The woman hesitated.

Lloyd turned to Marjorie, shock written all over his face. 'What does she mean? You're not Gee's milliner?'

'Oh, give it up, Lloyd,' Thornton Thripp huffed. 'This was as much your idea as it was mine.'

'What?' Marjorie suddenly felt ill. She looked at her fiancé.

'Miss Plunkett, we know about Fiona. We heard Mr Thripp and Miss Broadfoot – I mean Treadwell – talking about it and then we found an old mainframe in a strange room in the very bottom of the hunting tower, beneath the cellar,' Alice-Miranda explained.

'Fiona told us everything,' Edgar said with a proud grin.

'And what exactly did she say?' Marjorie asked.

'That you were her boss and that Fiona 2.0 was located at SPLOD HQ,' Caprice said.

Queen Georgiana stared at Lloyd. 'So is it true the abdication papers weren't witnessed?'

'She stole them from HQ,' Lloyd said, pointing to Treadwell. 'And he got Fiona to verify them once I'd taken over the system.' Lloyd glared at Thornton Thripp. 'No, they're not real. She couldn't find the real ones.'

'But we did.' Alice-Miranda produced the original copy from the tower. 'Caprice found it in a drawer in the room Fiona was in, along with a whole lot of old documents.

'Thank heavens for that.' Her Majesty exhaled. 'But what were they doing up there?'

Marjorie turned to her fiancé. 'You knew all along that I wasn't a milliner?'

Lloyd shrugged.

'Did you ever love me, or was I just part of your evil plan?' A tear wobbled down Marjorie's cheek.

'I don't know. You would have made a lovely queen, Marjorie,' Lloyd said. 'And you would never have been any the wiser.'

'How could you?' Marjorie sobbed. 'You're certainly not the man I fell in love with.'

Queen Georgiana shook her head. 'Why, Lloyd? I don't understand. You've never expressed any interest in being King before.'

'Because I'd rather anyone be King than that feeble-minded son of yours,' Lloyd hissed.

'Steady on. That's our father you're talking about.' Edgar walked over to Lloyd and poked him in the chest.

'I know Freddy can be a bumbling twit at times but this is so extreme. You were the best of friends when you were boys. What happened between the two of you?' Queen Georgiana asked softly.

'He pushed my sister from the tower and ruined her life – *that's* what happened,' Lloyd fumed.

'No, he didn't,' a tiny voice said from the back of the room.

'Lydie?' Lloyd breathed. His jaw dropped and he looked completely shell-shocked.

Alice-Miranda ran around behind the footmen.

'Are you all right, Miss Lancaster-Brown?' the child asked. Lydie nodded. Alice-Miranda held the woman's hand and led her to the centre of the room.

'But . . . how?' Lloyd stumbled backwards and steadied himself by grabbing hold of the desk.

'It doesn't matter. But you owe Cousin Gee and Freddy an apology,' Lydie said. 'I didn't remember that day until now – until Braxton came to see me and things started to fall into place. He took me to the tower, Lloyd, and it was as if all the missing pieces were there. You and Freddy were so awful to me. You told me you'd ruin every-thing if I married Braxton. You said that he wasn't good enough for me. We argued, then you stormed off and Freddy stayed. I was so cross with both of you.'

'He pushed you,' Lloyd said, tears swimming in his eyes. 'He was like my brother and he pushed you out of the tower and ruined your life. I hated him from that day on. I hated him even more because he lied about it.'

Lydie shook her head. 'But he didn't push me. It was *my* fault. We were arguing and I ran upstairs to get away from him. Then I spotted a nest in the tree outside. Three little baby birds were chirping for their mother but I saw her lying on the ground. Freddy followed me. I told him to leave me alone but he just kept at me. He said it would be a disgrace for me to marry a farmer's son. But I wasn't listening. All I cared about was getting to that nest and rescuing those tiny creatures. I leaned out of the window and that's the last thing I remember about that day.'

Lloyd looked at his sister bewilderingly. 'All this time I've wanted to find a way to ruin Freddy's life the same way he ruined yours.'

'Well, you've done a very good job of ruining your own life, Lloyd.' Her Majesty shook her head at the man and walked over to his sister. 'Lydie, darling, welcome back to us, welcome back.' She embraced the woman warmly.

Alice-Miranda strode over to Lloyd Lancaster-Brown and stood in front of him. 'You're lucky you committed treason now and not a couple of hundred years ago. Now you'll only go to gaol. Back then you would have lost your head.'

Lloyd's bottom lip trembled.

'Take Thripp, Lloyd and Bunyan – or whatever her real name is – to the dungeons,' Queen Georgiana ordered.

Braxton Balfour nodded at Her Majesty. He and five footmen marched forward and positioned themselves in pairs beside each prisoner.

'The dungeons!' Caprice looked at Alice-Miranda. 'I thought you said there weren't any dungeons at the palace.'

Alice-Miranda grinned. 'I guess Aunty Gee can never be too careful.'

'Oh, darling girl, you're right about that,' Queen Georgiana said, and hugged Alice-Miranda tightly.

Millie raced over to the desk where Her Majesty's abdication paper was sitting. 'What would you like to do with this, Aunty Gee?' the child called.

'Tear it up, Millie,' Queen Georgiana said with a nod. 'Tear it to pieces.'

And just in case you're wondering . . .

Lloyd Lancaster-Brown, Thornton Thripp and Rowena Treadwell, also known as Miss Broadfoot and Frank Bunyan, were all sent to prison for their treasonous plot. Though none of them would admit whose idea it was in the first place, each blaming the other as the mastermind behind the evil plan, their roles became more apparent over time.

Rowena had been clearing out some old filing cabinets at SPLOD HQ when she came across the unsigned abdication document. Marjorie was away at the time, so Rowena had taken it to Thripp in his capacity as the Queen's chief advisor. He'd told her to sit tight and had hatched a plan to interrupt the line of succession and stop Freddy from becoming King. In return for her cooperation, Thornton promised Agent Treadwell the position of Chief of SPLOD as soon as Marjorie became Queen. This suited Rowena perfectly as she'd always resented Marjorie getting the top job over her.

Lloyd had hacked into Fiona, taking control of SPLOD's master computer. Agent Treadwell switched the surveillance in Millie's camera and took the photographs of Alice-Miranda while she was at school and, much to Her Majesty's disgust, Thripp was the poet and author of the appalling notes. When she later questioned Thripp about his reasons for committing his treasonous acts, he said that he simply couldn't bear the thought of Freddy ascending the throne after the reign of his gracious and elegant mother. Queen Georgiana couldn't believe his stupidity.

Lloyd was desperately sorry for being such a fool and apologised to his sister Lydie, and cousin Freddy. He even tried to make it up to Marjorie by creating a completely hack-proof shield for Fiona 2.0.

Vincent Langley was given the option to retire on a very handsome pension. To everyone's surprise he leapt at the chance, allowing Braxton Balfour to achieve his lifelong dream of becoming head butler at Evesbury. He and Lydie rekindled their romance and planned to marry the following spring. As time went by, her memory grew stronger and stronger. Lydie was more than happy to continue making Her Majesty's hat too. Marjorie Plunkett had only ever known that the person who lived in the cottage provided her cover – she had never known who the woman was.

After breaking off her engagement with Lloyd, Marjorie chose to focus on her professional career for the moment and work on making SPLOD a more transparent organisation. She even agreed to be interviewed by the famous talk-show host Michael Frost about her role and the responsibilities of the organisation. That way, she no longer had to pretend that she was Her Majesty's milliner. Marjorie was stunned to find a whole host of important original documents stored in the tower vault and promptly had them safely moved to HQ.

Together with Her Majesty, Marjorie turned the hunting tower into a tourist attraction and charged visitors to view the very first SPLOD computer, Fiona 1.0. They even had Fiona reprogrammed to answer the public's questions – to a certain extent, of course.

The Prime Minister of Samoa's visit to the palace had been part of Thripp's plan to create yet another diversion. Fortunately, by the time dinner was served that night, order had been restored to the palace and the man was none the wiser.

Queen Georgiana decided that it was much safer to keep a close eye on Edgar and Louis and their inventions, and set them up in the attic. Though, their gadgets constantly caused her to question her decision – particularly after a stink bomb went awry and the entire palace had to be evacuated and the bomb squad called in.

Caprice's grandfather recovered from his stroke and, though her mother was annoyed that Caprice had chosen to stay at the palace instead of going to be with her family, Venetia was pleased to hear that her daughter had played a positive role in apprehending the threesome that would have brought down the Queen.

Her Majesty took Hugh's advice and gave Freddy more responsibility. He and Elsa had just represented her on a trip to the Pacific Islands. Apart from mispronouncing Prime Minister Tuitua's name as Prime Minister Tutu, Freddy didn't fare too badly.

Queen Georgiana appointed Mrs Marmalade as her chief advisor on top of her services as lady-in-waiting. Marian couldn't wait for Dalton to return and realise what had gone on in his absence. Never mind the answer when he applied for leave again.

Alice-Miranda and her friends had the most wonderful week with Aunty Gee and Mrs Marmalade. As promised, Aunty Gee took Alice-Miranda and Millie riding, and Caprice tagged along too. Even Millie had to admit that the girl was a very accomplished rider. The children had picnics and midnight feasts, and they used the clothes from the attic wardrobe for a play they presented to the palace staff on their very last night. Of course, they insisted on Aunty Gee and Mrs Marmalade performing in it too. It wasn't a stretch for either of them, though, playing a queen and lady-in-waiting.

ROYAL
FAMILY
TREE

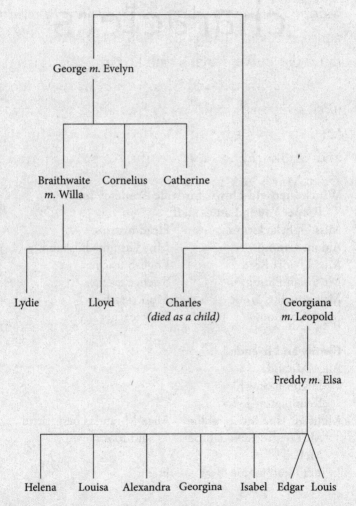

George *m.* Evelyn

Braithwaite   Cornelius   Catherine
m. Willa

Lydie   Lloyd   Charles   Georgiana
                          (died as a child)   *m.* Leopold

                                                      Freddy *m.* Elsa

Helena   Louisa   Alexandra   Georgina   Isabel   Edgar   Louis

Cast of characters

Winchesterfield-Downsfordvale Academy for Proper Young Ladies staff

Miss Ophelia Grimm	Headmistress
Aldous Grump	Miss Grimm's husband
Miss Livinia Reedy	English teacher
Mr Josiah Plumpton	Science teacher
Mr Cornelius Trout	Music teacher
Miss Broadfoot	New teacher

Family and friends

Alice-Miranda Highton-Smith-Kennington-Jones	
Millicent Jane McLoughlin-McTavish-McNoughton-McGill	Alice-Miranda's best friend and room mate
Jacinta Headlington-Bear	Friend

Sloane Sykes	Friend
Sep Sykes	Lucas's best friend and brother of Sloane
Lucas Nixon	Alice-Miranda's cousin
Cecelia Highton-Smith	Alice-Miranda's adoring mother
Hugh Kennington-Jones	Alice-Miranda's adoring father
Ambrosia Headlington-Bear	Jacinta's mother
Charlotte Highton-Smith	Cecelia's younger sister and Alice-Miranda's aunt
Lawrence Ridley	Famous movie actor and Aunt Charlotte's husband
Marcus and Imogen Ridley	Twin babies of Charlotte and Lawrence
Valentina Highton-Smith	Alice-Miranda's maternal grandmother

Royal Family and staff

Aunty Gee	Queen Georgiana
Mrs Marian Marmalade	Queen Georgiana's lady-in-waiting
Thornton Thripp	Queen Georgiana's chief advisor
Vincent Langley	Head butler at Evesbury Palace
Braxton Balfour	Under butler at Evesbury Palace
Frank Bunyan	Butler at Evesbury Palace
Freddy	Queen Georgiana's only child
Elsa	Freddy's wife
Louis	Twin son of Freddy and Elsa
Edgar	Twin son of Freddy and Elsa
Lady Sarah Adams	Cecelia and Charlotte's cousin
Lord Robert Adams	Lady Sarah's husband

Lord Herbert and Lady Lisbeth Luttrell	Guests
Lord Tavistock	Guest
Lord Lloyd Lancaster-Brown	Queen Georgiana's second cousin
Tom	Kitchenhand at Evesbury Palace

Others

Venetia Baldini	Famous television chef

Caprice Radford	Venetia Baldini's daughter and
	    student at Winchesterfield-
	    Downsfordvale

Marjorie Plunkett	Head of the Secret Protection League of Defence

Agent Rowena Treadwell	Operative of the Secret
	    Protection League
	    of Defence

Lydie	Queen Georgiana's milliner

About the Author

Jacqueline Harvey taught for many years in girls' boarding schools. She is the author of the bestselling Alice-Miranda series and the Clementine Rose series, and was awarded Honour Book in the 2006 Australian CBC Awards for her picture book *The Sound of the Sea*. She now writes full-time and is working on more Alice-Miranda and Clementine Rose adventures.

www.jacquelineharvey.com.au

Jacqueline Supports

Jacqueline Harvey is a passionate educator who enjoys sharing her love of reading and writing with children and adults alike. She is an ambassador for Dymocks Children's Charities and Room to Read. Find out more at www.dcc.gofundraise.com.au and www.roomtoread.org/australia.

Want to know how it all began?
Read on for a sample of
Alice-Miranda at School

Chapter 1

Alice-Miranda Highton-Smith-Kennington-Jones waved goodbye to her parents at the gate.

'Goodbye, Mummy. Please try to be brave.' Her mother sobbed loudly in reply. 'Enjoy your golf, Daddy. I'll see you at the end of term.' Her father sniffled into his handkerchief.

Before they had time to wave her goodbye, Alice-Miranda skipped back down the hedge-lined path into her new home.

Winchesterfield-Downsfordvale Academy for

Proper Young Ladies had a tradition dating back two and a half centuries. Alice-Miranda's mother, aunt, grandmother, great-grandmother and so on had all gone there. But none had been so young or so willing.

It had come as quite a shock to Alice-Miranda's parents to learn that she had telephoned the school to see if she could start early – she was, after all, only seven and one-quarter years old, and not due to start for another year. But after two years at her current school, Ellery Prep, she felt ready for bigger things. Besides, Alice-Miranda had always been different from other children. She loved her parents dearly and they loved her, but boarding school appealed to her sense of adventure.

'It's much better this way,' Alice-Miranda had smiled. 'You both work so hard and you have far more important things to do than run after me. This way I can do all my activities at school. Imagine, Mummy – no more waiting around while I'm at ballet or piano or riding lessons.'

'But darling, I don't mind a bit,' her mother protested.

'I know you don't,' Alice-Miranda had agreed, 'but you should think about my being away as a holiday. And then at the end there's all the excitement of coming home, except that it's me coming home to you.' She'd hugged her mother and stroked her father's brow as she handed them a gigantic box of tissues. Although they didn't want her to go, they knew there was no point arguing. Once Alice-Miranda made up her mind there was no turning back.

Her teacher, Miss Critchley, hadn't seemed the least surprised by Alice-Miranda's plans.

'Of course, we'll all miss her terribly,' Miss Critchley had explained to her parents. 'But that daughter of yours is more than up to it. I can't imagine there's any reason to stop her.'

And so Alice-Miranda went.

Winchesterfield-Downsfordvale sat upon three thousand emerald-coloured acres. A tapestry of Georgian buildings dotted the campus, with Winchesterfield Manor the jewel in the crown. Along its labyrinth of corridors hung huge portraits of past headmistresses, with serious stares and old-fashioned clothes. The trophy cabinets glittered with treasure and the foyer was lined with priceless antiques. There was not a thing out of place. But from the moment Alice-Miranda entered the grounds she had a strange feeling that something was missing – and she was usually right about her strange feelings.

The headmistress, Miss Grimm, had not come out of her study to meet her. The school's secretary, Miss Higgins, had met Alice-Miranda and her parents at the gate, looking rather surprised to see them.

'I'm terribly sorry, Mr and Mrs Highton-Smith-Kennington-Jones,' Miss Higgins had explained. 'There must have been a mix-up with the dates – Alice-Miranda is a day early.'

Her parents had said that it was no bother and they would come back again tomorrow. But Miss Higgins was appalled to cause such inconvenience and offered to take care of Alice-Miranda until the house mistress arrived.

It was Miss Higgins who had interviewed Alice-Miranda some weeks ago, when she first contacted the school. At that meeting, Alice-Miranda had thought her quite lovely, with her kindly eyes and pretty smile. But today she couldn't help but notice that Miss Higgins seemed a little flustered and talked as though she was in a race.

Miss Higgins showed Alice-Miranda to her room and suggested she take a stroll around the school. 'I'll come and find you and take you to see Cook about some lunch in a little while.'

Alice-Miranda unpacked her case, folded her clothes and put them neatly away into one of the tall chests of drawers. The room contained two single beds on opposite walls, matching chests and bedside tables. In a tidy alcove, two timber desks, each with a black swivel chair, stood side by side. The furniture was what her mother might have called functional. Not beautiful, but all very useful. The room's only hint of elegance came from the fourteen-foot ceiling with ornate cornices and the polished timber floor.

Alice-Miranda was delighted to find an envelope addressed to 'Miss Alice-Miranda Highton-Smith-Kennington-Jones' propped against her pillow.

'How lovely – my own special letter,' Alice-Miranda said out loud. She looked at the slightly tatty brown bear in her open suitcase. 'Isn't that sweet, Brummel?'

She slid her finger under the opening and pulled out a very grand-looking note on official school paper. It read:

Winchesterfield-Downsfordvale Academy for Proper Young Ladies

📖

Dear Miss Highton-Smith-Kennington-Jones,

Welcome to Winchesterfield-Downsfordvale Academy for Proper Young Ladies. It is expected that you will work extremely hard at all times and strive to achieve your very best. You must obey without question all of the school rules, of which there is a copy attached to this letter. Furthermore you must ensure that your behaviour is such that it always brings credit to you, your family and this establishment.

Yours sincerely,
Miss Ophelia Grimm
Headmistress

Alice-Miranda put the letter down and cuddled the little bear. 'Oh, Brummel, I can't wait to meet Miss Grimm – she sounds like she's very interested in her students.'

Alice-Miranda folded the letter and placed it in the top drawer. She would memorise the school rules later. She popped her favourite photos of Mummy and Daddy on her bedside table and positioned the bear carefully on her bed.

'You be a brave boy, Brummel.' She ruffled his furry head. 'I'm off to explore and when I get back I'll tell you all about it.'

Winchesterfield-Downsfordvale Academy for Proper Young Ladies
School Rules

1. Hair ribbons in regulation colours and a width of $^3/_4$ of an inch will be tied with double overhand bows.
2. Shoes will be polished twice a day with boot polish and brushes.
3. Shoelaces will be washed each week by hand.
4. Head lice are banned.
5. All times tables to 20 must be learned by heart by the age of 9.
6. Bareback horseriding in the quadrangle is not permitted.
7. All girls will learn to play golf, croquet and bridge.
8. Liquorice will not be consumed after 5 pm.
9. Unless invited by the Headmistress, parents will not enter school buildings.
10. Homesickness will not be tolerated.